HUNT◆KILLER®

PERFECT SCORE

POLICE LINE DO NOT CROSS POLICE LINE DO NOT CROSS POLICE LINE DO NOT CROSS POLICE LINE DO NOT CROSS POLICE LINE DO NOT CROSS POLICE LINE DO NOT CROSS

AN ORIGINAL NOVEL BY A. M. ELLIS

SCHOLASTIC INC.

For DeJesus, Kairi, and Aaliyah. Always speak your truth. —AME

Copyright © 2022 by Gnomish Hat Inc.

All rights reserved. Published by Scholastic Inc., *Publishers since 1920*. SCHOLASTIC and associated logos are trademarks and/or registered trademarks of Scholastic Inc.

The publisher does not have any control over and does not assume any responsibility for author or third-party websites or their content.

ISBN 978-1-338-78402-2

10 9 8 7 6 5 4 3 2 1   22 23 24 25 26

Printed in the U.S.A.   131

First printing 2022

Book design by Katie Fitch

Photos © Shutterstock.com

ONE

MONDAY, FEBRUARY 21, 9:18 A.M.

CHLOE ST. JAMES stared up at me, her stormy-gray eyes pleading for me to save her. Unfortunately, she was already dead, her entire existence reduced to the contents of a banker box stashed away in the back row of Chicago PD's records room.

I flipped through a few of the tagged items—a modest engagement ring, old playbills, bloodied silk scarves. The forensic photographer managed to capture the last glint of light in Chloe's gaze, even with her left pupil blown. Another stack of photos focused on the ligature marks around her neck, rope burns at her wrists, and her left ring finger— broken. The lead detective had given up after a matter of days, the death of an understudy from the South Side swept under the red carpet of the historic Chicago Theatre.

I snapped my own photos with my phone. Cautious not to leave any trace of my presence, my gloved hands removed and replaced every piece of cataloged evidence with care. My phone buzzed, making me almost drop an engraved cuff link. I checked the alarm that I'd silenced one too many times.

Shit. Late for AP Calc.

Tucking the cuff link back between the bagged, bloodied scarves and unrequited love letters, I resealed the banker box and heaved it up onto the shelf above. I grabbed my Irish-cream coffee, my saving grace from the overwhelming smell of mildew and wet cardboard, and made my way out of the storage locker. I passed row after row, shelf after shelf, all of them full of banker boxes, tagged and forgotten.

How many of these cases sat here, cold?

The concrete walls and dim fluorescent lights sent a shiver trickling down my spine.

Too many, I thought to myself.

It was that fact that had set me on the path to starting my own PI firm one day, whether my parents approved or not. Too many families were in need of closure—justice. They're what kept me coming back every week. I wasn't going to sit around and wait for these cases to be solved. And I didn't see anyone else rushing to be the voice of the silenced.

At the end of the last row, I knocked for Officer Hal to buzz me back through to the basement's hallway. He sat behind the guard desk in front, chowing down on the pastrami sandwich I'd brought him from Manny's, spicy brown mustard somehow smeared high on his freckled cheek.

I grinned. "Appreciate the assist, as always."

He lifted his sandwich as if to say ditto for the meal, his sandy-blond hair spiked at odd ends. That, combined with his third cup of under-brewed joe, meant another night spent on the couch. Not sure what he did this time to wind up in the doghouse—most likely out too late drinking at McNally's, based on his bloodshot eyes. One thing I did know: Marjorie wasn't packing his meals in the meantime.

"Did you find it?" he asked, mouth still full.

"Exactly where you said it would be. I took pictures of everything, and"—I peeled off the black latex gloves and tossed them in the trash bin—"I already have an angle to explore."

He winked, goofy as ever. After a year of me wandering into police headquarters during my lunch break back when I still attended school across the street, Hal had developed a soft spot for me. He claimed I was the spitting image of my mother. It was possible that he needed his eyes checked. I may have inherited my mom's curiosity, but my complexion was a good couple of shades lighter than her deep mahogany, I had my daddy's hazel-green eyes instead of her pecan brown, and my hair was more frizz than curl, though I tamed it this morning with a few too many passes of my flat iron.

"Well, you keep supplying Manny's, I'll keep moving you to the front of the access queue," he said. "Happy to help with that dream of yours."

I stole a chip from his desk and slid on my backpack. "Operation PI is well on its way."

"Jolene Kelley, private investigator. Has a nice ring to it." He smiled. "And by then, Junior will be in college and can intern with you."

I shook my head as he waggled his brows. Junior was all of eleven to my sixteen.

"What can I say, we Halligans like our older women."

"You just focus on getting off the couch. Buy Marjorie some flowers, pink tulips."

"How did you—"

"It's the little things, Hal." I swiped another chip and waved, turning down the hallway. My phone buzzed for the umpteenth time as I stepped into the elevator. I hit the button for the lobby before peeking at the screen. Four unanswered texts.

Frankie:
Did you get it?
Sabrina:
👀

Frankie:

???

Sabrina:

This is not the type of suspense I signed up for.

A smile tugged at my lips. Frankie was the one who found the case. His sights set on attending Columbia, he spent all his free time in the library scrolling through old newspapers, perfecting his craft for a future in investigative journalism. When he came across the unsolved murder of a forgotten Black girl from the same street we grew up on in Englewood, he knew it was a case that would pique my interest.

Jolene:

You were right. Case went cold back in '89. Hanging in Chicago Theatre, but not a suicide. Detective chalked it up to a jealous ex, but he didn't put in the effort to actually track down the guy.

I shared the photo album with Frankie and Sabrina, already knowing what Sabrina was going to say.

Sabrina:

Oooh, this is giving me Michelle Gray vibes.

Frankie:

Everything gives you Michelle Gray vibes.

Sabrina:

What was that cold case she went up to New York to solve a few years ago? That one had a cuff link, too! There was an actress from the 1930s, a fancy theater . . .

I rolled my eyes as the elevator doors opened. Light flooded into the lobby from the floor-to-ceiling windows that faced South Michigan Avenue. Shoes echoed against the marble tiles, a steady rhythm as the city's finest moved through the space. I nodded to a few familiar faces, a couple of lieutenants, deputy directors, and Chief Ryan making his way around security and out the door. Frazzled, he was oblivious to my greeting as he rushed outside, his assistant running behind to hand him his coat. *Must be late to another press conference.* He usually liked to hear what I was up to. I'd have to pick his brain about the cold case another time.

My gaze landed on the clock behind one of the desk sergeants. I sighed. One of these days I was going to be on time for calculus. Today was not that day.

At least I was consistent.

I shot back a text to Sabrina.

Jolene:

Great detective work, Bri.

Sabrina:

😑 You follow Michelle just as closely as I do. You know the case—you remember the killer?

"Jo?"

I glanced up at hearing my name. Reya Morales passed through the metal detectors, channeling every bit of Meghan Markle's Rachel Zane—her dress perfectly tailored, her silk press flawless. No one would ever know her outfit was from the discount rack at Target the way she pulled it off. Except for me. I was with her when she bought it last weekend.

"Hey! New case?" I asked, nodding to the papers in her hands. "Anything good?" I rocked on my heels, hoping she wouldn't notice the time. No such luck.

Reya raised her glasses as she checked the watch at her wrist. She looked at me, then back to her watch. Then back to me. She held up the files. "Need a few signatures for the state attorney's office. What brings you south of the Loop during school hours? Trouble with calc?"

That's what made running into Reya different from everyone else. She'd known me since I was in diapers and, with that, my class schedule. Everyone else was used to me coming over from De La Salle High during my lunch break or before school, but not everyone knew my parents made me transfer to a fancy academy in Lakeview for sophomore year. They had big dreams for my future, ones that didn't include community college and opening my own PI firm. The fact that the classes were harder now—many of them pointless (who needs a semester studying Gothic literature?)—and that I was now the weird girl who ate lunch with her guidance counselor didn't seem to bother my parents one bit.

"Calculus is still a breeze," I lied as I held up my phone. "Grabbing a new case for the gang."

"Let me see." Reya flipped through the photos. She loved the cases as much as I did, shadowing my parents at the public defender's office for years before choosing the paralegal route to save up for law school.

"She was from the neighborhood. The department just let it go unsolved, it seems."

She nodded. "Come by tomorrow—*after* class. I'll see what I can help you with."

I let out a sigh of relief, making a mental note to pick us up some frappés for fuel.

Reya handed back my phone with a raised brow. "Your friends are asking you to skip and meet them at the Chicago Theatre in an hour."

I flipped back through the messages. Sabrina had already hit the forums and wanted to check to see if there were any employees left from the time of the murder. Not surprising considering how much she enjoyed interviews and undercover work. Any opportunity to gossip—that's where she thrived.

"I already turned in all my assignments for the week, and studied for the pop quiz in AP Spanish that Mr. Perez thinks no one knows about." Only one half of that statement was true, but I put on my pouty lip and hoped for the best.

Reya crossed her arms. "Okay, then," she said before

narrowing her eyes. "But don't tell your peeps I'm letting you skip. I'm supposed to be a model adult."

"Not a word!" I sent off a quick text to Sabrina and Frankie.

Reya turned to the elevators, calling over her shoulder. "If you can wait a half hour, I can give you a ride."

"I'll catch the Green Line. Thanks, Rey!"

Pulling my coat out of my backpack, I hurried out the door and headed to the L. For a moment I almost forgot it was February in Chicago. The wind slapped me in the face, back and forth from multiple directions. A familiar nemesis. Mounds of dirty snow lined the streets, too stubborn to melt in the hazy sunlight, and cold air bit at my legs. Every winter, Mom huffed about us needing to move somewhere warm, but Dad and I knew she would never leave. Both their families went back generations, roots planted firmly in this city.

I rushed down the block and over to Thirty-Fifth and Bronzeville, slipping inside the station house before letting myself navigate to a podcast for the ride. I slid on my headphones. *Behind True Crime* was next in my queue. This week's episode went behind the scenes of a failed homicide investigation in Mississippi—the lead detective obsessed with an innocent man.

Heading up the steps, I passed the familiar stench of paint remover used for the now-faded graffiti on the walls. Other people passed me on the way down. A train had just let out.

As I reached the platform, I spotted Mr. Medina stepping out of a southbound train, the only guidance counselor I had ever known to rock a man bun. I froze at first but then remembered if he was here, he was skipping school, too.

Mr. Medina was part of the reason I now attended North Shore Preparatory. He used to work at Kershaw Elementary, where I spent kindergarten through eighth grade, and he even helped me through some tough times with my mom. But then he left for his fancy new school right after my eighth-grade graduation. After a year at North Shore, he decided to convince my mom and dad I needed to do the same. Him, I had forgiven. My parents . . .

I pulled my phone out of my pocket.

Jolene:

Just saw Mr. Medina.

Sabrina:

Bring him with you.

Frankie:

REUNION OF THE ORIGINAL KERSHAW
MYSTERY BOOK CLUB

Sabrina:

Does he have the man bun today or is it more
Keanu Reeves/John Wick type vibes?

I looked up, hoping to catch his attention before he left the platform. I waved and lifted my headphones.

"Mr. Medina!" I took a few steps closer. It was hard to

hear much of anything with the wind whipping in my ears. He didn't notice me. Instead, he was gesturing wildly, deep in conversation with someone I couldn't see—one of the platform's steel columns was blocking my view. Based on his body language, I got the impression they were talking about the papers he held tight in his hands. He looked pissed.

A few stragglers walked between us, including a couple who looked lost. They huddled together over one of those tourist maps, mumbling about the Bean. This was definitely the wrong stop.

My phone buzzed again.

Frankie:

Tell him about the case!

Sabrina:

Still waiting on the man bun update.

A scarf flew by me, and my fingers grazed the soft wool as I failed to catch it. Dark blue with an orange-and-white crest. I didn't have to see it clearly to recognize the design. North Shore Preparatory Academy.

A horn wailed as another southbound train streaked into the station, followed by a screech—metal on metal. The conductor was applying too much pressure to the brakes. I glanced up just as Mr. Medina went flying off the platform.

Time slowed as I clocked every beat of movement before my eyes. Mr. Medina's body folded over as if he had taken a forceful push to the gut, his eyes growing wide in disbelief. The papers he held only moments before fluttered around him like a snowstorm.

The train was moving too fast.

And I was too far away to do anything.

No one reached out to pull Mr. Medina back to safety. No one even seemed to notice what was happening. There was only the one person I saw stepping away from the tracks. A dark figure that slipped back behind the steel column, shielding themself from view.

Then the world was going full speed again. I flinched and squeezed my eyes shut as Mr. Medina hit the front of the train with a sickening crack.

TWO

MONDAY, FEBRUARY 21, 9:32 A.M.

SCREAMS CUT THROUGH the nerve-grating shriek of the train's brakes. One of the voices grew hoarse as my throat started to burn.

Wait.

Was I the one screaming?

Unable to move, to breathe, I stood frozen. The train had stopped, but my view was blocked by those who moved in front of me, hands over their mouths, shocked expressions on every face.

"Did he jump?" someone muttered.

"He just fell back, I think," another answered. "That damn wind."

I took a step forward before a hand curled around my wrist.

"You don't want to do that, baby." An old woman tugged lightly for me to follow her, ushering me to the closest bench to sit down. I forced one foot in front of the other, making my way over. A man in a dark double-breasted coat rushed to the platform's exit, followed by the tourist couple from earlier. My eyes followed the wife's fingers as she dialed three numbers on her cell phone: 9-1-1.

My mouth opened, and then closed, no words forming on my lips.

That didn't just happen. I didn't just see that.

The crowd thickened, too dense for me to see anything, and everything around me faded into the background. My body tingled—heart pounding against my ribs.

This isn't— I can't. No.

Station guards rushed the platform, pushing back onlookers.

Another light touch, this time on my cheek. The old woman guided my gaze over to her. I stared at her face, my eyes tracing the deep wrinkles set in her golden-tan skin. My focus wavered, Mr. Medina's body soaring through the air still fresh in my mind. I blinked it away. The woman's silk floral scarf fluttered, and she pulled it tight to cover her graying hair. Her plum-colored lips moved, but the voice in my head didn't match the movements; the husk of a man was whispering in my ears. My headphones hung around my neck, the podcast still playing.

"The killer acted with no remorse, no fear of being caught. Each time leaving the body in public venues for the world to gawk and see . . ."

I muted the voice.

"Did you know that man?" she asked again.

I tried to turn my head to see what was happening at the tracks, but she pulled me back to stare into her eyes. They were brown, upturned, and filled with sorrow.

Did you, she had said. Not *do you*.

"Yes." I swallowed. My throat still burned. "He's my guidance counselor." The words came out barely above a rasp.

People on the train banged on the doors to be let out. "What's going on?" someone shouted to those of us still on the platform.

A voice came over the loudspeakers. "There's been an incident on the track. Please wait."

Sirens blared. The police were arriving.

I blinked again. Everything moved too slow and too fast all at the same time. My breath came in shallow spurts, and I clenched my fists, only to notice something soft graze my hands.

"I saw you reach for it," the woman said as she placed the blue scarf in my lap. She gestured to where she had found it—caught on a gate at the end of the platform.

I traced the school's crest with my fingertips. North Shore Preparatory Academy.

This is his scarf.

I'm late for AP Calc.

I frowned as the thought crossed my mind. School. We were both supposed to be at school. Why was he here?

My phone buzzed.

Frankie:

???

Sabrina:

Earth to Jo!

Sabrina:

I bet she's wrapped up in another podcast.

Frankie and Sabrina still waited for an answer.

Officers walked past, muttering to one another. "Another jumper?"

I squeezed my eyes shut. The hunch of Mr. Medina's body, his brown eyes wide. The O of his mouth in a soundless scream. He wasn't arched back like a slip or fall. Wasn't facing forward like a jump. Hunched, like he was hit with force. And the arguing voices . . .

He was pushed!

But the words wouldn't leave my mouth.

"Jo!" Reya ran up the platform, flashing her ID to be let through the barricade meant to close off the station. It took no time for her to cross the space between us, swoop down, and pull me to her. "There were so many patrol cars when I drove past. And you weren't answering your phone."

The old woman squeezed my hand. "I'll leave you with your friend. Promise you won't look, baby."

I nodded over Reya's shoulder as the old woman stood to leave.

Reya turned to offer a grateful smile before facing me again, tucking the wild strands of my hair behind my ears. "I thought something happened to you."

I unlocked my phone screen. Three missed calls. *How long has it been?*

A few papers flitted by with the school crest.

Someone needs to get the papers. Mr. Medina will need them—

Reya pressed her hands to my cheeks. "Are you okay?"

I tried again to turn my head to see the front of the train.

"You don't want to do that. It's . . . It's not the same as looking at a photograph."

"It's Mr. Medina," I whispered.

"From school?"

I nodded.

A small gasp escaped her lips as she covered her mouth. She knew him from all my stories about his club at Kershaw. Remembered all the books I dragged her to the library to help me find. They had even met briefly at the last parents' night at North Shore, my own parents too busy with work to attend themselves.

More papers blew about the ground, student records from the looks of it. I caught the name of one student as the cover sheet of his file found itself wedged under our bench: Julius James. He had a smile in his school photo where one side of his mouth quirked up higher than the other. A gloved hand snatched up the paper. I didn't look up to see who it belonged to.

A metallic stench wafted through the air, and the Chicago wind whipped again. Blood. My stomach lurched. Reya was right; this wasn't the same as my cold cases.

"I'm going to call your parents to take you home." Reya waved an officer over, a middle-aged man handing out blankets to those who remained on the platform. He wrapped the scratchy thing around my shoulders. I'd seen him before, in the lobby this morning. My gaze flitted to his badge. Lieutenant Charles.

"Do you think you'll be able to give a statement?" he asked.

I opened my mouth to speak, and again, nothing came out.

Reya held up a hand. "Give her a minute."

For the next thirty minutes, I sat still as the scene moved around me. Officers and EMTs passed through the station as trains single-tracked on the northbound side, not stopping to receive or unload passengers. This was a crime scene, after all.

"I can't reach your dad, but your mom can meet us at the house."

Right. Dad was in court today. I could have told Reya, but I wanted him to be the one to answer the phone, not my mom.

"Let's take you home." Reya pulled me to my feet.

"I—I haven't given my statement. About what I saw."

"Do you want to wait? I'm sure we can work it out for you to go down to the station later. You're a minor, and your parents aren't here, so it should be okay."

My eyes flicked up to the platform overhang. Security cameras in fixed positions.

Rolling my shoulders back, I straightened up. "I can do it. I want to."

I didn't see who Mr. Medina was arguing with, but it had to be on the station's security cameras.

Reya left to find the lieutenant while I tightened the blanket around me. The old woman was gone, along with the tourist couple and most everyone else. All had given their statements. Someone had to have had a better view of the argument. I glanced around one more time. Only one other kid was waiting for his parents to pick him up.

Did they already have the suspect tucked away?

Reya made her way back. "They have all the statements they need. Did you see him fall?"

"Fall?"

Reya frowned, searching my eyes. "Lieutenant Charles said the statements they've taken so far indicate this was just an unfortunate accident."

"Taken so far"? Shouldn't they get all the statements before making a call on what just happened?

"No." I shook my head. "No, he was pushed. He flew through the air. His face—" My voice cracked, my breath caught in my throat.

"Are you sure? Did you see someone push him?"

"No. But he didn't fall. I saw his body in the air . . ." Brows furrowed, I forced myself to picture it again. He was too high off the ground to have fallen.

Reya looked back at the police officers before wrapping an arm around me. "Let's get you home, Jo."

I stumbled at first, not wanting to leave but unable to do much else. It was like I had forgotten how to move without someone nudging me in the right direction.

My mind drifted back to the sound of screeching train brakes, metal on metal. I shook my head as though that action alone would quiet the memory. It didn't.

To get to the stairs, we had to walk past the portion of tracks now taped off. I snuck a peek, only to see a bloodied white sheet covering Mr. Medina's form. It still felt so unreal. I wanted to see a finger move, someone to yell out he was okay. But nothing happened.

Turning away, I locked my eyes on the security camera pointed directly at me.

The police will see who did this on the footage. They have to.

At home, Mom made lemon and lavender tea and threw on a pot of chicken stock. We had rotisserie last night, which meant chicken and wild rice soup for dinner tonight. She and Reya spoke in hushed voices at the stove, Mom sneaking a glance at me here and there. After the third look of pity, I slipped away and went upstairs to my room.

My hands shook as I placed the now-folded scarf on my desk. The desk was old and wooden, covered with a mix of schoolwork and printouts from the last cold case I worked with Frankie and Sabrina. Photos dotted my wall. We took selfies every time we went somewhere new to investigate a case. My favorite photo was from eighth grade—the three of us with Mr. Medina celebrating the third anniversary of our inaugural book club session. He'd taken us to the movies, and we all wore cream cable-knit sweaters to channel Chris Evans's character from *Knives Out*. It was one of our many investigations, Mr. Medina challenging us to figure out who the killer was. None of us got it right, but it was all we needed to spark our love for mysteries outside of just books. We started researching cold cases soon after that. All because of Mr. Medina.

Looking down at the scarf, my thoughts wandered. Would this go in an evidence box? Will the police forget about Mr. Medina like all the others in the records room? Will his case go cold?

But this wasn't another case. This is—*was*—Mr. Medina. And it wasn't an accident.

My phone vibrated again.

Crap. I never answered my friends.

Sabrina:

We heard what happened.

Sabrina:

😣 😣 😣

Frankie:

I just . . . Damn, are you okay? Want us to come over?

I started to respond, but nothing I tried to say came out right.

"Argh!" I threw the phone across the room and flopped onto my bed, screaming into my pillow. My cheeks hot and wet with tears.

Finally. It had taken long enough for me to cry. This was real. It was happening.

It happened.

Mr. Medina was dead.

THREE

THURSDAY, FEBRUARY 24, 7:49 A.M.

MR. MEDINA'S DEATH hit me differently compared to others who had come and gone from my life. It wasn't as if this was the first time I'd lost someone. My great-grandmother Nana Josette was the sweetest old lady, made the best potato salad (the only potato salad I would ever eat), and had been, on most days, my best friend. When she passed two years ago, I put on my white dress for her going-home service, shed a few tears, and spent the week after making all her recipes with my mom while she told stories from her summers with Nana. We didn't let ourselves mope. She had lived a full life and left behind a legacy that would be forever unmatched.

Mr. Medina was different.

He didn't get to live a full life. Someone took that from him.

In the past three days, I'd barely gotten out of bed, argued twice with my mom about missing class, and binged more episodes of *Criminal Minds* than I cared to admit. I didn't want to move past Mr. Medina's death with the swiftness everyone seemed to think I should. How could I? This was murder. But it felt as if no one else believed that.

A knock came at my door in the tune of the Dolly Parton classic my dad named me for. I paused the TV, framing Dr. Reid in mid–aha moment as he started to unravel the unsub's book cipher.

My dad inched open the door. "Hey, kiddo."

He was already dressed for another day in court—a pressed gray suit and his signature skinny silver tie. His superhero costume he called it. He always wore it for closing arguments. I scooted over in my bed, brushing a few candy wrappers to the floor to clear a space for him.

Plopping down next to me, he grabbed one of my Red Vines. "Which episode is this?"

"Beginning of season two: 'The Fisher King: Part Two.'"

"And these are one-hour episodes? Have you done anything else?" He raised a brow.

"Technically, they're only forty-five-minute episodes. No commercials on stream."

"Fair enough." He pulled another Red Vine from the bag and watched the TV screen as I unpaused the show, allowing Dr. Reid to continue being the investigative genius I hoped to one day become.

We managed a few minutes of silence before Dad finally spoke up. "You know, Mr. Medina meant a lot to me, too."

I tensed. I suspected he was here to talk but had hoped he just wanted to steal from my candy stash. "Dad—"

"Ah—let me finish. Now, I didn't grow up running with the best crowds, and I got tangled up in a few things. I was lucky to snag your grandfather as my arresting officer. But the city out there has changed so much since then. I remember a few years back having friends from out east call and ask me, 'What's going on in Chicago?' Multiple homicides every day. The city had become this murder capital as the world just sat and watched." He shook his head at his words. "Your mom and I even thought about leaving a few times."

I paused the TV again.

Leaving Chicago was something Mom always joked about. Dad was content with only living in cities where they dyed the river green during his favorite holiday. He never mentioned wanting to go anywhere else.

"Then Frankie's little brother got clipped with that stray bullet while playing in his own yard, two doors down from us," he continued. "There was a PTA meeting at Kershaw, and all the parents asked for the school to do more, provide after-school care to keep the young ones off the streets. Most of our cries were met with empty words. Mr. Medina, though, he did something. He started that book club for you and Frankie and Sabrina, and he got a few other teachers to start their own programs. He knew ending at five wasn't enough time for most families to make it home from work, so he took you all to the library, or to one of the neighborhood aunties, just to make sure you were somewhere safe. I owe a lot to that man. A lot of parents do."

His voice wavered as he wrung his hands together. "Are you sure this wasn't an accident? Someone pushed him?"

I lifted my head to meet his eyes. I'd shared my version of the incident with my parents that first night at dinner, only for Mom to brush it off as me grieving in my own way, a coping mechanism. The two of us had barely spoken in three days. (Not that that was anything new.)

Dad stared back at me now, caring eyes and an open expression. He actually wanted to hear my answer.

"He wouldn't jump. And the wind might have been a beast that day, but he wasn't at the edge of the platform when it happened. I'm sure of it."

Dad ran his fingers through his fading red hair, his mind working on something as he let out a sigh. "There are two things I've tried to pass on to you."

"Be a voice to the voiceless," I recited.

"And always speak your truth." He nodded. "We're listening now."

My door creaked, and there was my mom, her briefcase in hand. She wore her own pressed suit, her coily hair pinned up in a tight bun. "I put in a call. Reya's picking you up in a few minutes to take you down to headquarters. You have an appointment with the lead on Mr. Medina's case, Lieutenant Charles. But—you have to go back to class tomorrow," she said pointedly.

I faltered. That was not what I expected. Not from her. "I thought the officer didn't need any more statements?"

"He's willing to take one more. I'm still not sure about what *may* have happened on the platform or if your account will change his report"—she looked over to Dad, a skeptical look on her face—"but we know you need to do this. So you can move on."

I took in her words. She still didn't believe me. She was wrong, though. My statement *would* change things. The police just needed to be pointed in the right direction.

My throat tightened, and I swallowed the emotions trying to escape. I didn't have time for that right now.

"Thank you," I murmured. I pulled Dad into a hug before hopping out of bed. Glancing down, I remembered my pajama onesie. "Dang. I gotta get dressed."

"No, you need to shower first," Mom corrected.

I scrunched up my nose at her before shooting down the hall to the bathroom. Ten minutes later, I was outside, shimmying my way into, as Reya referred to it, her *vintage merlot* Toyota Corolla. Taylor Swift blared in the speakers, going on about another heartbreak.

"*1989?*"

"Nope, *Reputation*." Reya turned the radio down to a

legal volume as I buckled myself in. Her album choice combined with her siren-red wrap dress could only mean one thing.

"Trouble with Damon?"

"Damon is no more. Couldn't handle it," she said, waggling her brows.

"At least he was better than Stefan."

"Mmm. Well, I've moved on to Elena." She passed me her phone to see her newest squeeze, with long dark hair and doe-like eyes.

"Ooooo. I approve of this upgrade."

Reya smiled—the kind of smile that reeked of pity because you remembered the person you're smiling at locked themselves in their room for three days. "You all right?"

"I will be." I broke my eyes away from her gaze. I was fine as long as I didn't have to talk about my emotions. Talking about them would just mean more tears. I cried once—that was enough.

Reya leaned over and sniffed. "Your mom wasn't lying; your hair does smell like red licorice and corn chips."

I rolled my eyes. "It's not that—" I took a whiff of my ponytail only to pull out some body spray from her purse. I gave my hair a spritz. "I was rushing, and my mom only gave me ten minutes. You know my hair takes an hour on its own. I'll wash it when I get home. Sabrina owes me a braiding session anyway."

She laughed. "Hey"—she looked over to me—"I'm proud of you."

The corners of my mouth lifted just a smidge. "You think Mr. Medina would be?" I asked her. "Proud, I mean. Would he be proud?"

"Now that you are out of bed? Yes."

I stuck out my tongue and settled back in my seat. Reya turned up the volume, singing "End Game" at the top of her lungs. She couldn't carry a tune if she tried, but I found it oddly comforting.

I'm giving my statement. And it will *change things. My truth* will *matter.*

It had to, for Mr. Medina's sake.

———

Wrapping Mr. Medina's scarf around my neck, I stepped onto the curb outside police headquarters while Reya circled for parking along the street. Snow melted from the last few days of flurries, leaving puddles on the sidewalk. I wiped my feet at the entry before walking through the lobby to the elevator bank. It was hard not to feel like all eyes were on me. Add that to the wait outside the lieutenant's office, and my right leg wouldn't stop shaking.

What if he turns me away, again?

What if he doesn't believe me and no one answers for Mr. Medina's death?

Somewhere in the car ride over, my confidence had dropped and the weight of my statement fell on my shoulders. No one else at the platform had claimed to see anything. I was alone in this.

Reya sat beside me in the waiting area, giving my knee a squeeze to bring me out of my negative thoughts. My phone buzzed in my pocket.

Dad:

Proud of you, kiddo.

I locked my screen and shut my eyes.

"This isn't a big deal," I mumbled. I'd helped close plenty of cold cases. I knew exactly what the police needed to hear. Mr. Medina wasn't going to become another forgotten banker box in the basement of police headquarters. My statement would see to it.

A few minutes later, the office door creaked open, and Lieutenant Charles walked out. Black freckles splayed across the officer's light brown cheeks alongside a look of determination. "We'll have it squared away in the next day or so," Lieutenant Charles noted as he shook hands with the man who exited behind him. The stranger wore a sleek suit, tailored to a tee, the navy-blue fabric popping against his stark-white shirt and olive complexion. His dark hair stood up high in a pompadour, defying all laws of gravity.

"Appreciate it, Wendell," Sleek Suit replied. His grin was one of those fake plastic smiles with teeth bleached too white.

"You've done so much for me and Amita. I—" The

lieutenant's gaze fell to me. "Ah, my next appointment is here."

Sleek Suit turned around, his grin widening. I didn't think that was possible. "Oh, you're the Kelleys' kid?"

I couldn't help but frown. "Yes? Sorry, are you here for our meeting with the lieutenant?" I looked back to Reya, who looked just as confused.

"No, no apologies needed. Wendell here mentioned you were coming in. I've met your parents a few times at the courthouse. It's admirable what they do, and I see you're following in their footsteps, making sure you give your statement for that horrific accident."

"It wasn't an accident," I replied a little too quickly, my voice sharper than intended.

But what I said was true.

His mouth twitched into an amused smile. "I see." Reaching into his pocket, he handed me his business card, navy blue with a matte finish, white and gold lettering. "I'm Alderman Jay Corben, city councilman over in Lakeview. Mr. Medina was a good man, and he did a lot for the community through his work at the academy." He eyed the scarf at my neck as I crossed my arms to cover the North Shore crest. "My condolences. If you ever need anything, don't hesitate." With that, he nodded to Reya and turned to leave, his heavy footsteps muted by the gray carpet tile.

Awkward silence followed before Lieutenant Charles remembered we were waiting on him.

"Are you ready for us?" I asked, looking between the now-empty hallway where the alderman had disappeared and back to the lieutenant's empty office.

"Yes!" He motioned toward his open door. "Yes, come on in."

Guided by his sweeping gesture, Reya walked over to the worn leather chairs that sat opposite his ornate cherry-wood desk. "Thank you for seeing us."

I slipped into the seat next to her, tucking my hands under my legs to keep myself from squirming. The lieutenant's office was surprisingly clean. Very few files were visible, and most of the space was filled with family photos—a few recent ones from last year's CPD holiday party, showing his right hand in a cast, and tons of candid shots of his son playing Little League and holding up a second-place ribbon at an eighth-grade science fair.

"He's at Morgan Park now, top of his class." Lieutenant Charles nodded to the photo. "With any luck, you'll see him next year at North Shore. My apologies for my behavior on the platform Monday. If I had known you had a personal connection to the victim, I wouldn't have brushed off your request to make a statement before. I thought I was saving you from getting involved in a police investigation, especially at such a young age." His eyes became unfocused. "Such an unfortunate accident," he muttered.

Clearing his throat, life came back into his gaze, and

he pulled out a notepad and pen. "Now, tell me what you remember."

As I spoke, the fountain ink scratched across the paper in elaborate flourishes, loops that seemed to travel to the ends of the earth, the pen's sound and movement holding my attention. There was a lot of nodding and mm-hmms—his reactions exaggerated, overdone. He stopped writing as soon as the last word left my lips.

"That was brave of you to come in and share, Miss Kelley."

I tried to look at his notes, but I was too far away.

Did he get it all down that fast?

"Does that match what the conductor saw?" I asked.

He knitted his brows together, tilting his head to the side. "Who?"

"I couldn't be the only one who saw what happened. Mr. Medina's body would've crossed right into the conductor's line of sight. And the train camera—it should've caught it all."

Confusion still covered the lieutenant's face.

"The person driving the train," I continued.

"Ah." He nodded. "We're giving everything the proper attention on this case, don't you worry. I appreciate you coming in." He stood a bit too fast, his chair tilting back as it caught on a few loose carpet threads.

No follow-up questions?

I sucked in a breath and counted to five. "Thank you for listening." I shook his hand, and he barely matched my grip. I stole a quick glance at his notepad.

My heart sank.

"And you too, Ms. Morales." He turned to shake her hand.

Reya smiled and snuck me a look. We were ushered back out into the hallway without any other acknowledgment and waited until the elevator doors closed behind us before speaking.

"That was—"

"Patronizing," Reya finished for me. "I know this case isn't his area of expertise. He's not a beat cop anymore and far from a detective, but that felt off. I thought his head would fall off his neck from all the nodding."

"He didn't write it down."

She spun to face me. "What?"

"The notepad. His movements were too exaggerated, and his pen stopped with my last word. He can't write that fast. There was a picture of him with his dominant hand in a cast not too long ago, and he struggled to hold the pen firmly. Same with his handshake. It was weak."

Reya smiled to herself. "Well, I agree with your parents on one thing."

"What's that?"

"You might be dreaming too small with this private investigator thing. You should set your eyes on Quantico.

Introduce me to that cutie from Chicago who's on that crime show you're always watching."

I shrugged, trying not to smile. My breakdown did sound impressive. "I snuck a look at the pad, too. It was a bunch of scribbles."

She grinned. "Never tell 'em your secrets."

The elevator doors opened, and we stepped out into the hustle and bustle of the lobby, uniformed officers passing us by. Outside, it was overcast, leaving no sun to filter in through the windows. The gloom matched my mood. Everything with the lieutenant was nothing but a show.

Reya slipped on her coat, and I could feel her eyes on me. "Hey." She gave me a light nudge. "He's working in the administrative department and had no plans of catching a case. I'm sure he just wants to close it out. I looked him up before we got here. He's aiming for a promotion soon. He might believe wrapping this up quickly will help with that."

My heart crashed against my chest. The lack of files, all the photos highlighting achievements. *Protect and serve* was obviously not his immediate focus. "Are you saying we should move on?" I stopped walking.

"Never." She tipped up my chin so I would look her in the eye. "They have the cameras and the conductor, like you said. Whatever happened will come to light."

I nodded. We stepped outside, the wind making the scarf at my neck dance in the ice-chilled breeze. I don't know why I grabbed his scarf to wear, but I was glad I did. I needed Mr. Medina's presence today.

Reya fished her car keys out of her oversized purse. "Should we stop somewhere for breakfast before I drop you back at home? I could go for some pancakes."

I stared up the street toward the train station. I had to trust that Lieutenant Charles was going to do as he said: give everything the proper attention. But how could he do that if he faked taking my statement?

"Can we check the platform? I want to see something."

"Of course. Let me grab my flats from the car, and we can walk over."

Walking into the train station at Thirty-Fifth and Bronzeville, everything was as it was before, and at the same time, it wasn't. Something dark stained the concrete platform near the incident, and a lone saint's candle burned at its edge. The frankincense aroma blended with the crisp smell of the winter and a hint of bleach. A train idled on the southbound tracks, allowing passengers to board. Memories began to flood my mind, and I rushed to push them back down.

"Jo?" Reya's voice snapped me back.

I shook it off. "You stand here." I moved her to stand under the camera that would've seen everything. Running over to the column where the figure arguing with Mr. Medina stood days before, I looked over to her, unable to see much more than the sleeve of her coat.

"Can you see me?" I called out.

"Not really. Maybe if you stepped out a bit. The way the columns divide the platform, I would need to peek around."

My shoulders dropped. These cameras were stationary. There was no *peeking around*. "The cameras have blind spots."

Reya nodded. "It's been a problem in a few cases for the police. There's a contract out to get all the stations upgraded surveillance."

The wind blew again, and the cold prickled against my skin, turning it to gooseflesh. The train left the station, revealing the trash-covered southbound tracks full of the usual food wrappers and someone's lost Ventra transit card that had slipped from their grip.

Reya joined me at the platform edge.

"Everything okay?"

My eyes watered from the cold, pushing tears to fall, but the wind dried them as quickly as they formed.

The cameras might be a bust. But there's still the conductor's statement.

Just give it time, I told myself. *My truth will matter.*

I hooked my arm through Reya's. "I got what I needed for now. Let's go."

FOUR

STANDING IN FRONT of Mr. Medina's office the next morning was a surreal experience. Flowers and well-wishes blocked his door, along with stuffed animals and heart balloons. Pools of hardened wax dotted the floor where I assumed someone had tried to burn candles only to have them replaced with fake flickering tea lights.

I gripped the straps of my backpack, staring at it all, trying not to show emotion in a hallway full of faces I barely knew. They walked by in their cliques: jocks, theater kids, society's elites, and those already high out of their minds before first bell. I didn't have anyone at this school without Mr. Medina. Coming into this building only cemented that truth.

A student stepped into my periphery. Khaki slacks fell over his brown loafers. He wore a pressed white button-up under his midnight-blue sweater with the orange-and-white school crest at his heart. Julius James: the same boy whose file I saw on the ground at the train platform Monday morning. He gave a quick nod in my direction and added a saint's candle to the growing mass, lighting it with a quick prayer before leaving. The comforting scent of frankincense wafted through the hall—the same candle from the train platform.

"Who keeps—" The dean of students, Mrs. Lawson, walked by, snatching up the candle. "Please stop leaving lit candles in the hallway!" she bellowed. "We have announced this many times!" Her face grew red, though her over-processed blond hair didn't shift an inch, that French twist of hers held in place by what smelled like an excessive amount of hair spray—a likely fire hazard.

"I'll take that, Mrs. Lawson," a voice from behind offered.

We both turned, surprised to find Mrs. Medina, formerly Ms. Salvatore, perfectly prim in her dark tweed skirt and black kitten heels. New wrinkles crinkled at the corners of her eyes, though her concealer hid the shallow bags underneath. I don't know what it says about me that I didn't think of Mr. Medina's widow until now. Didn't think that there was someone grieving more than I could ever understand.

"Of course." Mrs. Lawson nodded and continued down the hall. She stopped short at the end. "Are you still sure you don't want a few more days at home? If you need more time—"

"I'll be taking the afternoon and next week. I like it here, though. The kids keep my mind busy," Mrs. Medina replied.

Mrs. Lawson nodded again and turned the corner as Mrs. Medina stepped in place next to me, her dark waves falling over her face, a sad smile peeking through. "She's tough on you students, but she sat with me that day when the officers came to deliver the news. We had been in meetings all morning, prepping for the next alumni fundraiser, and then the police arrived . . . She held my hand and prayed the rosary with me even though that isn't her faith." She blew out the candle.

I motioned to it. "Saint Daniele?" I asked.

"Patron saint for strength and courage. Missionaries, too. Manuel never missed Sunday Mass, something my Sicilian parents would've appreciated." She traced the saint's painted features on the candle's glass casing. "Your parents said you were having a rough time. That you were there?"

I nodded. "Yes, ma'am."

"Was he meeting with you?"

"No, I—I don't know why he was there." It was a question I'd asked myself over and over, as if answering it would solve everything.

Her shoulders fell, and her eyes glazed with tears she

didn't try to hide. I hadn't given her the closure she needed. Why her husband was so far from where he was supposed to be—at school with her.

"Well, I'm glad to see you in class today," she said, kneeling to pick up a few of the cards and one of the large teddy bears dressed up like a classic Sherlock Holmes. "I've decided to spread his ashes privately with his mother at her home in Spain. But there will be a small memorial service at our loft tomorrow instead of a formal funeral. You're welcome to stop by. And your other friends from the club at Kershaw Elementary. Frankie and Sabrina, right?"

"Wait, his ashes?" *They're releasing the body?* "The investigation isn't over, is it?"

"I believe it is? I'm supposed to pick up his remains later today. It was recommended to cremate . . ." She sniffled as she looked up. "Sorry, I didn't mean to bother you with those details."

"It's okay." I placed a hand over hers. "Who—"

"Nic?"

At the end of the hall stood the same man from Lieutenant Charles's office—Alderman Corben—with the same suit and same towering hair.

"The memorial is at one o'clock tomorrow. I would love to see you there," Mrs. Medina whispered before joining the alderman. He placed his hand at the small of her back, leading her around the corner to her office in admissions.

I stood there with no words, dumbfounded. The late

bell rang, and I was left in an empty hallway, save the mementos at my feet, antique glass cases full of academic achievements, and marble busts of dead headmasters.

The case can't be over. My statement and the conductor's— they had to be enough to bring up new questions, new theories.

And the alderman. How does he know Mrs. Medina?

"What the actual hell?" I muttered.

———

"The officer really just scribbled nothing?" Sabrina pulled at my hair, dragging her comb along my scalp to add another part. "Hey! Head straight!"

"Ow! Gentle, gentle," I squealed, trying to get comfortable between the squeeze of her short winter-white legs. I still wore my school uniform, a high-waisted box-pleat skirt and long-sleeve sweater, both in the North Shore midnight blue, but I'd peeled off the two layers of dark knit tights. My mom had the heat on high, and it was too hot for that compared to the freezing hell outside.

Frankie sat at my desk, his feet up and hanging off the corner edge so as not to dirty the papers scattered across it. His tall, scrawny self was almost lost in the folds of his oversized hoodie, his hickory-brown fingers peeking out his sleeves as he tossed back my stash of almond M&M's. It was Friday night, which meant the three of us would be up late going over our latest case. Sabrina lived too far to walk home alone at night, so she always stayed over.

"You asked for individuals," Sabrina argued.

"I asked for some braids. You wanted to get fancy." I readjusted myself between her legs.

"All right." Frankie swung his feet down from my desk, rubbing his hands over his short buzz cut. "Back on topic. Your texts yesterday were vague. Did you literally mean he wrote nothing?"

I started to nod my head but already felt Sabrina ready to tug my head back into place. "He wrote nothing. And Reya and I went back to the platform. The cameras wouldn't have caught anything. There was a blind spot."

"Well, that was convenient," Sabrina muttered.

"So, what next?" Frankie asked.

Sabrina tapped my shoulder, letting me know she'd finished the last plait.

I turned around to face her in her unicorn pajamas while she went to twisting her own mousy-brown hair into two high buns. "I'm thinking the conductor had to see something. What do you think?"

She chewed on her cheek while squinting her eyes. Her tell for when she was thinking hard on something.

"And the alderman, you sure that was him at your school?" Frankie questioned.

"Yes."

"Also, convenient," Sabrina noted.

"I think you mean a coincidence. It's not really convenient— Oomph! Really?" I cried out as I received a pillow to the face.

"You know what I meant." She and Frankie locked eyes, sharing a look. The look they always share whenever they thought I was overanalyzing.

I waved my hand between the two to break their stare. "Look, Mr. Medina was pushed. I know what I saw."

Frankie held up his hands. "We aren't arguing."

"And this one person was at police headquarters with the lead officer on the case *and* at my school, meeting with Mr. Medina's wife."

Silence fell, no one wanting to debate me. I didn't blame them.

I was fixated, yes. But with reason.

"I think it's weird his wife got him cremated. I didn't think Catholics did that." Sabrina glanced over to me for confirmation.

"My dad only drags us to Mass on Easter and Christmas, so I'm not sure. But I was thinking it could be a way to get rid of evidence? She said someone encouraged her to do it." I looked back and forth between them.

"There are other reasons." Frankie squirmed in his seat.

"Like what?"

"Jo . . . he was hit by a train. He could've been . . ."

I cringed, not wanting him to finish that sentence.

"Well, you know my grams used to work for the Chicago Transit Authority," Sabrina started. "She was on the CTA janitorial crew that cleaned the tracks every Sunday night, but she had a lot of friends who were conductors. A few are still there, and they gossip like crazy. Maybe I can poke around."

Frankie sat up. "Yeah, and I can check the camera feeds."

I whipped my head in his direction. "This isn't the same as hacking into the school's grading system to give Bri an A in phys ed." Another pillow to the face. "Ow!"

"I can do it," he said. "Investigative journalism is my thing, right? I was able to find the scanned records for the Chicago Theatre case in the CPD online database. Their firewall is surprisingly weak."

"Are you two continuing that case?" I hugged the pillow to my chest, dropping my gaze. Anything to avoid eye contact. I hadn't forgotten about the cold case, but Mr. Medina's felt so much more important.

He hesitated. "Yeah . . . we would've called you, but—"

"We needed a distraction while having to sit through class this week," Sabrina finished.

I shrugged. The reminder that they still had each other at De La Salle while I was alone at North Shore Prep only stung a little bit, but it was still a reminder I didn't have Mr. Medina to talk to during lunch anymore. I didn't have anyone at that school. "What do you have so far?"

"We're going to work the angle of the ex-lover the detective abandoned. Her left ring finger was broken, and the engagement ring they found doesn't match her tan line. Then there's the love letters."

"Ex-lover, eh?" Frankie's words sparked a thought.

Alderman Corben had called Mrs. Medina by her first name—well, not even. It was a nickname I'd only heard used by Mr. Medina. (The other teachers used her full name, Nicolette.) Then the alderman had placed his hand on her lower back, below her waist. That would suggest familiarity, but was it intimate?

I pictured the dark figure who made sure to stay behind the steel column. An alderman would know where to stand to stay out of camera view if he kept up with the city contracts.

My wheels turned. "Looks like we have two cases. Let's get to work."

––––––––––

It was two in the morning before Sabrina fell asleep and Frankie headed out, my dad walking him home. After working through bits of the cold case, we had settled on watching *Doctor Strange*, Frankie and Mr. Medina's favorite MCU movie. While mysteries are what first brought us together, we all agreed with Mr. Medina that Benedict Cumberbatch was the best Sherlock and one of our favorite Avengers.

Sabrina lay spread-eagle across my bed. There was no moving her. She might've been a petite size two, but when she slept, she was dead to the world. Grabbing my favorite satin pillow, I walked down the hall to the guest bedroom that used to belong to Nana Josette only to notice a light on downstairs. I wandered down the steps and into the kitchen. My dad sat at the round wooden table in his plaid red pajamas, a newspaper from a few days ago in hand as he sipped on a glass of ice water.

"Trouble sleeping?" I asked.

"Your mom just about sweated me out of the room with the heat on so high. And she turned on the space heater." He raised his glass. "Just needed a cooldown. That and catching up on some news I've missed."

I smiled. I used to love climbing into their bed during the winter just to have that blast of hot air in my face. It always helped me go to sleep when there was too much on my mind, melting away my worries.

Dropping my eyes to the paper, there in black and white, was a large photo of Chief Ryan.

Section 1 | Tuesday, February 22

CPD Chief Commanding Officer John Ryan.

BUREAU CHIEF ANNOUNCES BID FOR CPD SUPERINTENDENT, KEY CITY POLS BACK MOVE

By Angelica Monai

On Monday morning, at a press conference held at McCormick Place, Bureau Chief John Ryan, a veteran of the Chicago Police Department, announced his campaign for police superintendent. Chief Ryan joins the police superintendent race as an immediate favorite with overwhelming support from key city figures from both sides of the aisle.

I'd almost forgotten. The same day of Mr. Medina's death, Chief Ryan had announced his bid for police superintendent, seeing as Superintendent Donahue planned to retire this summer. The article called out how the chief was the only candidate with support from almost all fifty aldermen.

"He was running late that day," I noted, grabbing my dad's drink for a sip. "I remember seeing him rush out of headquarters."

"You were up there grabbing a cold case? Is that how you ended up at the station? Your mother and I assumed, but . . ."

We both fell silent. This was *not* a conversation I wanted to have right now. "Well, I'm going to go—"

"Wait. Jolene." Dad reached out to touch my arm. "You know this tension between you and your mother . . . She just wants to see you get out of this neighborhood. It can be hard to break generational cycles. Your Nana Josette moved up here from Mississippi during Jim Crow. My ancestors came here long before then, settling for low-paying jobs at the meatpacking plants. It's time for our family to leave the South Side. We may not have the means, but you—" He tapped his temple. "You got those smarts."

"But I'm stuck at North Shore *alone*. When I was at De La Salle—"

"At De La Salle, you would skip, play hooky, and still had straight As. We both know you weren't challenged. Look at you now, a sophomore with a full AP schedule. You might even finish high school in three years, instead of four.

"Your mom and I want to push you to be the greatest

you can be. Just like Mr. Medina did. That's why he wrote you that recommendation, helped us get you that partial scholarship with the Chicago Police Scholars—"

"I didn't need all that. I like the cold cases. I like helping out the people here—the ones who get ignored by everyone in uniform. *You* understand that. But Mom—do you remember how she reacted when she saw my first murder board? The things she and I said to each other? What she did?"

He folded up his paper slowly. "She's worried about you—your future. Do this for us, for *me*. Four-year college. You don't have to go to some East Coast Ivy. It can be a state school nearby if you wanna stay close. I just want you to open yourself up to more. I'll work on your mom about the PI thing."

I crinkled my nose, not wanting to give. "I'll think about it."

"That's my girl." He smiled, picking up his drink.

"I'm keeping your ice water, though." I swiped the glass before heading back up to the guest room. I settled into bed, guzzling down the cold liquid. The ice clinked in the glass. One simple clink, and my mind flashed back to the screech of metal on metal. Squeezing my eyes shut, I turned on the space heater to blow in my face and wished for it to take the memories away.

FIVE

BY THE TIME I woke up the next morning, Sabrina had gone home to change for the memorial. I sent a quick text to Reya double-checking the status of Mr. Medina's case after everything I had learned at school the day before. Reya's response was one I didn't want to hear. She confirmed that the final police report ruled Mr. Medina's an accidental death.

Case closed.

Everything about that was wrong. And now today I had to say goodbye to the only adult who ever encouraged me to pursue my dream.

"Are you sure you don't want your dad to go with you?" Mom asked. Together, along with too much Eco Style gel, we had managed to lay my edges and weave my braided hair into an elegant knot at my nape. Mom slid a few gold bobby pins by my ear to restrain potential flyaways as I stared at my reflection.

I couldn't help but notice she offered for Dad to come with me, not her. She must've realized her presence wouldn't exactly be a comfort right now. "I'll be okay. I'll have Frankie and Bri."

I rubbed my hands over the dark wool dress that fell to my knees, smoothing out a small wrinkle at my waist. It was a size twelve, but surprisingly I had a little room. With black tights and a pair of Reya's high heels, I almost didn't recognize the girl in the mirror. But this was for Mr. Medina, and I would be my best self.

I will not break.

A notification alert pinged on my phone as I pulled on my coat. "That's probably Sabrina. She's borrowing her girlfriend's ride for us to use today."

Mom tied my—Mr. Medina's—scarf at my neck. "Text me when you arrive."

I nodded, letting her kiss my cheek before heading out the door. I lived for these little moments, when things between us didn't feel so strained. My thoughts shifted for a moment, wondering if Dad had talked to her already about my dreams to become a PI. And he was right: With the track they had me on at school, I could graduate early, get a part-time job to save up for my own space—

"Jo?"

I turned around at the edge of the driveway to see my mom standing at the door.

"Today is about you saying goodbye, all right? Reya told me the case is closed, so it's time for you to move on. I'm sure that's what he would have wanted." She gave a light smile, holding her arms around herself in the cold.

And just like that, the moment between us was gone.

She knew nothing about what he would've wanted.

I dropped my eyes to the ground, no energy to argue with her, and turned back to hop into the old Volkswagen minibus. Opening the side door, I was greeted by Frankie sitting in the passenger seat in a dark suit while Sabrina sat behind the wheel in her pink faux fur. She'd curled her hair into bouncy ringlets held back with a black satin bow.

"Everything okay with you two?" she asked as I slid the door closed with a bang.

I shrugged, watching my mom disappear back in the house. "I mean, I know she's not all bad. She just doesn't get why this is important to me—making sure Mr. Medina's case isn't just swept away . . ." *The possibility of him becoming another cold banker box in the police records room.* I shuddered, shaking off the thought.

"Let's get going. It's almost twelve thirty, and we gotta survive Bri's driving all the way uptown." Frankie pointed to my seat belt as Sabrina stuck out her tongue at him.

He threw a look at her as she rolled over the curb while backing out the driveway.

"I forgot to ask." Frankie shifted in his seat to face me once we got on the road. "Was it hard going back to school yesterday?"

I tightened my seat belt as Sabrina missed a stop sign. This was going to be a long ride. "I guess. There were all these cards and teddy bears and condolence wishes outside his door, but by the end of the day, they'd been cleared away. Now his office is just dark. I think it's taking me a while to accept that he's gone."

He nodded. "I can get that. It's different for us. We didn't see him every day like you did. And it had been a while since we all got together to talk mysteries. After you left De La Salle, it kinda turned into you and him bouncing ideas around during your lunch period while me and Bri did our own thing." Frankie looked over to Sabrina.

"We keep each other busy," she replied, speaking more to herself than to anyone. She kept her eyes on the cars in front of her. "Do you think—I don't know if this is weird to ask, but—will your parents let you come back to De La Salle? It was Mr. Medina's idea for you to go to North Shore, right?"

I sucked in a breath. The one thing I used to always dream about hadn't crossed my mind once since the incident. My focus had shifted to Mr. Medina's case, and to leave the one place he worked so hard for me to get into . . .

"It feels like that would be a bit disrespectful at this point."

"Yeah. Yeah, you're right." She caught my eye in her rearview, forcing herself to smile.

"Hey. We still have our Friday-night hangouts. And you know I have no problem skipping class to grab new cases." My words were more for me than her. With Mr. Medina gone, it was like I'd lost one of the last threads tying me to my old life before North Shore. I still had my investigations with Frankie and Sabrina, though at times, it felt like that was slipping away, too. We didn't do nearly as many cold cases as we used to.

The three of us slipped into random small talk for the rest of the ride, with Frankie shuffling through his dad's Spotify playlist of Carrie Underwood; Earth, Wind & Fire; and BTS. (Pops had range.) A half hour later, we managed to find parking on the street, miraculously.

"This is what he left the South Side for?" Frankie glanced up at the high-rise. The exterior was a mix of dark steel and frosted glass, modern luxury at its finest. A man in a charcoal-colored wool coat and white gloves held open the door as we walked in. The lobby was immaculate, accents of dark wood, gold, and black marble. We could see our reflections in the elevator doors, it was that shiny.

"This was Mrs. Medina's place before she married Mr. Medina. Her parents left it to her. I've been here a few times to go over North Shore's admission requirements with my parents." I pressed the button for the top floor.

"Oh, before we get up there—" Sabrina shimmied out of her coat. Underneath, she wore a tailored blazer over dark slacks. It was a little low-cut, but she was always the most fashion forward of us all. "Grams had gossip when I called her this morning. One of the conductors was suspended for the incident, but a city official helped him get a nice retirement package instead."

Frankie raised a brow. "That seems backward."

"She gave me the name; I typed it in my phone. I couldn't remember who you said the alderman was, Jo." She scrolled on her phone as the elevator opened.

Mrs. Medina was in the foyer, shaking hands with one of Illinois's state senators and his husband. She looked exquisite as always in her black lace ensemble, but she couldn't hide her blotchy cheeks and red eyes. I stared at the man standing next to her, greeting guests as they entered the loft. He wore a navy three-piece suit with a white rose tucked in his lapel, his coifed hair at a reasonable height.

"Alderman Corben," I muttered.

Sabrina looked up from her phone. "Yes, that's it!"

I nodded to where he stood with Mrs. Medina.

We stepped off the elevator, passing our coats to an attendant, and within moments the alderman had his hand out to greet us. "Miss Kelley, we meet again!"

"Yes, yes we do." I shook his hand, pressing my lips together.

Mrs. Medina offered a polite smile as she pulled me in for a hug and a quick peck on the cheek before moving on to my friends. "Thank you all for coming."

"Of course, Mrs. Medina. If there's anything you need, well, anything we can help with—"

"That's sweet of you, Frankie. I'm so glad you all made it. I have a few things of Manuel's I think he would want you to have, but please, make yourself comfortable in the meantime." She gave my hand a quick squeeze before turning to greet the next batch of arrivals.

"So that's the same alderman?" Frankie asked as we moved into the main hall.

"Mm-hmm. Still thinking coincidence?"

"Convenient," Sabrina answered, waggling her brows. "And they do look pretty cozy."

Behind us, the alderman had his hand at Mrs. Medina's back again—this time right above her hip—whispering something in her ear.

"Reminds me of another Michelle Gray case."

I opened my mouth to respond, but Frankie pulled us away toward the food. "Let's grab a bite. Watch the room a little."

"Are you thinking the killer is here?" I darted my eyes around, ready to confront anyone looking sus.

"I'm thinking you're thinking you already have an idea

who it is. You know how we work. Figure out motivations, create a pool of suspects, then whittle them down one by one using means and opportunity."

I sighed, letting myself relax a little. "Fine."

"You guys eat. I'm going to go gossip with the neighborhood aunties." Sabrina walked off toward the edge of the loft where the sliding glass windows faced a snow-covered terrace. She joined the two women who stood there, huddled close together, whispering excitedly with red wine in hand.

Everything looked how I remembered it from the last time I was here. Myrrh- and chrism-scented candles made the Medinas' home smell like a cathedral. Dark hardwood ran the length of the space, lush sofa chairs and mahogany side tables strategically placed. Abstract paintings in gilded frames covered the walls while crystal chandeliers hung from the fifteen-foot ceiling. Today, a long table ran through the center of the loft filled with fancy hors d'oeuvres that looked questionable at best, and a few dishes inspired by Mr. Medina's Spanish heritage. The night I was here last, he had made us his mother's paella—crispy rice, mussels, and saffron. Whatever this soupy rice dish was in front of me, it was not paella.

"What are you thinking about?" Frankie piled his plate high with bacon-wrapped scallops and cucumber slices with salmon mousse.

I cringed at the pink mush. "Do you know what that is?"

"No," he replied, popping one in his mouth. "But Deputy Mayor Khara's wife has been throwing these back like ballpark peanuts with her pinkie high in the air. Gotta blend in."

I rolled my eyes, sticking to the fruits and cheese as we walked around for a while.

"Think they have a library here?" Frankie asked. "It's probably filled with all his old mysteries."

"It's down the hall."

Right as I said that, Mrs. Medina snatched her arm away from the alderman, stomping off in that very direction. Visibly annoyed, he followed not too far behind her.

Frankie noticed it, too. "Well, I'll give it to you. That's—"

"Suspicious," I finished.

"She could just be overwhelmed with all the people." He shrugged. "Could be nothing."

"Could be," I muttered. It took all my effort not to follow after the two of them.

Sabrina took that opportunity to waltz back over, breaking my view as Mrs. Medina slipped out of sight on the other side of the room. "The aunties had all the tea as usual. They think Mrs. Medina moved on *way* too fast. Apparently, she and *Jay* knew each other in school, former flames. They had some opinions about his presence here."

"I mean he's an alderman, right? Don't they make sure all their constituents are happy? Maybe he's just helping a new widow through a tough time. She doesn't have any other family here to comfort her."

Sabrina and I both glared at Frankie.

"He's too touchy," I huffed.

"And he's trying to make her *too* happy," Sabrina added.

"Okay, okay. I just want to make sure we're looking at it from all angles," he surrendered, but not before downing a cracker with a vibrant orange smear across it. "Oh, you gotta try that one. It tastes like the ocean."

The three of us settled for walking around a little more, looking at all the pictures Mrs. Medina had out on display of her husband. I found myself constantly checking the entryway. No one else from Kershaw had shown up, or Englewood for that matter. And there were no other students from North Shore. Only me. I did recognize a few state politicians, other aldermen, and the CPD's bureau chief. But where was everyone else? All those lives he'd touched?

"This feels less like a memorial service and more like a city officials' social hour," I mumbled.

"You're not wrong," Frankie replied, somewhat distracted. He eyed the food display as if deciding whether he had room for more. He always had room.

Sabrina bumped my hip with hers. "At least we're here."

"I guess." I stopped walking and stared at a photo of Mr. Medina with some of his old friends at a Cubs game. He had a wide grin, his hair tied up, and was wearing one of those fake tuxedo shirts with the printed bow tie.

"I'm going to miss that man bun," Sabrina whispered.

The corner of my mouth tipped up. "At North Shore, the faculty dresses more formal, but he always had on sneaks with his slacks and tie. The dean hated it."

"He did teach us a bit about style along with how to solve a mystery," Frankie quipped, popping the collar of his suit jacket.

Sabrina pressed his collar back down. "Sweetie, no. That style died a decade ago."

I stifled a laugh. It felt good to smile, yet weird since we were in a room full of strangers. It was a small reminder that Mrs. Medina was new to her husband's life. I couldn't fault her for not knowing his past, but it nagged at me. She could've asked someone, leaned on some of his friends that she did know. Instead, she had turned to the alderman.

"Why don't you go see what you can find?" Sabrina nudged me toward the hallway, interrupting my thoughts.

I frowned. "You sure? You don't mind me snooping at a funeral?"

"We know you have a theory ruminating in that head of yours, and you won't stop until you figure it out. Go snoop," Frankie added before biting into another orange-smeared cracker.

At that moment, Alderman Corben walked back into the main room and tapped a small knife to his glass, gathering the guests together. Mrs. Medina hadn't returned with him.

Speeches without the widow?

I didn't wait any longer. I nodded to a few people as I moved to the back of the crowd. Once I was sure everyone's attention was on the alderman, I slipped into the hall without a sound.

It didn't take long to get to the library. It was the dream of any bibliophile. Hundreds of volumes shelved on antique white bookcases lined with gold filigree. It felt very *Beauty and the Beast*–esque. I'd be lying if I said I didn't want to hop up onto one of the sliding ladders and channel my inner Belle.

"Like it?"

Startled, I turned to find Mrs. Medina patting the corner of her eye with a dark handkerchief. "I used to joke with Manuel that he married me for my books. My father had a first edition of *The Hound of the Baskervilles*."

"Mr. Medina's favorite," I said. "You might be right. This library is beautiful." My eyes flitted from shelf to shelf. Pure heaven. I turned back to Mrs. Medina as she watched me with a hint of smile. I twirled my fingers at my lap. "Sorry for wandering—"

"Here," she interrupted, setting off toward the other side of the library. "These are his."

Following behind her, I passed so many shelves. Book after book, memory after memory, it all flooded back. Reading and tracking all the clues in each story, trying to guess the killer before reaching the end of the novel.

"Do you want them?" We'd reached the bookcases filled with antique volumes. Mrs. Medina gestured to three of the four Sir Arthur Conan Doyle masterpieces.

I tried to keep my jaw from dropping. All three, first editions. "I couldn't—"

"I think he'd want you to have them. I can have them couriered to your home tomorrow."

I stammered, "You—you don't have to do that."

"Yes, I do." She pressed the handkerchief to her nose before speaking again. "I think I mentioned how he spoke so highly of you and your friends. The first cohort of young Englewood detectives. It meant a lot for him to be able to create a safe space for students to gather after school. Away from outside influences."

My eyes glinted over the books, and I stepped closer to the shelf. "*The Hound of the Baskervilles* is missing."

"I believe he kept it at the school for your club?"

I froze, almost teetering back on my heel.

"You all met so often in those last few weeks. But he said you and Julius loved it, and we both know how much Manuel enjoyed sharing his mysteries."

Julius? My thoughts went straight to the swarm of papers flying around Mr. Medina at the train platform. "Julius James?"

"Yes. He was there with you two, wasn't he? I know I saw him waiting in Manuel's office a few late afternoons."

I stood there with no words.

There was no mystery book club at North Shore. But looking at Mrs. Medina right now, barely holding it together as she pulled her black lace shawl around her shoulders, I couldn't tell her that.

But why would Mr. Medina lie about it? And how was *Julius James* involved in all this?

"Yeah," I finally answered. "Of course."

She traced her husband's face in a nearby glass picture frame. Flipping over the photo, she removed it and handed it to me. "I think he'd want you to have this, too."

Frankie and Sabrina stood on either side of me and Mr. Medina, all of us dressed as characters from Clue for Halloween. I was Colonel Mustard. Mr. Medina was Mrs. Peacock.

"Thank you." My gaze traveled back to the bookcases. So many memories. "Do you mind if I look around a bit more?"

"Take your time. Anything you or your friends want, let me know."

"Actually . . ." I paused. I couldn't stop thinking about the gossip Sabrina shared: Mrs. Medina and the alderman as former flames. "Alderman Corben, is he—was he a friend of Mr. Medina's?"

"Jay? I've known him for quite some time." There was a light smile on her lips, her eyes glossed as if she was lost in a memory. "He's always been there for me. Like you have Frankie and Sabrina."

"Right." I frowned. She hadn't answered my question.

"He's been a tremendous help. It might sound insensitive of me but . . ." She took in a breath. "I just need to move through this. Him stepping in to make sure the city's investigation went along smoothly, being able to just have my husband's ashes to give him a proper goodbye—" Her voice wavered.

"Oh." *They rushed the investigation on purpose? The two of them?*

"You just come find me if you need anything, okay?" Another light smile and she turned back to join the others at the memorial.

Her heels clacked softly against the hardwood as she left, and I waited until they faded into nothingness. Her response left me with a pit in my stomach. The Medinas' marriage had looked perfect on the outside. But now all I could think about were the photos she had laid out, her tears—was any of it real?

Pressure built up inside me, and I wiped my eyes, grateful for waterproof eyeliner. Being here, in Mr. Medina's home, with everything Mrs. Medina just said, it was overwhelming.

I leaned against one of the shelves. *Inhale, exhale. Now focus on why you're here.*

I looked to the bookcases surrounding me. There were so many. A back shelf held old yearbooks and encyclopedias while another held memoirs and nonfiction. I searched around the library for anything out of place—anything that could give me a single clue as to why Mr. Medina was dead—and why Alderman Corben was here in his place. He might've grown up with Mrs. Medina, but I'd seen photos of her younger years around the loft. He wasn't in any of them.

Another book sat on an end table, a historical romance with a thick piece of card stock sticking out of the top. Curious, I flipped open the volume to find not a bookmark but the business card of a divorce attorney.

Thomas Mitchell

President, Mitchell & Mitchell

Divorce and Family Law

(309) 929-9014
www.mmdivorceattorneys.com

"Well, crap."

I hurried back to the main room as quickly as I could in Reya's heels, and found Frankie where I'd left him, along with a brown-haired boy flirting shamelessly with Sabrina. "We need to go."

"You missed some of the speeches." Frankie was still eating, having moved on to the mini desserts.

"Now." I tugged at Sabrina to follow and led the way to the coat check. The back of my neck tingled, the prickling stare of eyes following us down the hall.

"Did something happen?" she asked, slipping on her faux fur.

"We can talk outside," I muttered.

"Leaving so soon?" Alderman Corben approached, his politician smile fixed on his face.

"Yes!" I winced. *That was a bit too loud.* "Yes. Please tell Mrs. Medina we appreciated her hospitality."

"Of course." He shook each of our hands in turn. "Remember if you need anything, don't hesitate. The Medinas and the Salvatores have long served this great city, and any friend of theirs is a friend of mine."

I cringed at his touch and slipped my hand from his grip. I managed another thank-you before booking it to the exit.

"Are you going to tell us what has your Spanx in a bunch?" Sabrina asked as I called the elevator, pressing the down button far more times than was required.

"I found a business card for a divorce attorney," I whispered.

She gasped. "You really snooped?! At a funeral?"

"You told me to! And were you not flirting? With a boy? Which is weird, but whatever you like. Safe space."

"He's the alderman's son, home for a long weekend from Yale. I was *trying* to get info for your affair theory. But he said his dad really is old friends with Mrs. Medina."

The elevator doors opened, and in my rush to leave, I ran right smack into whoever was stepping off. "Dang, sorry about that." I bent to grab the bouquet of calla lilies the stranger dropped.

"No need, I got it."

Straightening back up, I stepped into the elevator and mashed the lobby button. I didn't notice the stranger's head of dark curls and black suit until the doors began to shut.

Wait. Is that Julius? I tried to catch the door but was too late. *What was he doing here?*

Sabrina poked me in my side. "He was cute."

Ignoring her, I mashed the lobby button a few more times until we found ourselves back downstairs. I could worry about Julius later. For now, I just needed to get away from the alderman. Shaking the hand of Mrs. Medina's boyfriend at her husband's funeral left me feeling slimy.

"Frankie, can you google Mitchell and Mitchell? It should be a law firm."

A few swipes of his phone, and he had the homepage pulled up. "It's a husband-wife team of divorce attorneys." He scrolled through a few more pages. "They have a Facebook page."

I looked over his shoulder. "People follow law firms on Facebook?"

He navigated to the photo gallery. "Looks like they had a gala last fall for their twenty-year anniversary . . . and look who's in attendance."

The alderman's creepy bleached-white smile stared up at me.

"Why is he everywhere?"

He shrugged. "Rich people often move in tight circles."

I took in a few breaths to calm myself. An affair . . . ? Could that mean Mrs. Medina was involved in her husband's death? My gut instinct was no, but I couldn't be sure anymore.

I nodded to Frankie's phone. "The alderman is the reason the case closed so quickly. Mrs. Medina, she said he was helping make sure the investigation ran smoothly so she could go ahead and pick up Mr. Medina's ashes."

"If he and Mrs. Medina are having an affair, that would give him a reason to get the case closed. They could move on together, keep people from snooping around, and avoid a scandal. He *is* on the city council," said Sabrina.

"Yeah, but does that explain what you saw on the platform, Jo? Does an affair give him motive to kill Mr. Medina?" Frankie questioned.

"I mean, we've seen it in our cold cases. There are so many things politicians will do to avoid losing their power. But in this instance here, I don't know . . ." I trailed off, replaying everything I'd witnessed at the memorial. I took another breath as my heart raced. This case felt different—real. This was someone I knew. I didn't have the luxury of being wrong. The police already closed the case. I only had one chance to prove them wrong.

"Another thing." I pulled on my coat and tied the scarf around my neck. "Mr. Medina told his wife we had book club meetings at North Shore."

"Y'all had a club without us?" Sabrina asked.

"There's no club, Bri." Frankie sighed.

"Oh. Why would he lie about that?"

"I think I see where you are going with this, Jo, but we need to slow down."

"He was hiding something. Maybe he knew about the affair? Planned to out them—"

"Jo."

"Frankie."

"Sabrina," Sabrina chimed in.

"Look, he was near the police station, during school hours, with a bunch of files. I'll admit that the card for the divorce attorney and the alderman's behavior is worth investigating, but we can't breeze past the first part," Frankie challenged.

I sighed, picturing the hurricane of papers flying through the air. "No, you're right."

"I know," Frankie said, popping his collar only for Sabrina to once again fold it down.

"We need to break into his office at school," I continued.

"That's not what I—"

I started toward the door leading outside. "If he was hiding something from his wife, he might've kept it there. I'll work on getting a copy of the police report in the meantime."

"Reya will get it for you?" Sabrina hurried behind me.

The wind whipped my face as the doorman let us out into the Chicago cold. "I'll ask her, but I'm probably going to need to figure out a way to get it on my own."

"Hey." Sabrina pulled me to the side, taking out a tissue to dab the corner of my eye. "Your eye makeup is smudged a little. Are you sure something else didn't happen? I feel like you're moving too fast."

I swatted her hand away. "I'm fine."

"Jo—"

"Sabrina." Steeling myself, I met her gaze with a lie on my lips. "I. Am. Fine."

SIX

MONDAY MORNING, I found myself standing in front of the state attorney's office with two ice-cold French toast Frappuccinos, one of which had an extra sprinkle of cinnamon dolce powder. It didn't take long for me to navigate to Reya's quiet office, eager to defrost my hands with her space heater.

"Knock, knock," I announced, setting her favorite morning wake-me-up in front of her.

Her eyes lit up. "Ooh . . . wait, did you go to the one where Stefan works?"

"He gave you extra cinnamon and two pumps of hazelnut."

She hesitated for a moment before opening her drawer to

grab her metal straw. "Who am I to deny such a gift." She let herself indulge in a long sip. "Mmm. Are you skipping today?"

"Nope, I still have—" I checked my watch. "Thirty minutes before late bell. I realized I never properly thanked you for taking me to give my statement the other day." I sat in the seat across from her, balancing my drink at the edge of her desk.

"That's sweet of you. I thought you might've been mad at me after Saturday night's conversation—the whole 'me saying no when you asked for Mr. Medina's case file' thing."

I squirmed in my seat. She wasn't wrong. "I know you're just looking out for me. Mom's right, I guess. I need to move on," I lied.

She reached her hands across her desk to hold mine. "I'm so sorry about the case."

"I know." Still, I didn't let myself meet her eyes. Instead, I stared at the photo of us she kept in the corner, both of us decked out in green wearing too many shamrock-themed accessories for last year's Saint Patrick's Day.

I hated having to do this, but I needed that file.

As I turned back to her, my hand managed to knock my eight-dollar frappé to the ground. "Oh! Crap, sorry."

"Don't worry about it." Reya was already on the floor, patting up some of the mess with her stash of recycled take-out napkins. "Let me grab some paper towels from the bathroom." She stepped over the spill in her nude stilettos, making her way down the corridor.

I tapped my fingers against my leg, counting out five more beats before sliding myself into her seat, wiggling the mouse for her computer to come alive. "You got two minutes, Jo," I muttered to myself.

I typed in a few password guesses, managing it on my third try, using her usual formulas. "ReyaHeartsElena-4ever" for the win. Very elementary, but Reya was a sucker for romance.

I scrolled through her email, opening the most recent message from Lieutenant Charles.

From: Charles, Wendell
Sent: Friday, February 25, 10:44 a.m.
To: Morales, Reya
Subject: CPD CASE 35BRZ0207

Ms. Morales,

While I appreciate Jamila Kelley and her daughter reaching out, the investigation has already been completed. There was no evidence of foul play and the testimony of other witnesses, including the rail conductor, corroborated this. Please find my final report attached.

—WTC

Lieutenant Wendell Theodore Charles Jr.

Office of Constitutional Policing & Reform

Chicago Police Department

What? How did the conductor's statement not *point to foul play? Is this why Alderman Corben helped to get him a retirement package? A bribe to close the case?*

Not having time to react to the email, I forwarded the file to myself, erased the sent mail, and swooped down to clean up the rest of the spilled frappé.

Moments later, Reya stepped back into the room. "Oh, looks like you got most of it up."

I grabbed the paper towels from her hands and soaked up the last bits of the hazelnut-and-cinnamon concoction. "Well, at least your office smells like your favorite drink." I grinned.

She inhaled, her smile growing. "Yum. I should find some candles in this scent. Hey, I can walk you to the corner and buy you another."

"No, no need. I don't want to take advantage." The words stung.

My phone pinged.

"My Lyft is outside." I wrapped Reya in a hug. "Thank you."

"Always, Jo. I'll swing by tonight for dinner. Your mom said she's making Nana Josette's smothered pork chops and brown sugar apples."

My mouth watered. We might not have the best mother-daughter relationship, but her cooking? Couldn't argue with that.

By the time I slipped into the rideshare, guilt choked my neck like a yoke.

I scrolled back through my phone, rereading the conversation I had had with Reya Saturday night, after the memorial.

Reya:

I don't think sending you the report is a good idea . . .

Jolene:

Why not? You share files with me all the time.

Reya:

For your cold cases. You shouldn't investigate when it's personal. There are too many emotions involved.

Jolene:

I'm not going to seek revenge or anything, c'mon, Rey.

Reya:

You didn't see the daggers you were throwing at that lieutenant w/ your stare. If looks could kill . . .

Reya:

I know you're not the revenge type, but I can see you telling Mrs. Medina to not let his son into NS.

> **Jolene:**
> . . . I didn't think about that. Great idea.

> **Reya:**
> JOLENE OLIVIA KELLEY

> **Jolene:**
> jk jk (probably)

> **Reya:**
> Wait, what was that "probably"?

> **Reya:**
> Jo?

> **Reya:**
> Chica, don't leave me on read!

Abusing Reya's trust and friendship wasn't anything I wanted to do again.

It left me sick.

After that, school was rough, to say the least. Sabrina messaged that she tried to deliver cookies on Sunday to the rail conductor under the guise of a present from her grams, only to find out the guy had already started his retirement—in Florida.

And Frankie had actually managed to hack the CTA surveillance like he said he would, but there was nothing on the security cameras aside from a pixelated blur of movement that no amount of Photoshop could sharpen.

I went back and forth between wanting to open the email and find the conductor's statement in the attachments, to wanting to ask Frankie or Sabrina to do it for me. I remembered the flashbulbs of forensic cameras at the train platform, the pictures taken before the white cloth went on. Those would be in the file.

I threw up a little thinking about it.

AP Spanish was the usual bore. I was the only sophomore in the class, but with Reya speaking Spanish to me since I was three, I had breezed through the prerequisite exam. In the back of class, Madison Ryan, North Shore's own version of Cheryl Blossom, gossiped with her minions. If they didn't look so much alike, I would never have known Maddie was the youngest daughter of the police's bureau chief—soon-to-be police superintendent if everything went his way. Their family came from old money, and Chief Ryan could probably have coasted on that, but he chose a blue-collar job anyway. Where he treated others around him with a kind heart, Maddie acted as though she was auditioning for the role of the one-dimensional nineties mean girl. But both had the same porcelain skin, deviously dark blue eyes, and thick brown hair they consistently dyed a frosted blond. If only personalities were hereditary, too.

Swiping open my screen, I stared at the list of afterschool activities on North Shore's website for the hundredth time. No mystery book club. I knew there wasn't one, but I kept checking. Mr. Medina's lying to his wife didn't make sense if *she* was the one being unfaithful. And the card for the divorce attorney was in one of her books, not his.

I'd worked up my own convoluted motive: The alderman killed Mr. Medina over his wife. But there were holes in my theory. How did they both end up at that station? Based on the alderman's business card, Thirty-Fifth and Bronzeville was three stops from his office, and it was even farther for Mr. Medina. And like Frankie said, Mr. Medina had all those files with him. They swirled in the wind as he fell, adding chaos to the hell unfolding.

Then there was Julius James. His name was in the files, and Mrs. Medina mentioned him as being part of the non-existent club. How did he play into everything?

"He's dead. Don't worry about it."

I stiffened before realizing the words weren't directed at me. My ears perked up. It was Maddie's voice.

"I have my acceptance letter to Brown," she continued with a smug tone. "And you're good with Yale. We got in early decision like we planned. Antonio got the short end having to wait until April to confirm if they're going to New Haven with you and Sheetal."

"But what about—"

"Let's not talk about that here, Nat. Scum might be listening."

I turned my head to meet Maddie's eyes. Her lips twitched up into a smirk.

"He's dead. Don't worry about it."

What the hell did that mean?

A low hum broke me away from her stare. A text.

Sabrina:

Anything?

Right. She and Frankie were waiting on news about the police report.

Jolene:

I haven't opened the email yet.

Sabrina:

We understand. We're moving really fast with this. We can stop and breathe for a minute. It's only been a week.

I let out a breath, shutting my eyes as I leaned back in my chair. *She doesn't get it.*

Jolene:

The longer we take, the colder the case gets.

Sabrina:

Sweetie . . .

Frankie:

It's fine, Jo. So, what's next?

The bell rang, and Maddie stood to leave. *He's dead,* she had said.

Jolene:

You made a good point after the memorial. We need to figure out why Mr. Medina was at the train platform with those files.

Frankie:

So we're going to do it? Break into his office?

Frankie:

And just to go on the record, the B&E was NOT my idea.

Frankie:

But I'm game.

I switched back to the North Shore events page. The varsity basketball team had a home game tonight against Lake Forest. I snapped a screenshot and sent it to the group chat.

Jolene:

You always said you wanted a tour of the school. Tonight seems like a good night.

When my last class ended, I still had four hours before Frankie and Sabrina arrived. Four hours to do one of my favorite things: snoop.

I paced the halls in front of Mrs. Medina's office, but the crowd of students never thinned out enough for me to try to get inside. Her office was dark, but I managed to spot pictures of her and Mr. Medina all over her desk and on the shelves behind it, along with a calendar with yesterday's date circled.

Would she have those pictures up still if she was moving on with Alderman Corben?

I leaned against a locker, tapping my thigh. *How do you prove an affair?*

I unlocked my phone and navigated to my Favorites. "I need help," I admitted to Sabrina as FaceTime connected.

"Frankie and I will be there in a few hours. Unless you want us to come earlier? Do you need to talk?"

"No, not that." I sighed. "I'm blanking on how we can go about proving this whole affair thing. Usually, couples are caught in the act, right? We don't have that type of evidence. And unless Mr. Medina is hiding photos from a PI he hired, I don't think we're going to be able to get it."

"Oh. Well, we do the same thing I did at the memorial. We chat up the right people. Gossip makes the world go round—or destroys it. Depends on the occasion."

I stopped pacing. *Chat up the right people.* I pulled the alderman's card out, tracing the letters of his address. "Can you give me a quick lesson?"

Sabrina grinned. "I've been waiting for this moment. Jolene Kelley, welcome to the dark side."

Within thirty minutes I found myself downtown. It felt a little weird not having Sabrina with me, but I couldn't wait. And it wasn't like last year when we could easily just hop on the CTA together after class. I had to do this on my own.

The office space of an alderman turned out to be much fancier than expected. It looked a bit like an HGTV special—without the allure of six-foot-four twin brothers. The walls were the same signature navy blue the alderman wore, the ceilings and baseboards a stark white. Gold light fixtures crisscrossed above me in an elaborate geometric pattern while bamboo hardwood ran the length of the floor beneath my feet. The space was scented heavily with French vanilla. And this was just the lobby. I could only imagine what the offices held.

A text alert went off in my pocket, and I peeked at the screen before turning it on silent. A message from Sabrina, outside of our usual group chat.

Sabrina:

I just realized—you aren't going to go talk to anyone alone, are you? We always go in pairs and we NEVER approach our suspects. You don't need to rush this.

Sabrina:

Jo?

I slid my phone back into my coat.

"Can I help you?" An older woman wearing a blush tweed blazer over a pale pink blouse sat behind the reception desk. Her tortoiseshell frames balanced precariously at the end of her sharp nose.

My goal was easy enough: chat up the alderman's receptionist to see if she'd let anything of interest slip. I'd watched Sabrina do it dozens of times, and her tips were simple: stay engaged, focus on one topic, and smile.

Here's hoping Alderman Corben hired a gossiper.

I started with the smile. "I'm hoping you can help me with—"

"Miss Kelley!" The alderman's voice filled the space as he turned around the corner in his usual attire. His dark hair was gelled up into another pompadour with extra height. "I'm off to a late lunch, but what can I help you with?"

I found myself wondering how many suits he had in the same color before realizing I hadn't planned to speak to him directly. My cheeks grew hot. I had half a mind to send up a prayer asking: What Would Sabrina Do? "Hi, yes—"

"Hold that thought." He tapped on the face of his watch before pressing his AirPods into his ears. "Hello? John! I was just about to call. Charlotte, put Miss Kelley on my calendar. I have to take this call. But we'll talk. I said to reach out if you needed anything, and I meant it. I keep my promises." He winked at me, then continued out the door, talking as loudly as ever.

Charlotte placed the mail she was sorting to the side—a pile of bills, something from the transit authority, a letter from the governor's office, and other junk—and pulled out one of those spiral planners. "Now, let's see here."

"He seemed like he was in a rush," I started, *relieved*, and leaned onto the elevated counter of her desk. "And he's looking exceptionally sharp today. Dressed to impress. Must be a lunch date."

"Oh, not today, but he is ever the charmer." She nodded to the fresh flower arrangement next to her. "Those were just because he wanted to make me smile this week." She beamed.

"Wow." I gave the flowers an exaggerated sniff. I knew I would hate the smell, but it felt like a Sabrina thing to do. "I can only imagine how he treats his lucky someone."

"Well." Charlotte looked around before lowering her voice. "Every Tuesday, he and the missus have their standing late lunch. Thursdays he sends her a single rose—"

It couldn't be that easy. I coughed. "I'm sorry. Did you say 'the mistress'?"

"God, no!" Her face twisted in horror. "The *missus*. His wife, Samantha."

"Oh." *Dang, need a quick rebound.* "That's so sweet of him. Does she ever come here to visit him?"

"Mm-hmm." She motioned for me to come closer. "When she pops up here, I have to tune them out. These walls are thin if you catch my—"

I held up a hand. I didn't want to catch her drift or any drift.

"He seems like a passionate man," I managed to get out without gagging. The visual—I was struggling with the visual. "Mrs. Medina said he helped her a lot after her husband's death."

"Yes, that was so unfortunate. As soon as he heard about it, he was at her side. Childhood friends and all."

"So I've heard." I drummed my fingers against the desk. I needed more than that. "Did she ever come around?"

"Mrs. Medina?"

I nodded.

"No, can't say that she ever did. Last week was the first time I'd heard her name in quite some time. But let me stop gossiping and get you a spot on his schedule."

She flipped to later this week, pulling a silver pen out of her gray top bun. "Let's see, you have the North Shore colors peeking out from under your coat. Blue plaid skirt and that vibrant orange sweater. They let out at three, correct?"

I nodded again.

"How about two Thursdays from now, the tenth?" She started penciling me in before I could respond.

"I guess that works." My mind churned, the alderman's schedule within my reach. "Can I ask you a favor?"

She tucked the pen back into her hair. "Whatcha need, dear?"

"My friend Frankie, he's really into city politics. Dreams of becoming the mayor one day. He goes to De La Salle."

"Well, that's a good start! A few mayors have come from there," she noted.

"Yes! Exactly. He's been trying to take pictures with all the aldermen for his scrapbook, and he claimed he took a photo with Alderman Corben last week at an event. But I say it wasn't him. He didn't have on his signature blue." I pointed to the walls.

"He loves his power suit. Let's see. What was the date?"

"February twenty-first." I held my breath as she flipped back to the day of Mr. Medina's murder in her planner.

FEB 21

MONDAY

8	
9 9:30 AM-12:00 PM	1 1:00 PM-2:00 PM
Press Conference	Lunch with Council
10 for John Ryan at	2 at Lou Mitchell's
McCormick Place	
11	3
No Driver	4 4:00 p.m.
12 ↓ Needed	Private Alumni Dinner,
Evening	5 Northwestern University
	Driver Requested

TUESDAY

"He could've gotten it! The event went long because Chief Ryan was over an hour late to his own show. But if Mr. Corben wasn't in that power suit, he might want to take a better picture." She reached up to her hair. "I can pencil him in—"

"No need! I'll let him know. He'll be happy with your confirmation."

I gave a wave as I turned to leave. The press conference was set to start right around the time Mr. Medina was pushed. And with the details Charlotte just overshared about the alderman's marriage, an affair was seeming more and more unlikely. It was too weak a theory with no concrete evidence. I was walking down the wrong path.

I looked down to my watch. Three more hours until the game and I had no other leads.

You're missing something, Jo. And it's right in front of you.

SEVEN

LATER THAT NIGHT, my two best friends pulled up to one of the most prestigious private schools of the Midwest in a Volkswagen minibus decked out with a paint job reminiscent of an assorted neon highlighter pack.

Sabrina squealed as she hopped out the passenger seat. "This place is giving me such *Truly Devious* vibes. Fancy kids, dark secrets . . ."

"Won't argue with you there. Hey, Aiko!"

Aiko waved through the open door. With her black tresses braided into a crown and expertly painted red lips, she was the only person I knew who rivaled Sabrina's fashion sense. They were perfect together.

"Don't get arrested," she yelled over as Frankie slid out

the side door. The minibus sputtered off down the driveway as we turned back to walk inside the school.

"You never mentioned you went to school in a castle," Sabrina whispered, shrugging off her faux fur.

"No big deal." I grabbed both their coats. "We can drop these in my locker. You brought your schoolwork?" I nodded at Frankie's backpack.

"Laptop. Thought I could poke around and see if I can access Mr. Medina's school computer through the Wi-Fi while you two look for physical evidence. It's a reach, but it won't hurt."

"Not a bad idea. All right, let's get to it."

We passed Mr. Medina's office, but too many students still wandered the halls. We would have to wait in the gym for the hallways to empty once the game was further along. We continued through the main building and took a shortcut through the humanities and arts wing to get to the gym.

Ten minutes later, we were sitting in the back row of the home-team bleachers, our voices drowned out by the screech of sneakers against the polished court.

"Okay, the seats are filling up. I'm going to try to get into Mr. Medina's office now. It'll be quicker if I go alone since I'll draw less attention. Frankie, you can hop on the school Wi-Fi."

Sabrina dropped her bobby pins into my open palm. "You sure I shouldn't come with? I'm better at picking locks."

"I need you to eavesdrop on that group of girls down

there." I pointed to Maddie, Nat, and a bunch of the other minions whose names I could never remember. "The chick with the dark roots and blue eyes said something in Spanish class earlier. I think she was talking about Mr. Medina."

"Gossip. Love it. Meet by the concessions in fifteen, then?"

"Works for me." Frankie lifted his laptop screen, his fingers already flying.

"Hey." I turned back to Sabrina before leaving. "Watch what you say so you don't accidentally end up on her bad side. I've heard a few horror stories."

Sabrina nodded. "Got it."

Back in the administrative wing, I let the moonlight streaming in from the windows light my way. Finally reaching Mr. Medina's office door, I jiggled the pins into the keyhole, trying to catch the lock trap. Sabrina was right, she was way better at this.

"Well. This is interesting."

I cursed under my breath. Based on the voice, it had to be a student, so I wasn't too concerned. Ready to lie on the spot, I spun around to greet whoever had caught me.

My breath hitched. "You."

Dark curls fell over his almond-colored eyes as the corners of his mouth curved into the same lopsided smile I'd seen in his school photo. "Me," Julius replied. "I figured we would meet soon enough."

I stared at the boy in front of me, unsure what to make of him. He purposely stood in the shadows with only his face lit by the outside light. His bright eyes and white slit of a smile popped against his bronzed complexion. He looked every bit the bad boy, and a little voice in the back of my head told me to run.

Instead, I decided to interrogate him. "What are you doing here?"

"Not breaking into my mentor's office." He leaned against the wall, hands tucked into his sweatpants pockets. "I followed you. Mr. Medina's favorite teenage detectives reunited? Gotta admit, it piqued my curiosity."

"And you know about us because . . . ?"

"There's a photo of you all in matching sweaters inside his office. But you know that. You used to eat lunch here before Mr. Medina . . ."

"Was murdered," I finished his sentence. It was the first time I had said it out loud.

Julius nodded, not flinching at my words.

He agreed? Did he know what happened?

A key in his hand reflected bits of starlight. "You can pin your hair back up." He stepped forward, and I moved aside, letting him approach the door. Unlocking it, he flipped on the light switch. Mr. Medina's office sat untouched. The picture from our *Knives Out* adventure was still atop the set of drawers along the back wall, next to the photos of Mr. Medina and his wife and other kids he'd mentored over the years.

"How do you have a key?" It was one thing for him to follow me to Mr. Medina's locked office; it was another thing for him to happen to have a way inside. A thought crossed my mind—what if he was on his way here to snoop, too? Or remove evidence?

He propped himself up against the door frame as I wandered farther inside. "Work study. Sometimes Mr. Medina would have to leave me here to finish my filing, so I needed to be able to lock up."

"Work study? Isn't that like one step above suspension for students here?"

He shrugged, not answering my question.

After-school work study. That would align with the fake mystery book club he and I supposedly attended. Though it was still strange for Mr. Medina to lie about it.

I opened one of the drawers, and then another. "Are they all empty?"

"Mrs. Lawson had to assign his students to other counselors. Couldn't let the files sit."

"So, his computer?" I pressed the power button on the iMac only to be greeted with "Welcome" in five different languages. "The school wiped it."

Damn it.

"It's not that weird. The only reason his belongings are still here is because of Mrs. Medina. She's in Spain this week with his family."

My eyes caught on the blinking red light coming from the desk phone. I stared at the voice mail button, every inch of me wanting to press play.

He followed my stare. "I mean, if you aren't going to." Crossing the room in two smooth strides, he hit the flashing light.

"New voice mail for 309-929-2050 left on Sunday, February twentieth, at nine forty-seven p.m."

"That's his cell phone number," I muttered.

Julius shrugged. "He probably routed it here. He hardly ever answered his cell."

"Stay away from this," a man's voice rasped in the phone's speaker. "It's a losing battle. I mean it, Manuel. Don't think I won't do what's necessary to protect what's mine."

The phone clicked, and the voice operator cycled through the options of save and delete.

The man's voice had sounded familiar, though distorted. *If I could listen to it again with Frankie and Sabrina*—I reached over to forward the message to myself.

"What are you—" Julius swatted my hand away, causing it to slide across the dial pad.

"Message deleted."

"Damn it!" I fumed. "What was that for?"

"You don't want to get involved in that."

"That?" I pointed to the phone. "How do you know what *that* is?"

"I know that Mr. Medina died twelve hours later." He stared down at the floor, his lopsided grin from before now gone.

Frustrated, I took out my cell, quickly typing away what I could remember. "We could've given that to the police."

"Don't you think he tried that?"

I froze.

Of course. The station at Thirty-Fifth and Bronzeville is walking distance to police headquarters. We assumed he was there about the files he had on him, but maybe he wasn't. Maybe he was there because of this message.

The realization was a punch to the gut. *What did he get himself into?*

My gaze fell to the small bookcase. I flipped through the volumes, looking for something, anything. He had to have left a clue, a paper trail. My eyes caught on *The Hound of the Baskervilles* on the middle shelf. "You definitely know a lot about him," I replied, picking up the novel. *Too much, really.*

"I didn't share his love for mystery, but I make it a habit to know everything going on around me. People are quick to backstab and throw others under the bus. It's a different type of ruthless up here at North Shore. Honestly I preferred school on the South Side."

My mouth quirked up a little at his last comment. Feeling his stare on me, I squared my back to him and closed the book, my fingers grazing a raised edge on the inside back cover. Out slipped a USB. It was nothing more than a thin black strip, barely the size of a thumbnail. Small enough to be overlooked by anyone.

Except me.

"He loved a good hidden compartment," I mumbled to myself.

"Find something?"

"Nope." My phone vibrated. Time was up. I turned back around to face Julius. "Thanks . . . for ah, letting me in."

He nodded. "See you around? Maybe we can swap Mr. Medina stories."

I opened my mouth to reply with a quick *no* but hesitated. The way Julius's name kept popping up, his reaction to the voice mail—he knew something. My heart beat faster as everything inside me warned me not to cross this line. But it was too good an opportunity to pass up.

"I'd like that." I let my lips curve in a smile like Sabrina taught me. I needed to know what he knew. And his offer didn't come off as innocent as he might've believed. Maybe he was using me as well. *I can play that game, too.*

He flashed one last lopsided grin as I left the office.

Walking back to the gym, the threatening voice mail replayed over and over in my thoughts. The possessive tone and choice of words: "protect what's mine." The affair theory was all but dead at this point. Even if we paired the message with the card from the divorce attorney, there still wasn't enough evidence to make it true. The suspicions of the neighborhood aunties at the memorial wasn't proof.

But now we had whatever Mr. Medina had stored on the hidden flash drive.

Up ahead, Frankie already had two hot dogs smothered in yellow mustard and sport peppers, sandwiched in the bun with a pickle spear. He offered one to me. "No onions, just like you like it."

"Thanks." I took a bite. "Where's Bri?"

He nodded to her as she separated from Maddie and crew, a smile plastered on her face as she made her way to us. It dropped as soon as she was out of their range.

"Anything useful?" I asked.

"It was just a lot of bragging about the Ivy Leagues they're attending in the fall. Nothing big to note. She's bitchy like you said, though. One of the boys on the team dumped her. When I walked up, they were planning how to make his new crush's life a living hell. Basic ideas, but still."

"Brutal," Frankie said. "Well, my sleuthing was less eventful. I couldn't find Mr. Medina's computer on the Wi-Fi."

"Mm-hmm. And I know why. I found something in his office, but I think we should get back to my house first."

"I'll call a Lyft after I get another order of nachos." Frankie got back in line, leaving me alone with Sabrina. She pursed her lips together, watching Maddie and her friends.

I frowned. "Is something wrong? Did Maddie say some—"

Sabrina threw her hands up, cutting me off. "This place is *amazing*. Some of the classes those girls were talking about— did you know there's a textiles focus? Fashion, Jo. Your school teaches fashion! You've been so mad at your mom for making you transfer here and so focused on leaving—I'm surprised you haven't realized how good you have it. You have two parents emptying their savings to get you into the best school in Chicago. Have you looked at the chemistry coursework here? You could easily get into any school you wanted, study forensic science, and really rock the PI thing."

I shifted back and forth on my feet. Mr. Medina had made a similar point to me once. "How do you know what classes are offered at North Shore?"

"I might have peeked once or twice. I didn't know about your textiles department, though. And, I mean, I do like fashion, but working these cases with you two, that's my favorite. I just think you could take advantage of the school's opportunities a bit more."

I wrapped my arm around Sabrina and rested my head on her shoulder. "Yeah, maybe. Though this place is still missing you and Frankie."

"You don't need us as much as you think you do, Jo. We're still solving cases. Nothing is going to stop that."

Our moment was interrupted by Frankie crunching loudly on his nachos, throwing his arms over both our shoulders. "Y'all should get some chips before we go. The vendor said they're homemade."

I stifled a laugh. These were the moments I missed.

"I can't believe he defaced a first-edition *The Hound of the Baskervilles*," Frankie muttered as he examined the USB.

"I wouldn't say 'defaced.' The edge of the back flap was already kind of loose. He just wiggled it in."

"But why would he hide it in a book? And why that one?"

We sat in my room huddled around Frankie's laptop. I'd just finished recapping my failed stealth attempt and run-in with Julius.

Sabrina plucked the drive from Frankie's grip and plugged it in. "Won't know until we look."

A window popped up asking for a password.

"Damn." Frankie typed in a few attempts, failing each time. "Birthday, favorite sports team, favorite author . . ."

"Try 'Nicolette.' That's Mrs. Medina's first name. And their anniversary, I think it was this month." I went over to my planner, flipping through the pages. My mind flashed to the circled date on Mrs. Medina's calendar. "Wow, yesterday was their two-year."

"That's rough." Frankie typed in a few more combinations. "It's not the password, though."

We sat there for the next hour, a mixture of silence and randomly calling out password attempts. Nothing. "Well, it feels obvious, but he hid the drive in his favorite Sherlock book," Sabrina pointed out. "What was the inspector's name? Or maybe it's Dr. Watson?"

Favorite Sherlock. I thought on it. "Benedict Cumberbatch was his favorite Sherlock."

"True." Frankie tried another password and shook his head.

"I still think he ties with Robert Downey Jr.," said Sabrina. "He does the whole method-acting thing. That man is literally Tony Stark."

I rolled my eyes. "Back on topic—" I paused as Sabrina and Frankie delved into their own back-and-forth about RDJ's filmography.

"Come on, Bri. Did you see him in *Dolittle*?"

"Well, did you see him in *Tropic Thunder*?"

Benedict Cumberbatch, I thought to myself. Favorite Sherlock *and* favorite Avenger.

"Try 'Doctor Strange,'" I interrupted.

"I know for a fact it's not 'Doctor Strange,'" Sabrina countered.

"No." Frankie spun the screen around for us to see a bunch of file folders. "That was it. How'd you figure that?"

"Benedict Cumberbatch. Played his favorite Sherlock and his favorite Avenger. The book—he must've chosen it as a red herring. It would be easy enough for us or anyone to get lost in trying to connect *The Hound of the Baskervilles* with his password choice. That was pretty smart of him." I sat back down on the bed. "I don't think that many people would've guessed 'Doctor Strange,' though. Not even his wife. What was he trying so hard to hide?"

Frankie opened a few of the files, but it didn't seem like much more than student records, test scores, and college acceptance letters.

"These files over here are locked." He hovered his cursor over a folder with a padlock at its corner.

I stared at everything. They looked like the same papers fluttering about Thirty-Fifth and Bronzeville only a week ago. "Wait, go back." I pointed to Maddie's folder. "Click on her practice scores from last May. North Shore has this setup where you can take a practice exam in the guidance offices before the real one. Mr. Medina must've kept the records."

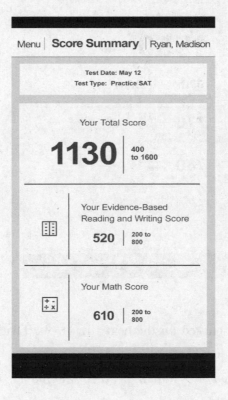

Menu | **Score Summary** | Ryan, Madison

Test Date: May 12
Test Type: Practice SAT

Your Total Score

1130 | 400 to 1600

Your Evidence-Based Reading and Writing Score

520 | 200 to 800

Your Math Score

610 | 200 to 800

"Huh, 1130. Not bad, but I thought you would need more to get into Brown," said Sabrina.

"A lot more," I agreed. "Now go to her June SAT scores."

Menu | **Score Summary** | Ryan, Madison

Test Date: June 5
Test Type: SAT

Your Total Score

1550

400 to 1600

99th
Nationally Representative
Sample Percentile

99th
SAT User
Percentile National

770 | 200 to 800
Your Evidence-Based
Reading and Writing Score

99th-99th+
SAT User Percentile—National

780 | 200 to 800
Your Math Score

99th-99th+
SAT User Percentile—National

Frankie clicked on the next file. "1550. That's a jump. But it's not just her."

He clicked on Natalia's file, then Antonio's.

My mouth dropped.

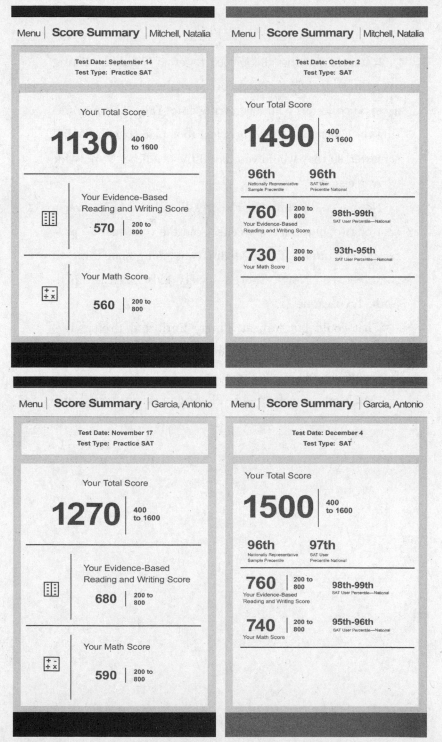

Test Date: September 14
Test Type: Practice SAT

Your Total Score

1130 | 400 to 1600

Your Evidence-Based Reading and Writing Score

570 | 200 to 800

Your Math Score

560 | 200 to 800

Test Date: October 2
Test Type: SAT

Your Total Score

1490 | 400 to 1600

96th
Nationally Representative
Sample Precentile

96th
SAT User
Precentile National

760 | 200 to 800

Your Evidence-Based
Reading and Writing Score

98th-99th
SAT User Percentile—National

730 | 200 to 800

Your Math Score

93th-95th
SAT User Percentile—National

Test Date: November 17
Test Type: Practice SAT

Your Total Score

1270 | 400 to 1600

Your Evidence-Based Reading and Writing Score

680 | 200 to 800

Your Math Score

590 | 200 to 800

Test Date: December 4
Test Type: SAT

Your Total Score

1500 | 400 to 1600

96th
Nationally Representative
Sample Precentile

97th
SAT User
Precentile National

760 | 200 to 800

Your Evidence-Based
Reading and Writing Score

98th-99th
SAT User Percentile—National

740 | 200 to 800

Your Math Score

95th-96th
SAT User Percentile—National

I started putting the pieces together. Maddie talking about how *it* didn't matter because she already had her acceptance letter. Natalia getting into Yale. Antonio getting the short end—Antonio's test took place late in the fall semester, so they would've missed the deadline to apply for early decision.

No one could jump their scores like this. Maybe over a year or two, but in a few weeks? And the voice mail—"protect what's mine." If Mr. Medina was doing something to come between North Shore's society kids and their path to the Ivy League . . .

That could put him at Thirty-Fifth and Bronzeville, hands full of evidence, ready to make their lives crumble. But someone took his life instead.

"Mr. Medina uncovered a college admissions test scam."

EIGHT

I STARED IN disbelief as Frankie continued to scroll through the student records on Mr. Medina's flash drive. Eight seniors had increased their test scores by hundreds in a matter of weeks. Ivy League scores.

"Ooo, it's the cute boy from the loft," Sabrina cooed.

Julius's photo flashed on the screen.

So that's how he fits in. He's in on the scam.

"So that's Julius," she continued. "His scores are different. There's only one, a 1600, but it's old. No practice scores, and nothing else in his file. How did they manage all this?"

I took the laptop from Frankie and clicked through the files again. "I mean, we can run through a hundred scenarios, but I'm thinking it has to be either someone hacking in and changing their scores, or the tests are being taken by another student. With a perfect score in the file, it has to be a hack job, right? But no one has ever hacked the College Board. It's impossible."

Frankie ran his hands over his head. "This is wild."

"It's not that weird. Scandals like this have happened before, right?" I opened all the different acceptance letters: Yale, Brown, Cornell, and Harvard. There were copies of each student's reference letter, Dean Lawson's signature on every single one.

"So, we're looking for a murdering Aunt Becky or a desperate housewife?" Sabrina questioned. "I'm not trying to make light, but, like Frankie said, this is wild."

Frankie paced. "Let's pause on the 'how' for a minute. What's the 'why'? Why fake test scores? You make it into the school, then what?"

"They do it for clout," I answered. "School reputation. Family reputation. You don't go to a school like North Shore and then go to some random state school."

"Is that enough to kill over, though?" Sabrina asked. "Is it motive?"

"The kids at school, they thrive because of their names and the power they hold. If Mr. Medina revealed something like this, it would destroy that. Destroy the school, too. It has to be someone with a lot to lose. Someone willing to kill for what they have. This has to be the reason Mr. Medina was killed. The voice mail said, 'Protect what's mine.'"

Frankie nodded. "Okay. Okay, let's run with that theory for a moment. So, Mr. Medina uncovers all this and does what?"

Sabrina chewed on her cheek. "Goes to the dean? Or maybe he starts lower? Goes to the proctor?" She pointed to a file with the proctors' schedule cross-referenced against test dates. The schedule for the last test was missing.

"Or he goes to the student he thought he knew." I pulled up Julius's photo again. "Julius had keys to Mr. Medina's office, and Mrs. Medina thought the three of us had an after-school club. Julius and Mr. Medina must've been close."

Frankie spun the laptop back around to face him. "Solid theory, but go back to the proctor for a minute. Look at this." He pointed to the screen. "Mr. Medina kept all the proctor schedules, aside from the last one. Six of the seven tests were taken at whatever location a teacher named Mr. Callahan was overseeing that day. Do you know him?"

"Yes, but we're not going to be able to talk to him. He taught English, but he didn't come back this semester. I've had a sub for Goth lit since after Thanksgiving break."

"Maybe Mr. Medina spooked him? He became unhinged?" Frankie rooted around the room. "Where's the whiteboard?"

"Closet." I jumped up to grab the markers. "Okay, suspect pool."

Frankie wrote down "Julius" and "Mr. Callahan." "What's the name of the dean?"

"Mrs. Lawson," I answered. "All the reference letters are from her, but she has an alibi for the murder. She was with Mrs. Medina that morning. So, no means or opportunity."

"Guys, look at all the students." Sabrina scrolled back through the files. "Sheetal Khara. Is she the deputy mayor's kid?"

I nodded. "And Natalia Mitchell. I'm guessing her parents are the divorce lawyers from that card I found in Mr. Medina's library. And Maddie's dad is Chief Ryan at CPD."

Frankie scribbled down all the names. "Tight circles. Half these parents were at the memorial service."

"I remember seeing Mr. and Mrs. Russell there. They run Chicago's chapter of Jack and Jill and sit on the school's board of directors. Their kids are Jhamal and Whitney." I pulled up the school photos of two kids with perfectly maintained dreadlock twists. "And I think Kehlani's family works in real estate, Pekelo Construction? I feel like I've overheard him mentioning it during AP Calc. They hold a lot of contracts in the city, and the Garcias are wrapped up in the state government. Antonio makes sure everyone knows that."

"These are all parents who would have a lot to lose if they were caught up in a scandal like this. And the kids definitely couldn't have done this alone." Sabrina swiped her phone screen, quickly typing in a Google search. "In a similar scandal a few years back, those tests went for ten thousand dollars apiece. Everyone here has motive."

"Wait, are we writing down the students *and* the parents for the suspect pool?" I asked.

"Yep." Sabrina went over to the board to add more names. "You said he was pushed during an argument. Heat of the moment. There's our means. Everyone is capable."

"But they knew to stay out of sight. That's planned, premeditated," I countered. "And there was the threatening voice mail."

"We have to consider both possibilities," Frankie settled.

"Got it." Sabrina capped the marker. "Most of the adults on this board are public figures. We can rule them out quickly with alibis, call and sweet-talk assistants for their schedules that day. And the students—think you can check attendance records, Jo? Classic spill and snoop?"

"I'll go by the administrative office first thing."

"Good," she said, sitting back down. "So, what do we think is in the locked file?"

Frankie scratched his chin. "Maybe it's something to do with the hacker or details on however they managed to pull this off? Or a money trail? Something Mr. Medina wanted to make sure no one would be able to erase."

I frowned. "Can you unlock it?"

"I can run a key on it, but it'll take a few days. I'll pitch a few hypotheticals to my dad in the meantime to see what he thinks would be the best approach. His job is basically him trying to hack government systems all day to test their security, so he should have some good tips. And if you two have other password ideas, text me. I can research the hacking theory while the key runs in the background. See if I can replicate it. If they found a way to hack the College Board . . ."

Sabrina and I nodded in agreement. I looked over our suspect pool. It was larger than any of the cold cases we'd worked in the past. Everything about this was different. But now we were one step closer. The motive was clear. Next up, opportunity.

NINE

TUESDAY, MARCH 1, 8:31 A.M.

WALKING INTO THE school's front office the next morning, I carried the most expensive coffee drink I'd ever purchased. Behind the first desk sat a pale man with a thin nose and high cheekbones. He dressed way too chic to be an administrative assistant and he knew it; he looked more like a collegiate professor in his fitted, light gray knit cardigan with brown leather patches on the elbows.

"Hey, Emile."

He didn't look up.

I cleared my throat. "Hey, Emile," I repeated a little louder.

He stopped typing. "Can I help you, Miss . . . ?"

I clenched my jaw. As many times as I've had to come

into the front office, he knew my name. "Jolene Kelley. You've helped me a few times. You know, when I come in late, and you switch my absence over to tardy." I placed the coffee in front of him. "This is for you. I noticed your push thingy broke."

He turned up his nose. "This is French press?"

"It's Starbucks."

He moved the drink to the far corner of his desk. "I guess it's the thought."

I swallowed my retort.

All I need is for him to sign in; then I spill the drink, and he runs off for towels.

The office was set up with Emile's desk out front and a frosted glass wall behind him to give privacy to the other admins sharing the space. No one would even notice me at his computer. Most of the other assistants were consumed in their own tasks, clacking away on their obnoxiously loud keyboards.

"I was hoping you could pull up my attendance record? My parents have been getting on me about—"

"Form B221."

"Excuse me?"

"There's a form for all administrative office requests. Attendance—B221."

"I was hoping you could—"

"No."

"But maybe—"

"No." He glowered.

This bi—

I walked around and snatched the drink back. "I thought we were friends, Emile." I eyed his *Vogue Paris* magazine as I walked back to the student side of the desk, taking note of his screensaver showing his partner and their Maltipoo. "Obviously, I was wrong." I stomped back into the main hall.

You give someone a little bit of power and they just—

"Bad morning?" Julius stood leaning against one of the marble busts that lined the hall.

I took him in for a moment before turning to leave the administrative wing. "Is that what you do? Lurk in corners and elevators waiting to bump into me?"

"So you did recognize me at the memorial service?" He fell in step beside me.

I rolled my eyes. "Here." I thrusted the drink into his hands.

He blew on the steam before taking a sip. It took less than a second for him to choke and for spittle to fly. "This is the most disgusting coffee I've ever tasted."

"Well, it was expensive, and it didn't work," I snipped.

"You seem upset, Kelley Green Eyes."

I stopped walking. "Who's Kelley Green Eyes?"

"You." He pushed his hair back, out of his face. "Green eyes are very rare, and you, while you try to move around unnoticed, have always stood out. Works in my favor, though. Mr. Medina asked me to look out for you, before . . ."

I narrowed my eyes, trying to decide what to make of what he said.

Is this flirting? Is this what guys do to flirt? Annoy their victim?

I opted for ignoring him. I continued a little ways before passing through the glass corridor to the science and mathematics wing. I might actually be on time to AP Calc this morning.

After walking in silence—Julius following, not taking the hint—curiosity got the best of me. "When did he ask you that? To look out for me."

He smiled in my peripheral. "When you first started. It was a bit hard—seniors don't have that many classes with sophomores—but you take a lot of AP classes, so that means you have to be pretty smart. I know you watch for the little things and only speak on topics when you have all the facts."

"Your point?"

"I'm sure you can do anything you put your mind to. You just need to take a breath."

I frowned. He wasn't wrong. My run-in with Emile would've gone better if I'd put effort into it, did some recon beforehand. But I didn't have time for that. I can't let this case go cold. I won't.

I came to a stop a few doors away from my class, wringing my hands on the straps of my backpack. I didn't like Julius getting into my head. "What makes you think I need to take a breath?"

He smirked. Looking up at the hallway clock, he took a few steps back toward the classroom across the hall. "Follow whatever has your attention until it runs cold. Then you can free your mind up and not do dumb things like trying to bribe Emile with an overpriced Americano." He dropped the drink in the nearest trash can as the late bell rang for first period, then slipped into his classroom. "See you later, Kelley Green Eyes."

I kicked the locker next to me.

Deep breaths, I told myself. *I'm rushing, not focused.*

I never lost my cool during investigations. I'd also never struck out so badly trying to get information. I didn't even think to ask Julius any questions about the case, even though he's one of the names in our suspect pool. Stupid mistake. "Pull it together, Jo."

I'd been stuck on a single thought since I found the flash drive last night—Did Mr. Medina leave those files for me to find? He went to the police station, knowing there were threats on his life, and left a copy of his evidence in his favorite Sherlock book. Did he know I wouldn't be able to let it go if something happened to him? That I'd snoop through his office? Did he know that I'd be able to figure out his password?

The thoughts weighed heavy on me, the pressure to solve his murder.

I can't mess up anymore.

I sighed and dug around in the outer pocket of my

backpack where I kept my on-the-go candy stash. Sweets were the one way I knew to calm my nerves. I groaned. No Red Vines. The pocket was full of empty wrappers and two stale pieces of gum.

"Joining us today, Miss Kelley?" Ms. Taylor poked her head out of her classroom.

Ah, yes. Consistently late for AP Calc.

I flashed an apologetic smile and made my way to my seat. I knew what I needed to do to get my priorities straight: Treat this case the same as all the others.

It's just a puzzle to solve.

At home, I sat on my bed, staring at the list of suspects Frankie, Sabrina, and I had put together last night. I had wasted a whole day, not a single student's name crossed off. My eyes flitted to Julius's. He said Mr. Medina asked him months ago to look out for me, so why insert himself into my life *now*? Guilt? I thought back to the candle he left in front of the guidance offices last week. The same candle I saw at the train platform when I was with Reya. How had he known the exact spot where Mr. Medina was hit? There was the dark stain on the concrete that could've given it away—I shooed the memory away before it had a chance to fully form.

Taking a red marker from my desk, I uncapped it, blaming its aroma of rubbing alcohol and artificial raspberries on why my eyes started to water. Pushing down whatever was bubbling inside me, I took out my phone to find the list Frankie had sent over.

After telling my friends about the press conference the morning Mr. Medina died, Frankie—in all his Google-search geniusness—was able to find the recorded live feed on CPD's YouTube channel. It was a possible misuse of CPD's resources on the chief's end, but it helped us clock alibis for a few other parents we spotted in the audience—Kehlani's dad along with both of the Garcias. Frankie recorded the time stamp as each suspect appeared on camera. Chief Ryan was also in attendance (obviously), but he was definitely late enough to have been able to make a detour on the way. Deputy Mayor Khara had skipped the event all together. That left Sabrina to make some calls and track down the Russells and the Mitchells this afternoon. I scanned the whiteboard one more time.

"We never added Julius's parents," I muttered. I added "Mr. and Mrs. James" with a question mark. Julius had become an anomaly. His file was bare, he didn't seem to have come from wealth, and I had no idea if he even lived with his parents, or who they were. And his behavior in the last week—constantly popping up and dodging questions about Mr. Medina—was questionable to say the least. Stumped, I settled for slumping into my chair and drumming my fingers across my desk.

The vibrations shifted my computer mouse, and my MacBook screen lit up. The cursor still hovered over the blue-and-white mail icon from the last time I used my laptop. I hadn't been able to bring myself to open the police report yet. I drummed my fingers some more.

Treat it like a cold case.

Taking a breath, I counted to five and clicked.

Reya's forwarded email sat unopened in my inbox. At this point, I'm not sure what I expected to gain from the report. The cameras were useless, and Lieutenant Charles, in his rush toward a cushy promotion, hadn't put in any effort to actually investigate. But I had to go about the case right. No skipping evidence or brushing off leads.

I opened the attachment.

Inside was a zip file with one PDF and three folders: Witness Statements, Photographic Evidence, and Security Footage.

CHICAGO POLICE DEPARTMENT
CASE SUPPLEMENT REPORT
3510 S. Michigan Avenue, Chicago, Illinois 60653
(For use by Chicago Police – Bureau of Investigative Services Personnel Only)

35BRZ0207

Last Offense Classification/Re-Classification	IUCR Code	Original Offense Classification		IUCR Code
Accidental Death / Metro Rail	**XCTA**	**Accidental Death / Metro Rail**		**XCTA**
Address of Occurrence	Beat of Occurrence	No. of Victims	No. of Offenders	No. of Arrested
35th and Bronzeville	**SMI3**	**1**	**0**	**0**
Location Type	Location Code	Secondary Location		Hate Crime
Rail Train Station	**35B**			**No**
Date of Occurrence	Unit Assigned	Date RO Arrived / Fire Related?	Gang Related?	Domestic Related?
21-FEB 09:32	**OCPR**	21-FEB 09:34 No	No	No

Reporting Officer	Star No	Approving Supervisor	Star No	Primary Assigned	Star No
RYAN, John	**553**	**CHARLES, JR, Wendell**	**249**	**CHARLES, JR, Wendell**	**249**
Date Submitted		Date Approved		Assignment Type	
21-FEB 11:02		**24-FEB 16:02**		**Field**	

I sighed, relieved. The photos were in a separate folder. Opening up the PDF report, I skimmed the police report.

I glanced over the gathered testimonies and took a moment before watching the security camera footage. Then, after a few minutes of steeling myself and staring at the file, I pressed play.

The person who stood blocked by the platform column did well to stay out of sight. The grainy footage made it hard to even make out their height and build. I was quick to pause as soon as I saw the familiar arch of Mr. Medina's body folding over. My chest tightened. Holding my breath, I switched to the footage from the train's front camera—corrupted, nothing but static. Sabrina's voice echoed in my mind.

Convenient.

In the folder for collected testimony, mine was missing. Another big surprise. There was a pull in my stomach as I wondered if my mom knew the case was already closed when she arranged for me to give a statement. I didn't know if I wanted to find out the answer.

I scrolled through the various witness statements, stopping when I found the one I was looking for: the conductor. And it was as vague as ever: "Victim fell backward onto tracks."

I noted the date next to the signature. The statement was taken two days after the incident, not at the scene. His statement should've been taken immediately.

I did one last scan of the police report, my eyes catching

on the name of the first officer on the scene. Reporting officer: Ryan, John.

I sat up and read it again.

He couldn't have been the first officer on the scene.

And arriving only two minutes after Mr. Medina was hit?

I saw him leave police headquarters. He should've been well on his way to the press conference by then. Though the alderman's assistant did say Chief Ryan was over an hour late . . .

I dug into my memory. I would've recognized Chief Ryan if he was at the platform that morning. It was a ten-minute drive from CPD headquarters to where the press conference was staged at the McCormick Place Convention Center. There was nothing else in the report about his presence at the scene. Lieutenant Charles's own write-up noted he, himself, was called to the scene by Ryan. But how did two officers, neither on the beat, end up at the platform?

My mind raced as new theories formed. What if Chief Ryan wasn't rushing out to make it to his press conference? What if he was trying to catch someone at Thirty-Fifth and Bronzeville before they could ruin his bid for office with a scandal that would rock the city?

"How's everything going with school?"

My mom's voice broke my train of thought. She stood at my door, already changed out of her work attire, and had let her hair down out of its usual tight bun, her curls and coils surrounding her face like a halo. Crossing my room, she offered me a steaming hot mug of lemon and lavender tea.

Growing up, it was how she always calmed me down after nightmares. I wanted to be calmed by her presence now. Shouldn't tea from a mom make her daughter feel at peace? I couldn't shake it, though. My statement was missing from the report.

My truth was missing.

"Can I ask you about the call you made to Lieutenant Charles—so I could give my statement about Mr. Medina?" I closed my MacBook and took the mug with both hands. The smell of lavender hit my face, its aroma trying and failing to relax my nerves.

"Sure." She redid her robe's tie at her waist, fidgeting with the worn threads.

"Did you know the case was already closed?"

She opened her mouth, then closed it without speaking. A lie would come next. I steeled myself, waiting.

"Of course not," Dad answered from the hallway. He had just passed my open door on the way down the hall. His eyes fell to his wife, whose own eyes stared at the floor. "Millie?"

"I'm not going to lie to you. You've known my tells since you were fourteen." There was a light smile in her voice. She took a step forward as I pushed myself back farther in my seat. "You needed closure. I wasn't going to keep watching you mope—"

"Mope? I witnessed a *murder.*" My grip on the mug tightened, my nails trying to dig into the porcelain. Chest pounding, I attempted to focus on the floral and citrus scent as heat crawled up my neck to my cheeks. But I couldn't. Memories flooded to the surface. Me screaming at her as she ripped down the first murder board I created for a cold case. The words we said to each other. *Her* daughter wasn't going to waste her life playing Little Miss Detective. *She* had worked too hard for that. She wanted me to have something better—wanted me to choose a path different from the paths that had consumed my grandfather and uncle. Killed them.

But that didn't mean the same would happen to me. How could I choose any other path when being a "voice to the voiceless" was ingrained in my DNA?

That night, I had called her a few choice names a daughter should never call her mother, and she had slapped me across my face. She apologized after, but everything between us had already changed in that moment.

Two years later and the slap still stung.

"I'm trying to help you, Jolene. Losing Mr. Medina, it was like it broke you. When I look at you now—you remind me so much of my dad, my brother." She chuckled softly to herself. "They were always so ready to uncover the truth. If you didn't get out of bed that day, you probably would've tried to do something—start one of your investigations . . ."

My eyes flicked to the closed laptop.

She stopped. The light in her eyes faded. "That's what you're doing, isn't it?" One quick stride across the room and she was at the whiteboard reading off the names. "Politi-cians? Police officials?" Her face twisted in anger as she went to pick up the whiteboard right as I yanked it from her grasp. No. She wasn't going to destroy this. Mr. Medina needed me—

The mug of tea fell to the floor, shattering to pieces, and hot liquid splashed onto my legs.

"Ow!" I flinched, trying to wipe away the sting from my legs.

Within a second, Dad was at my side. "Jolene? We can get some cold water—"

"No. You said you would talk to her." I pulled away and tossed the whiteboard back in my closet before grabbing the USB off the desk. "This is me! I'm not going to magically wake up and not care about others around me, people who need someone to be their voice. Mr. Medina needs *me*. No one else is taking this seriously. You two obviously aren't." Anger burned over every inch of being, my body on fire. I wasn't going to be able to come down from this. If I didn't leave now, I would burst. *I can't do this. Not with her. Not now.*

I pushed past the two of them. "I'm spending the night at Bri's."

Mom reached out for me. "Jolene . . ."

No. She didn't get to turn on the sweet voice.

I left my parents to stand alone in my room and didn't look back.

"I'm so sorry, sweetie." Sabrina sat next to me at the bottom of her bed, wrapped up in her hot pink throw. I gripped her comforter, letting out slow breaths. I'd recapped everything, only for the anger to come flooding back through open gates I needed to weld shut. I focused on what surrounded us: posters of models, runway shows, and a corkboard full of fabric swatches.

Frankie sat at the top of the bed, his legs spread as he patted the space between them for me to sit. I joined him, leaning my back to his front as he pulled me into a hug. He squeezed tight, knowing the pressure was what I needed to breathe. He and I had known each other the longest. We used to stage weddings and play house in his backyard, and it almost felt inevitable we would go from childhood friends to something more, until puberty hit. He started to notice girls, and I noticed no one in particular. I didn't have physical attractions, at least not the way other kids our age did. I only wanted the emotional tugs that came with friendship. Needed it. Relationships with family and friends meant everything to me, and this thing with my mom tore at my heart. He understood that. I just wanted her to understand me.

He pressed his lips to my temple. "Your mom's going to open her eyes one day and see how amazing you are at this. She's just scared with what happened to her old man and your uncle when they were on the force. How things ended for them. Parents always want their kids to go one step further in life than they did themselves."

I turned around. "And when did you get so wise?"

Frankie smiled. "A few years back, my pops started reading all these self-help books for bonding with your kids. He'd leave them in the bathroom as reading material."

Sabrina scrunched her nose. "TMI."

I let out a laugh and moved back beside her. "Okay. I forwarded you the email with the report. Did you guys have a chance to read it?"

"Not so fast." Frankie scooted up behind me. "You're doing that thing where you put your emotions in a box."

I sighed, staring up at the ceiling. I didn't have time for this. Real detectives didn't let their personal life get in the way of their cases. I had to take this seriously.

"Have you tried talking to your mom about other things you are into?" Sabrina offered.

"Like what?"

"Well, these cases are our first love, but I have fashion. My mom doesn't have an ounce of style, but she lets me sew her new scrubs for work. She wants to catch the eyes of a certain doctor." She waggled her brows. "And Frankie has that hacking stuff his dad's teaching him."

"My mom's a public defender," I countered. "Cases should be an easy topic."

"But you know she wants more for you. You just gotta

show her there is more *to* you. That you won't let it con-sume you. I think that's what this is about."

I locked eyes with Sabrina. "Do you think I've let it con-sume me?"

She turned to share that *look* with Frankie.

I threw up my hands. "I'm over this. Let's move on. Did you guys read the report or not?"

Frankie broke his eyes away from Sabrina. "Yeah, we read it." Giving up on the previous topic, he walked over to Sabrina's craft table, where there was a stack of grilled cheeses and three bowls of tomato basil soup. Her mom had a double shift tonight, which meant dinner was fend for yourself. Lucky for us, Sabrina could work a panini press and spice up some Campbell's.

"I'm liking the chief for this," said Frankie, mouth full. "He had means and opportunity. Strong enough to push Mr. Medina, smart enough to stay out of the cameras, and we know he was there."

"Maddie's dad is a good lead, but we haven't crossed off any of the students as suspects," I reminded him.

Sabrina frowned. "But could a student really do this?"

"You've met Maddie, right? I don't even want to know what she's capable of in the heat of the moment. And Julius definitely knows *something* about what's going on."

"You have a point. But we need to at least put together a plan for how to get everyone's alibis. Then we can create suspect profiles on whoever's left." Sabrina tapped her chin in thought. "Tell me about Emile again."

I rehashed the story of my failed attempt to grab a look at the attendance records. Sabrina popped up with a smile spread wide, her cheeks pinching those electric-blue eyes of hers. "I've got an idea."

Within a couple of hours, we had a plan, and it was time for Frankie to leave.

He tugged at my sleeve as he stood up. "Walk me out."

I followed him down the worn carpeted steps to the front door. Pulling on his coat and gloves, he sighed. "I know you don't want to hear this, but I'm worried about you."

Rocking back on my heels, I tucked my hands into the pajama pants I'd borrowed from Sabrina. "I know." I avoided his gaze. "You and my mom are a lot alike."

"Hey, I gave up on trying to convince you to put a New York school on your list *and* agreed to add Northwestern to stay local as long as you do the same." He chuckled. "But I was thinking about how you're at North Shore alone. You haven't tried to make friends."

"I don't need new friends—"

"There's a bit more to it." He took in a breath. "Promise me you'll pace yourself with this case. And you won't do anything else without telling me or Bri."

I frowned up at him.

"You went to Alderman Corben's office by yourself

yesterday. If you had been right about the affair, that could have ended badly. You admitted you had no idea what you were doing."

"Oh. Right." I stood still, staring at the frayed carpet underneath our feet. He wasn't wrong. We always approached witnesses together in case something went sideways. But this wasn't the same. The two of them aren't around anymore, not the way they used to be. I had to learn to do things by myself.

"I know you haven't worked through your emotions surrounding Mr. Medina. It's causing you to try to steamroll through this case. But don't shut us out. You're very set in your ways, and when someone disagrees with you, you push away." He reached out to lift my gaze.

I nodded, choosing not to respond to the first part of what he said. "I promise."

"And relax a little. Go do facials and girly things. I told Bri to give you a manicure because those nails are looking jagged—"

"Bye, Frankie!" Opening the door, I shoved him outside and shut it behind him.

I looked down at my nails and frowned. They weren't that bad.

"Relax a little." Open my mind to new things. Everyone wanted me to do everything *but* solve Mr. Medina's murder.

"I can relax after the case," I muttered.

TEN

THE NEXT TIME I found myself standing in front of Emile's desk, I was prepared.

"And what does my little truant need today? Did you fill out the form and get a parent or guardian's signature?"

"Nope. Here for something else. I noticed the *Vogue Paris* on your desk. Do you know much about the fashion and textiles humanities focus North Shore has here?"

The blank stare of his beady eyes told me that was a dumb question. You would think working the front desk, Emile would have better people skills.

"My friend Sabrina, she's really into fashion. I thought I could see about getting her a tour. Maybe she could even shadow me so she can see some of the classes."

"That's a question for admissions." He waved me off and went back to typing.

"Yes, but Mrs. Medina will need to see a portfolio, right? I don't want to get Bri's hopes up if she doesn't have what the school is looking for."

He stopped typing. "And you thought to ask me?" His brow quirked up.

Now I had his attention.

"Well, honestly, you're much more approachable than some of the teachers in that department, and you obviously have an eye for it. I can arrange the visit with Mrs. Medina when she gets back next week."

He straightened his posture, rolling his shoulders back. "Well? Do you have her portfolio?"

"Yes." I flipped to the photo album in my phone Sabrina shared with me last night. "And the last one is the dress she made for her homecoming. The theme was Roaring Twenties."

"Mm-hmm, mm-hmm. Definitely inspired by the greats. Oh, twenties Dior. Very Daisy Buchanan." He met my eyes, looked back at the photo, and then handed my phone back. "It would be a shame if you *didn't* have her shadow you for a day. You know, this school feeds into FIT, Parsons, SCAD—if she's into southern hospitality."

"That sounds great. Thanks, Emile."

I stepped back, slowly turning away, waiting for the words I needed to hear.

"And do bring her by. I'd love to meet her."

Oh, I definitely plan to.

I let out a breath once I made it back into the hallway.

"I take it that went well."

Startled, I almost dropped my phone but managed an impressive juggling act to catch it before it reached the floor. This phone was not insured. "So, you *do* wait in dark corners for me to appear," I huffed out.

"Something like that," Julius replied. He handed me one of the two coffee tumblers in his hands. "Grabbed us some fuel from the teachers' lounge before third period."

I stiffened. *Coffee?* "Is this you flirting?"

He grinned. "That's your reaction to a kind gesture? This is me, trying to be your friend. That's all I'm looking for. Dating isn't really my thing."

"Oh." I let my shoulders relax. Friends. I could do that. Use it to my advantage.

I stared down at the drink and dared a taste, the dark roast warmed my body, notes of hazelnut and— "Irish cream? How did you know?"

"I didn't. Just seemed appropriate for Kelley Green Eyes. What's the case you're working?"

I almost choked on the next sip. "What makes you think I'm working—" I stopped after seeing his face. "Oookay. My friends and I, we research cold cases. We have one from 1989 with an off-Broadway star," I rattled off. Always good to keep lies as close to the truth as possible.

He raised a brow, interest piqued. "Why cold cases?"

"Because others have already given up on them, but not us. We're the voice to the voiceless."

He let out a low laugh as we turned the corner to the English wing. "You sound like Mr. Medina. He told me that was why he got into counseling."

I looked Julius over out the corner of my eye. He seemed genuine enough. He was still a suspect, though.

"How did you two meet?" I asked. "Besides the mandatory check-in. It seems like you were close to him?" I pried.

"Well, he has a soft spot for scholarship kids from the South Side. I think it's just me and you here."

"I guess." I tapped my fingers against the tumbler, thinking of how to get him to open up more. Give a little, get a little. "A stray bullet grazed my best friend's little brother when I was ten, and I had to go to counseling for it. Mr. Medina had board games in his office. Old ones from like the eighties and nineties. We played a lot of Clue and Guess Who? After a while, he asked if I liked to read." I took another long sip. Tension seeped from my neck. For the first time in a while, it felt good to talk about Mr. Medina. Not as painful.

Julius nodded quietly. "My mom died from breast cancer last Labor Day, two weeks before I turned eighteen. My dad has another family out west, but he wanted me to finish school here. He sends checks but . . ." He paused, scrunched his brows, and then shook off whatever emotion had just crossed his face. "The Medinas took me and my little sister in for a few weeks and helped with the papers to name me her legal guardian and keep her out of the system. I was close to Mr. Medina before, but that solidified it."

"Wow, he never mentioned that."

"Well, it's not necessarily something I wanted broadcast over the PA speakers. A bunch of rich kids learning that my mom died, my dad had all but abandoned me, and now I had a little sister to parent? Nah. No one needed to know that."

"He was like a father figure for you," I said.

He nodded again, and we fell in step together, turning another corner. That was telling. If he thought Mr. Medina betrayed him and the scandal came to light, he could lose custody of his sister. That's motive—a pretty strong one. Still, something made me hesitate.

"You know, you don't have to walk me to class. Won't you be late?"

He chuckled. "You've honestly never noticed me in your Gothic literature class?"

I frowned. "The kid who sleeps with his coat hood over his head?"

"At your service." He bowed. "It's a boring class, but I want to go into screenwriting. Most movies and shows are just new takes on classics. We wouldn't have Anne Rice's *Interview with a Vampire* without Bram Stoker's *Dracula*. And millennials wouldn't have their strange obsession with Stephenie Meyer's *Twilight* without Anne Rice."

"*Twilight*'s not just for millennials. My friend loves those movies."

"Uh-huh. Is she into vampires or werewolves?"

"I'm pretty sure she's into Kristen Stewart."

Julius grinned. "That's a legit team I can root for."

"Mm-hmm." I stopped outside the classroom door.

The sub stood at their desk fumbling with papers. There was a new replacement every week, and I couldn't keep up with them. This sub had added their pronouns next to their name on the chalkboard: she/they. "Do you know what happened to Mr. Callahan?"

It was quick, but it almost looked like Julius fought off a pained expression. Regret. He knew something. "Remember what I said about this place? Backstabbing and all? It wasn't his type of thing, and honestly it was above his pay grade. He teaches English to students in Okinawa now."

"Okinawa, Japan?" I asked, stepping inside as the late bell rang. *So* that's *what happened to the first proctor.*

"Yep."

"Who took over proctoring the SAT exams after he left?" I asked casually before he could walk over to his usual desk in the corner.

"Ms. Taylor." He answered without thinking but furrowed his brows after a beat. "Why do you need to know that?"

The sub cleared their throat.

Julius walked to his seat, leaving me to head to my own. For the next hour I sat in the back of class, wondering what to do with this new information. The proctor was a dead end, and Ms. Taylor had been teaching the AP Calc class I was skipping that morning. That alibied her.

I stole glances at Julius, wondering if I should ask more, but that last question of mine might have been too obvious. Digging deeper could shut him down, and I needed him to keep talking. Texting Frankie and Sabrina for advice got me nowhere.

Frankie:

Don't offer up anything to let him know what we know.

Sabrina:

It couldn't hurt? He seems nice enough from what Jo's said.

Frankie:

Bri, he's a suspect. He was at the memorial and he found Jo outside Mr. Medina's office. Classic inserting himself into the investigation. Killers do it all the time.

Frankie:

AND Jo said she saw a candle at the platform. Then the same candle in front of Mr. Medina's office. Sign of remorse. Guilt.

Sabrina:

Or grief.

Frankie:

Jo?

I bounced my leg, thinking. Frankie had a point. I'd already entertained the thought that Julius could be using me to see what I know about Mr. Medina's death, the same way I was using him.

Jolene:

If he's inserting himself, he knows something. He might slip up and say something we can use. I can be subtle.

Frankie:

Subtle isn't your strong suit.

Jolene:

But is that a no?

A few minutes passed as I waited on Frankie. The bell rang and students got up from their seats to leave class. Julius stood and stretched.

Frankie:

Be careful. And don't go anywhere alone with him.

"Hey, wait up." I packed up my books and hurried after Julius. He stood outside the door next to one of the school's newspaper stands. Picking up a paper off the stack, he handed it to me before starting out for his next period— lunch, I assumed, since he was pulling a bottle of pop out of his bag, along with salt-and-vinegar chips.

I looked down at the paper to see Maddie looking up at me.

MADISON RYAN: FIRST BROWN, NEXT VALEDICTORIAN?

North Shore Seniors Making Big Moves, Highest GPA Average to Date By Natalia Mitchell

With graduation season fast approaching, North Shore Preparatory Academy is sending a record number of students off to Ivy League universities, including presumed class valedictorian, Madison Ryan. Maddie (as she's known to her friends) will be joining the freshman class at Brown

I jogged up to catch him. "You know her well?"

"Four years together at North Shore."

"Did she really fill Whitney Russell's water bottle with vodka to get her suspended before homecoming queen nominations?"

Julius grinned. "You heard about that? I think it was more to deter Whit from applying to Brown. She ended up getting into Cornell, so I don't think the school reported the suspension either way."

I glanced back down at the paper. "I can't believe they put her on the front page."

He shrugged. "Maddie's the editor, so the news is a bit slanted."

"I have AP Spanish with her and there's no way her GPA is legit. She has to be bribing someone to do her work. Or paying for her grades."

Okay, maybe Frankie was right about me not being so subtle.

Julius hesitated, thinking for a minute. "A lot of the Ivy chasers in senior class do one or the other. But you don't want to get involved with Maddie, trust me."

"Because of her dad?" I stepped in front of him, trying to catch his eye. "Do you think it was him on the voice mail to Mr. Medina? I know I recognize the voice, but I can't place it—"

He stopped, looking around before lowering his voice. "I don't know why I let you into his office. Is this the case you're actually working? Not some off-Broadway star? You need to leave this alone. Seriously. Don't get involved."

"Is it because *you're* involved? Is that what the work study was for? Did you get caught cheating?"

He stiffened. "I've never paid for a single grade or test score."

"Then why do you care? What do you think you're protecting me from?"

"Aren't you the detective?" He nudged past, not looking at me. "See you around, Kelley Green Eyes."

ELEVEN

THURSDAY, MARCH 3, 8:40 A.M.

THURSDAY, I WAS five minutes early for AP Calculus. Unfortunately, so were a bunch of other students, doing some last-minute studying for a quiz I'd blanked on. By the time class ended, I felt confident I had at least a solid B based on my answers. I gave myself a pat on the back for only using my eeny-meeny-miney-mo technique on three questions.

I waited until the class filtered out before approaching Ms. Taylor. She was similar to Mr. Medina in some ways. Both had their own ways of pushing the limits of the faculty dress policy. Today she rocked high-waisted dark slacks and a cropped canary-yellow sweater, the smallest sliver of her dark brown midriff making an appearance whenever she moved.

"Ms. Taylor?"

She glanced up from her desk, her braids falling over her eyes. "Jolene. It was nice to see you before the late bell this morning."

My cheeks flushed a little. "Sorry about that. I've been working on it."

"I've noticed." She smiled. "What can I do for you today?"

"I heard you're one of the proctors for the SAT exams. I have another year before I really need to worry about my scores, but I thought I could start with study groups. Do you have one that you lead?"

"Changed your mind about community college?"

I faltered. "How did you . . . ?"

"I spoke with Mr. Medina about your attendance and commitment at the beginning of the semester. He told me about your postgraduation plans." She stepped around the front of her desk and leaned against the edge. "I'm not sure how you heard about me proctoring the SATs, though. I only did it once. It was . . . not for me."

"How so? I mean, I assumed teachers just graded papers or read during the exam."

"There's a bit more to it than that." She let her last words linger as she crossed her arms, almost as if to hug herself, as if my questions made her uncomfortable.

"I know of a few seniors who formed their own study groups in the past—Madison Ryan, Julius James," she continued. "If there are any other students asking around, I'll let you know."

"Thanks, Ms. Taylor." I turned to leave class, and lo and behold, Julius stood in the doorway. I pushed past him.

"You don't quit, do you?" he muttered.

"Nope."

My phone vibrated in my pocket as I left Julius behind.

Frankie:

Finally managed a hit on Deputy Mayor Khara and why he wasn't at the press conference. Family trip to Cancun. He took his daughter and two of her friends for her eighteenth.

Sabrina:

The privileges of the upper class.

Frankie:

I actually couldn't get an answer out of his office, but his daughter's IG had a highlights reel and plenty of photos. Check it out.

I clicked the link Frankie sent and found pictures of Sheetal, Natalia, and Antonio living their best life, drinking fruity mocktails with their manicured toes in the sand. The deputy mayor and his wife sat with their own drinks in the blurred background.

Jolene:

That alibis three of the students.

Sabrina:

I recognize Sheetal and Nat. Who's the third?

Jolene:

The one with the iridescent Speedo and flawless complexion? That's Antonio Garcia. Pretty sure they're also the one who stole Maddie's boyfriend.

Sabrina:

Jealous. Not about Maddie, but everyone's tans. I'm getting so pale this winter.

Jolene:

I love your priorities.

Jolene:

I have an update on my end with the proctors, btw. Things might have started falling apart once Mr. Callahan left. Ms. Taylor only proctored once after that, and I get the feeling she didn't want any part of it.

Frankie:

Do you think Mr. Medina poking around had something to do with it?

Jolene:

I think he spooked the first proctor. But maybe he warned Ms. Taylor next?

Sabrina:

That leaves us with five students, including Maddie and her DAD.

Sabrina:

Oh, and I did email Mrs. Medina about shadowing. She's going to set it up for Monday when she gets back. Okay if I spend the night Sunday, Jo?

Jolene:

Should be no prob. It'll give us an opp to go over your plan for Emile.

Frankie:

It's Thursday. What can we do for four days while we wait?

The hallway fell silent, the usual noise of kids running to class dying down. Without hesitation, I broke into a run. I had less than a minute to get to AP Spanish, and Mr. Perez was the type to lock you out. The late bell shrilled as I slipped into the room, him glaring as he closed the door behind me.

Mr. Perez was a round old man who always wore an off-white short-sleeve button-up, half untucked for reasons unknown, and a black clip-on tie. Today, he still had on his winter coat and a scarf wrapped around his neck. He pointed to his throat, then to the chalkboard.

"Did you lose your v—"

"¡Español!" he rasped.

"Dang, okay. Lo siento," I muttered. Heading back to my seat, I read the directions to break into groups of three for our discussion warm-ups. Maddie and Nat were the only ones not already paired with a third. Lucky me.

I scooted my desk over to theirs.

"Uh, perdón me, señorita." Maddie scrunched up her face as she spoke with the most offensive Spanish accent. She had curled her frosted hair to shape it into a bob, resulting in some weird framing of her face. She smacked her bubblegum-pink lips together.

"You said 'excuse me' wrong," I mumbled, then pointed to the board. "And it says groups of three."

Maddie squinted at the board as though she could actually read it.

"Didn't Mr. Perez just yell at you about not speaking Spanish?" Natalia retorted, flipping her auburn extensions over her shoulder before folding her arms over her hand-knit cardigan. As much as she annoyed me, I did admire how she always found a way to add style to the school uniform. It looked incredible on her curvy frame while my uniform felt boxy and did nothing for my pear shape. In another life, she and Sabrina would've been friends.

"If I said it to you in Spanish, would you have understood me?" That seemed to quiet them both. "I'm not trying to be rude. Congrats on Brown by the way, and Yale."

Maddie shrugged. "Thanks, I guess."

"I've been thinking about Harvard. Well, my dad has at least. He has some family in Boston," I started, trying to see what I could get them to say. Maybe I could make them think I needed in on the scam, too. "My PSATs are in the mid-1300s."

Maddie twirled her fingers through her hair. "You're going to need more than that for Harvard. And I'm pretty sure you can't afford it."

"Maddie!" Natalia shot her a glare.

"Relax. It's done."

I looked back and forth between the two, feigning ignorance. "Like a tutor? Ms. Taylor said something about study groups—that you and Julius had one."

"Sure. Julius was a tutor." She smirked. "He was a hot commodity once, but he's retired now. No more after-school activities after his close call with expulsion. Almost lost his scholarship, too, but the donor had pity on the *literally* poor orphan."

I clenched my jaw. Her tone was condescending, and she knew it. "What for?"

"Hmm?"

"What did he get in trouble for?" I gritted out.

"Oh, you didn't know? He took a swing at a teacher. When was that, Nat?"

"Ooo, I think it was, like, a month ago, maybe?"

I blinked. She had to be lying.

"You seemed surprised, Jolene. I just thought you should know about the people you're spending time with. Don't want to get too close to a boy like that. But then again, you are a little low on options and probably can't attract much else. I've seen your IG. Did your parents send you here to trap a trust fund baby?" She dragged her eyes over me. "You look like you could use a dollar, maybe a few thousand."

Hands shaking, I stood up, my chair falling back.

I can't be here right now.

A voice called after me in Spanish—I could only assume

Mr. Perez by the rasp—but I kept going, walking straight out of the classroom. I didn't stop until the cold winter air slapped me in the face.

———

When I finally peeled my eyes open after hours spent hiding in my bed, it was pitch-black outside my window. The tray where I'd left bits of crust from a smoked ham sandwich had been replaced with a bowl of frozen grapes.

I popped one into my mouth, the cool burst of juice calming my nerves. It had been a while since I let someone like Maddie bother me.

Being a scholarship student came with the usual jabs from entitled kids. I thought I was over it, but Maddie's tone, along with the low blows at Julius, my family—the things she insinuated—that didn't help. Pile that on top of the emotions I'd been bottling away and I was a wreck.

This investigation seeped into every part of my life. Cold cases I could box away. Not this, though. The investigation pulled at me, as though waiting for me to unravel and snap.

Snacking on the grapes, I freshened up and changed out of my school uniform before wandering downstairs, following the delicious, savory smell of collard greens slow cooking in our Crock-Pot. I stopped when I got to the kitchen. Mom sat at the table reading *Hollywood Homicide*, wearing an oversized tie-dye sweatshirt, dark yoga pants, and her plush corgi slippers—a gift from Dad last Christmas.

"You didn't wake me for dinner."

"I did not." She marked her place with a napkin before putting the book down. "Mr. Perez called to let us know you had walked out of second period, distraught. Dad came home early. He said you were closed up in your room." She stood, going to the refrigerator to pour two tall glasses of iced green tea. "We decided to give you some space."

"Thank you," I whispered as she handed me the glass before sitting back down.

"You know it took me a long time to get over losing Nana Josette. It's been two years and it still hurts."

I sat down at the table across from her. "You didn't cry, though."

"I cried every night. For weeks, after you went to bed, I walked myself down that hall to her room and cried until there was nothing left." She sipped her drink. "I don't want that for you."

"I know," I said. I tapped my fingers along the glass, the weight of this morning heavy on my shoulders. "That's not what made me leave school, though. I just . . . I want to be myself and for that to be enough. For you, the kids at school . . ."

My mom sat up. "Is something wrong at school? Is someone bothering you?"

I shook my head. "It's nothing. But—I . . ." It shouldn't

be this hard to talk to my mom, but all I could think about was our last conversation. "Why can't you accept this private investigator thing?" I whispered.

She leaned back in the chair. "Your grandfather *died* on the force, your uncle, too. It's like a cycle in our family. Dying while trying to protect others." There was a bit of sarcasm in her voice.

"I'm not going—"

"*I* chose to be a public defender, to take a different route. It might not have been much, but it was something. I wanted to break that pattern, and for you to just go back to it . . . I want more for you—better for you. I want you out of this place. You have so much potential. You're more than this." She gestured to the windows and what was beyond it. Our neighborhood.

I sat there quietly, staring into my glass and at the crushed ice swirling inside. A few hours ago, I had fallen asleep to the sounds of sirens and thought nothing of it. "But this is where we're from. What we do. Why is that so bad? We help others—"

"At a cost to ourselves. But you, my darling, are sixteen."

"How is it any different from what you do at the court-house? I want to help the people here. Who else is going to? I don't want to be like the stuck-up rich kids at school, looking down—"

She placed her hand over mine. "I'm not asking you to be like them. I'm asking you to look at those who came before you, how each generation took that one step to do better for the next. You don't have to forget your roots to do that. And you always, always, give back. But there's more than one way to do that, Jo. I'm trying here. I need you to try, too."

She gave my hand a squeeze before leaving me alone at the table. She meant well, but it didn't keep the anger from boiling at my surface. She still wasn't listening to me, hearing me. And she certainly wasn't "trying." Her words left me suffocated.

It was easier when Mr. Medina was here. But he left me—I sucked in a breath. Letting my thoughts go there was a slippery slope. I needed to scream, but I couldn't let it out. I couldn't give in. Not until this investigation was over.

———

"Knock, knock."

My door creaked open, revealing a tuft of red hair with graying roots before the rest of my dad's face appeared. "You have a visitor."

I sat up in my bed. "It's after ten on a school night."

"I know. Are you decent under there?" he asked.

I pulled off my covers so he could see me in the unicorn onesie Sabrina gifted me for my birthday in January.

Dad grinned. "Perfect." He opened the door the rest of the way, and Frankie stood behind him in a pair of sweats and a long-sleeve fitted Under Armour shirt.

"Thanks, Mr. K." He slipped through the door to sit on the edge of my bed.

Dad cleared his throat. "Ahem."

Frankie got up, moving to my desk chair.

"Great." Dad pushed the door open as wide as it could go. "Head home in about an hour, okay, Francis?"

"Heard, Mr. K."

Dad nodded, satisfied with Frankie's answer and our seating arrangement. He stepped back into the hallway, off to his own room.

"Your dad is hilarious. I thought you told your parents about the whole demi/ace thing."

"I did—it's just demi, but honestly I still don't fully understand it."

"A case that Jolene Kelley has yet to solve."

"It's a case that I can solve later. In another chapter of my life. Right now, my dad is a dad, and you're a teenage boy."

Frankie grinned. "Fair."

"What are you doing here?"

"You know how you said me and your mom are a lot alike?"

I groaned. "She called you?"

"You know it!" He leaned back and kicked up his feet over my desk.

"Well, that's not embarrassing at all."

The smile faded from his lips. "You didn't tell us you walked out of class. You just stopped texting."

"I thought you'd be happy I was taking a break."

Frankie moved to the edge of my bed. "Talk to me, Jo."

I sighed. "I want to be myself and not be judged for it," I whispered. "Not judged for what I like, where I live, what I want to do." I pulled at my plum comforter. "I'm alone at that school. I want to be alone in peace. And I can't even have that."

"I think this case with Mr. Medina, losing him, it's hardest on you. And I know why, and I think you do, too, but you don't want to say it."

I locked eyes with Frankie. "I don't—" I shook my head. "I can't think about that." I clenched my fists in the sheets.

"How about we think about something else?" Standing up, he walked over to my desk, clearing off the old evidence from the cold case we worked before the off-Broadway star.

"You still scrapbook each case?"

I nodded, sitting up.

"Put this entry in your book while I print out a few things."

I took the stack of photos and papers from him and pulled out my scrapbook from under my bed. It was an old canvas book, with plenty of pages yellowed with age. I'd found it at a secondhand shop and would never know the owner or who it was meant for, just that the first page, and only page written on when I found it, had my initials.

The mechanic whirl of my printer turning on and paper

cycling through it sounded behind me as I snipped photos and taped them onto the next blank page. I'd forgotten how much journaling calmed me down. When I finally turned around, I expected to see evidence from Mr. Medina's case. Instead, I found the stormy-gray eyes of Chloe St. James.

"She still needs you," Frankie murmured.

I walked over to the desk, eyeing the photos I'd taken of the evidence box contents mixed with playbills I hadn't seen before. It felt like that trip to see Officer Halligan at the records room had been months ago.

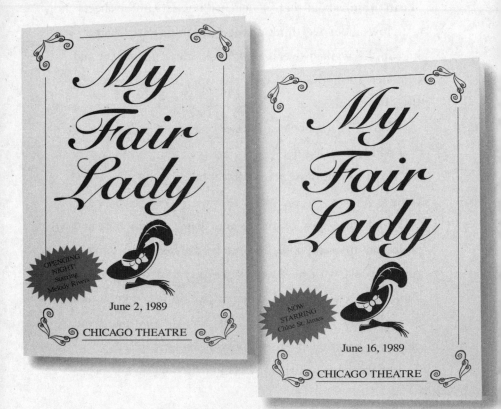

"It wasn't the ex-lover?"

Frankie shook his head. "Sabrina and I tracked him down. He was an officer in the Marines, deployed right before the Gulf War."

I nodded, slowly tracing my fingers over the crime scene photos. "And you found more playbills?"

"The theater kept pretty good inventory. We're thinking the motive has something to do with her quick rise to lead actress. But it only gives us one suspect: Melody Rivers, the former lead. She was known to be a diva with a mean streak."

"I didn't mean to leave you two to do this one on your own." I stopped, tapping on the photo of the victim as she was first found. "She was hanged center stage, right? But realistically, Melody wouldn't be able to overpower Chloe without help. I think we need to figure out how it was done."

"How she was killed?"

I nodded. "Look at the autopsy report. The killer hung her up to stage a suicide. The broken ring finger could have been done on purpose to throw police in case the suicide ruse didn't work. We need to take a closer look at everything. Understanding how it was done might unveil more motives and suspects."

Frankie smiled and shook his head.

"What?"

"That could apply to Mr. Medina's case, too. I haven't

figured out how they hacked the College Board. It really is impossible."

"I'm sure if it wasn't, more kids would try to do it. But actually—" I glanced over at the clock beside my bed. "He said an hour, but we probably have thirty minutes before my dad kicks you out, at most. Let's give Chloe some time. Back to Mr. Medina tomorrow."

OFFICE OF COOK COUNTY MEDICAL EXAMINER
2121 W HARRISON STREET
CHICAGO, IL 60612

REPORT OF INVESTIGATION

Name: Chloe St. James
Type of Death: Homicide

Description of Body

Hair: Brown   Eyes: Gray   Facial: None
Weight: 112 lbs   Height: 5' 6"   Body Temp: 89°   Date: July 29, 1989

Marks and Wounds

Handprint bruising around neck
Bruising at wrists
Rope burns at neck (postmortem)
Left pupil blown
Broken ring finger (tan line doesn't match ring found with body)
Foreign DNA under fingernails
Tox screen revealed unidentifiable substance ingested hours before death

CAUSE OF DEATH	MANNER OF DEATH	DESCRIPTION OF DEATH
Lack of oxygen to the brain—suspicious, unnatural death	violent	strangulation

Frankie and I examined the autopsy report, reading and rereading everything in the coroner's notes and what each bruise implied. One thing we learned: There was something in the tox screen that was inconclusive.

Frankie pointed to a photo of the theater stage. "There were drag marks, but no blunt-force trauma to indicate she was physically knocked unconscious. A roofie or some other drug seems like a good bet."

"I don't think there was a lot of information on roofies back then. And I doubt that's something forensics can reevaluate now, even if technology has improved since the eighties." I flipped through more of the evidence, showing Frankie one of the photos. "Here—there was an open bottle of champagne in her dressing room. Two glasses were printed. One was Chloe's, but the other had no match. The tox report might be a bust, but the police *can* rerun the fingerprints on the glass for a possible match. We could figure out who gave her the drink. And there was another print, too—a bloody one on the rope."

"Time to go, Frankie," Dad called out. I glanced at the clock. It took all of nineteen minutes for him to pop his head into my room, ready to walk Frankie two doors down to his own house.

"Sure thing, Mr. K." Frankie looked back to me. "We're close. I think we have the how—"

"Now we can narrow down the who."

TWELVE

FRIDAY MORNING, NO Julius. Not in the hallways before Ms. Taylor's class, or by the stairwell after AP Spanish.

"Didn't see you after second period yesterday, Jolene. Did you run off? Get lost on the train?" Maddie poked as she walked out of class behind me.

I didn't answer her.

"Those things are *so* dirty. Just a bunch of scum packed into metal boxes."

"And what do you know about the L train, Maddie?" I asked over my shoulder, annoyed.

It was Nat's voice I heard next. "I ride the CTA sometimes. The scenery can be nice."

"Ew, Nat. Take a Lyft. And what *I* know"—she nudged my shoulder—"is the cameras don't even work. My dad told me. You're probably going to get mugged by a homeless person."

I stopped walking. "What?"

"Did I offend your precious public transportation? Or are the homeless people your friends?" She smirked and turned down the opposite hall.

It wasn't her comment about who rides the CTA that bothered me.

Madison Ryan knew about the cameras.

My mind buzzed as I stopped by my locker before Goth lit. If Chief Ryan told his daughter about the cameras, was it possible some of the other students knew, too?

Lost in my thoughts, I pried open my locker—it was always getting stuck—only for a note to fall out.

YOU ASK TOO MANY QUESTIONS. STOP OR YOUR BLOOD WILL BE ON THE TRACKS NEXT.

A threat?

Ice trickled through my veins. I looked up and down the hallway. There was no way to tell when this was left for me to find. I hadn't had to open my locker since I walked out yesterday with all the books for my first two classes. I flipped the torn paper over—blank.

My heart pounded, blood pulsing in my ears. This case came with death threats. And with me asking so many questions this past week, I had no lead on who it could be from. Maddie? Julius? I had questioned Ms. Taylor yesterday. Could it have been her? I only knew one thing—I was getting close.

Too close.

Frankie:

If you're getting death threats, you need to tell someone.

Jolene:

It's not that serious.

Sabrina:

Did you tell a teacher? Should you take it to the police?

Jolene:

I'm sure that's what Mr. Medina was trying to do.

Jolene:

I just need to watch who I talk to. Obviously, it was someone I spooked this week. I won't question any of them again.

Frankie:

Julius overheard you talking to the second proctor.

Jolene:

I don't think he's the killer. This is premeditated, remember? Why would he kill his mentor? And there's no college acceptance letter in his file. I don't even see how he could have paid for the test, let alone a perfect score.

Frankie:

You're stuck on the idea of this being premeditated. We can't rule out that this happened in the heat of the moment. The camera angle could've been luck. And we don't even know if Julius has an alibi yet. You're forgetting that he also has a strong motive—custody of his sister.

Frankie:

I don't understand why you're letting him cloud your judgment. Julius said one thing about Mr. Medina wanting him to look out for you and now you trust him? For all we know, Julius made that up.

Right. I glanced up to see Julius in his usual corner of the Goth lit classroom, hood over his face. I didn't have the chance to tell Frankie and Sabrina about what Maddie said about Julius swinging at a teacher. If it were true, that would give him a violent history.

Jolene:

I'll be fine. We can take a break until Bri's shadow day on Monday. See what students still don't have alibis then and go from there.

"Jolene Kelley?"

The sub stood next to another kid with a hall pass in hand. "It appears you're being summoned to the dean's office."

Mrs. Lawson's office wasn't in the same area as Emile and the other admins. She had her own section in the administrative wing, and her assistant, Ms. Faiza, sat in a separate office you had to pass through first.

Ms. Faiza sat behind her desk wearing a lush, loose-fitting cream sweater, her hijab a cool ocean blue. I waited across from her, sitting on a hard wooden bench between a water cooler and a small table with an electric kettle and a ridiculous selection of herbal teas. I had half an urge to make my usual lemon and lavender to calm the nerves twisting my insides. Nothing good has ever come from getting called to the dean's office.

Did she know I discovered the scandal? If so, how? Who told her? Ms. Taylor?

"You can come in, Miss Kelley," Mrs. Lawson called from her office.

I wiped sweaty palms on my khaki skirt as I stood.

"Hey, Mrs. L.?" Ms. Faiza got up, slipping on her coat. "I'll be back in thirty. I'm going by the vegan place with the smoothies. Do you want me to pick one up for you?"

"Thanks, but I have a lunch date with George today. I'll lock up after this. We shouldn't be long."

Mrs. Lawson waved me over, and once inside her office, it took effort not to gawk. It was covered in Chicago Bears paraphernalia, with barely an inch of blank surface. Definitely not what I expected.

"Come sit down, Miss Kelley."

Dropping my backpack to the floor, I sat in one of the two leather guest chairs backed with the school crest. Laid out on her desk was a copy of my file, complete with De La Salle transcripts and my partial-scholarship letter.

"I called you here because there's been a small flag on your scholarship. Now, grades are always reported to scholarship committees a quarter behind, so this is based on second-quarter grades, but when we sent your transcripts for review to the Chicago Police Scholars, it came back that your GPA fell below requirements."

I swallowed, hard. "Excuse me?"

"Reading through everything and speaking with your teachers, I can see that your grades will be coming in higher this quarter, but you may have to reapply."

"I thought the requirement was a 3.5 GPA?"

Mrs. Lawson shook her head, not a single strand of hair moving. "This letter says 4.0."

Confused, I held out my hand. "Can I see it?" With the letter in my grip, I skimmed it over. My GPA had slipped to a 3.8 last quarter, but this was not the same requirement from when the scholarship was first awarded. My eyes flitted to the letter's date—today.

"Now, you can send over a teacher recommendation along with proof that your grades are rising, but next quarter your parents will have to pay in full. I understand this may be an issue."

I glanced down to the cochairs' signatures at the bottom. One was a name I didn't recognize, but the other—Chief John Ryan.

This has to be Maddie's doing somehow. The note in my locker, this letter.

What was happening? What did I say to tip her off?

I stared across to Mrs. Lawson. "Can't you write me the recommendation?"

She took the paper from my hands and placed it back in my file. Wheeling her chair over to her file cabinet, she blocked my view as she typed into a numeric pad and placed my records back into the drawer. "I only do college recommendations, and even then, that's a select few—only seven this year."

I nodded, my eyes still on the file cabinet. This was all wrong. I glanced to the door behind me. No dead bolt, just a single lock in the handle. Opening the outer pocket of my backpack, I picked through the empty candy wrappers. Found it. "Do you want a piece of gum?"

"Gum?"

I nodded again, popping a piece in my mouth while sliding another across the desk.

"I might as well. My husband's golf club always has the smallest lunch portions, and unsweetened tea." She twisted up her nose before smiling.

I smiled back.

"Now, Ms. Taylor has already offered to write you a

letter. Mr. Perez as well. That should be enough. Make sure you speak with them. There's also an alumni fundraiser tomorrow evening. I signed you up to volunteer with the student waitstaff. Many of the attendees often sponsor students for a quarter here and there, sometimes for the whole year. It will give you an opportunity to speak with a few donors. Someone may offer to cover this upcoming quarter's tuition."

I clenched my jaw. Selling myself to rich people wasn't high up on my list of things I wanted to do this weekend, but I could use it to my advantage. "Do you think Chief Ryan will be there? Maybe I could speak with him directly to iron this out?"

"Yes, he should be. His family is full of North Shore alumni."

I stood up from the leather chair. "Thank you, Mrs. Lawson." I glanced around the room one more time. "Go, Bears!" I added enthusiastically.

She laughed, turning around to one of the photos.

I slipped out of her office while her back was to me, pressing my chewed gum into the door latch.

THIRTEEN

FRIDAY, MARCH 4, 11:54 A.M.

A FEW MOMENTS later, Mrs. Lawson stepped out of her office, pulling what she thought to be a locked door behind her. I listened for the lock to catch. Nothing. I smiled. The gum was doing its job, stopping the door from latching.

Mrs. Lawson looked down to find me on my knees reaching behind the watercooler. She raised a thin manicured brow. "Everything okay, Miss Kelley?"

"I dropped my phone. I think it slid behind the watercooler here."

She checked her watch. "I'm late enough already. Once you find it, make sure to pull the door shut behind you as you leave."

"Will do!" I strained my arm behind the cooler, praying I wouldn't accidentally touch something gross. The main door closed with a click. I gave myself a few seconds before popping up and slipping into Mrs. Lawson's office. Back inside, I walked over to the file cabinet. Based on the drawer labels, the dean kept files on all the scholarship kids. I stared at the numeric lock replaying the beeps in my memory. Four numbers, first number a low tone, the rest on the higher end.

"Let's see, was it a birthday?" I took out my phone, typing in a few numbers on the dial pad, listening to the beeps. "First number had to be a one," I muttered.

Going over to the calendar on her wall, I flipped through the last months of the year, noting any and every day that had something written in its square. I typed in all the various combinations. Nothing—until something beeped and a little red light on the dial pad blinked.

What the hell?

I tried to type in another combination, but the numbers didn't budge. *No.* I looked all around the cabinet for a release and only found the serial number. I typed it into a quick search. "Fifteen-minute fail-safe." Shit. Ms. Faiza said she would be back in thirty minutes. How long ago was that?

I paced the room. I'd have time for one more attempt once the keypad unlocked again, if that. Until then I was stuck in a shrine to the Chicago Bears. I started to text Frankie for ideas, but I knew he would cuss me out for being in here without a lookout.

Fifteen minutes later I still was stumped, staring at the photo of a young Mrs. Lawson and her parents at a football game. She couldn't have been more than twelve years old.

And just like that, the cogs in my mind started turning. It could be jersey numbers, the team's founding year. I thought of my cousins from Boston, their obsession with their team's Super Bowl wins. (Yet the team couldn't make it to the playoffs their first year without their UGGs model, but enough on that.)

I googled the Bears' Super Bowl wins. There was only one: 1986.

First number a low tone, the other three on the higher end.

The lock chimed. Go, Bears.

I flipped through the folders and found my original scholarship letter along with the one dated today, and took pictures of both. Proof that criteria had changed without notice. Mrs. Lawson would've been able to see that. She might've had an alibi for the murder, but her behavior was still suspicious—especially considering those recommendation letters we found on the flash drive. Was she involved in what happened to Mr. Medina? Or was she just covering her tracks now that he was gone?

Closing the drawer, I dared to open another: James, Julius.

Voices sounded in the hallway: Ms. Faiza. I took a picture of whatever lay on top of his file and left the office, pulling the gum back out the lock. Keys fumbled in the door as I dropped to the ground.

"Yes, girl. I heard that— Excuse me, can I help you?" I looked up to see Ms. Faiza in the doorway on her cell and not far behind her, Maddie was entering the main administrative office across the hallway.

"Sorry, I thought I had left my phone in here. Found it, though." I held it up.

"No problem. I'm always leaving mine in random places, too." Ms. Faiza slipped into her chair and went back to gossiping with whoever was at the other end of her call.

I let out a breath, relieved.

Back in the main hall, I passed the glass doors of the front office to see Maddie sitting at the edge of Emile's desk, sipping a smoothie. Catching my gaze, she smiled.

I was not a vengeful person but, in that moment, I was ready to choose violence. She was playing with my life like a rag doll, carelessly. With her family's money, a scholarship probably meant nothing to her. For me, it was everything. In my mind, I could imagine what Frankie would say. *Stick to the high road. Inhale, exhale. This will all shake out soon enough.*

When I solved the case, she won't be smiling then.

Once I was around the corner, and alone, I looked down to the photo I'd taken of Julius's file. It was a copy of his SAT score and a student ID pinned to the top. There he was with his lopsided grin. But the name on the ID said Antonio Garcia.

With five minutes left in fourth period, the seniors' cafeteria was packed. I looked for Julius among the tables, finding him with a bunch of jocks. I dropped a book in front of him. "Time for a pop quiz."

"Kelley Green Eyes." He gave me a tense smile.

I didn't smile back.

"Guys, I'll meet you outside." He straightened up, and I sat down across from him.

"Didn't know you were a jock," I muttered as his friends left us alone.

"You mean you didn't assume that I, one of six Black guys in senior year, shot hoops and made the varsity team?"

A smile tugged on my lips. "You have the right build maybe, but you were *at* the game the other week, not *in* the game. And definitely not in uniform."

"I love how you notice the little things." He grinned. "Soccer. My mom had me dribbling as soon as I could walk."

I nodded, taking the SAT prep book and opening it to a random section.

"'Liselle finds a hostel for $99.95 per night, plus an eight percent tax—'"

"One, that's an expensive-ass hostel, and two, are you really quizzing me right now? Are you looking for a tutor, because we can go about this a different way."

"The tax is applied to the room rate plus a one-time non-taxed fee of five dollars—"

"Ah, I know. Someone told you my score and you think I paid for it."

I locked eyes with him. "Which of the following solves for Liselle's stay of X nights?"

"$1.08(99.95x) + 5$. Try a harder one."

Checking the answer key, I scanned the pages to find something else.

"Picture an isosceles triangle, the inner base is thirty-two feet, the inner length of the other two sides twenty-four feet. What's the value of cos x? I can show you the drawing—"

"Two over three."

Damn. I flipped to the next section for English questions.

"You don't have to do this," Julius started.

"The following passage . . ." I rattled off a few more questions, all of which he answered before I ever finished giving all the multiple-choice options.

"The answer is B. There's a reason I have a perfect score, Kelley Green Eyes. I've always had to work twice as hard just to stay a step behind everyone else here."

I closed the book. Everyone else in the cafeteria was gone, only the two of us left.

"I guess I can understand that." I stared at the table, clenching and unclenching my jaw.

"I know you do. You're the only sophomore with a full AP schedule across both semesters. You're actually the first in the school, but I doubt anyone told you that. Mr. Medina was waiting until the end of the year to celebrate it for you. He knew you would crush it here."

Of course he did. I kept my head down as my face grew warm. I still couldn't think of him without the flood of feelings. First sadness, then guilt from the anger that always followed.

"Why don't you ask me what you're really after?"

I cut my eyes to Julius, remembering how he didn't flinch when I said Mr. Medina's death was murder. *He knows.* My stomach churned with nerves. *Could it be him, though?*

Julius reached across the table, picking up my phone. Within a few moments his own cell rang. "When you want to talk—and I mean talk, not these interrogations that feel like I'm in a dark room staring at a one-way mirror—text me. We can talk about anything."

He stood up from the table and left.

I looked at his number in my phone, and then opened the group text.

Jolene:
It's not a hack job.

Frankie:
How'd you figure that?

Jolene:
I found the test taker.

FOURTEEN

FRIDAY, MARCH 4, 3:03 P.M.

OUR FIRST HINT should have been his SAT score. The 1600 was suspicious, but it was also during Julius's sophomore year—months before anyone else took their practice tests. Another alarm bell should've been only seven of the eight files having recommendation letters from Mrs. Lawson. Whatever the parents were paying to get their kids these scores had to include a letter from the dean, and Julius as the test taker wouldn't need one. He was smart enough on his own.

When the last bell rang, my legs couldn't get me out of the school fast enough. Friday nights usually meant meetups at my house, but Frankie had caught a break with the encrypted files, so we decided to meet at his place.

The wrought-iron gate groaned as I pushed past and approached the two-story redbrick. I took the steps two at a time, before ringing the doorbell. Frankie's mini me opened the door.

"Hey, RJ." I stepped past Frankie's little brother, ready to bound upstairs.

"Jo! Wait, I got something to show ya." He turned his head, pointing to the scar where the bullet had grazed his scalp and narrowly missed his eye. He used to hate it, the light-colored line burned into his dark brown complexion, but now that he was ten, he'd gotten into visiting the barbershop and having new designs cut into his fade, using the scar as part of it. Today, he had a shooting star.

"Looking fresh there, little man. It's cute."

"Cute?" he huffed. "Don't you mean . . . sexy?" He wiggled his eyebrows.

"Wha— RJ, what do you know about sexy?" I stifled a laugh as he started to moonwalk and groove to an invisible beat.

"Boy, stop harassing Jolene!" His mom rounded the corner from the kitchen, delivering a playful slap to the back of his head with one hand while handing me a platter of turkey sandwiches with the other. "Take these on up, dear."

"Thanks, Mrs. Palmer." I made my escape up the steps, entering Frankie's room right as he pulled on his signature oversized hoodie.

"Hey, Jo. Yes!" He bit into a sandwich before letting out a "Mmm . . . sammich."

I rolled my eyes as he scarfed down the half in two bites. "What's up with your brother?"

He grinned. "He found Dad's playlist he made for my moms called 'Sexy Time' and now he's been running around the house gyrating. He's gotten the talk already, so he knows exactly what the playlist is for, but I think he's just pushing their buttons for fun."

There was another ring of the doorbell, the creak of the front door opening, and a few moments later, Sabrina's voice. "Lil bro, you know I like girls and only girls, right?"

"Let me go get her." In a blink, Frankie was out the door, shouting at RJ.

I settled in the swivel chair at his desk. His room was such a contrast to Sabrina's. He had a board where he pinned old articles of cold cases we've solved, a corner full of Columbia paraphernalia, and another wall with sci-fi movie posters. (He preferred *Star Trek* to *Star Wars*.) Looking at the almost life-size photo of Uhura, aka Zoe Saldana, I wouldn't be surprised if she had something to do with it. There was also a poster of Gamora from *Guardians of the Galaxy*, and the blue chick from James Cameron's *Avatar*. Hard not to detect a theme.

Sabrina and Frankie walked through the door, the former plopping on Frankie's unmade bed. "Sweetie, it's been a *day*!"

Frankie opened his little mini fridge and handed us both an orange pop.

"Wanna talk about it?" I asked.

"Nope!" She popped open the can. "You washed these tops, right?"

Frankie narrowed his eyes. "You know my moms always washes and wipes down all the groceries that come through the front door. She read one article about rats in a warehouse and that was it."

She shrugged. "Just checking. Let's talk about Julius. Are you positive he's taking the tests, Jo?"

"Yes. And I've been meaning to cross his parents off the whiteboard, too. His dad is out west somewhere, and his mom passed away last year."

"Dang, that's hard," she muttered as she took a sip. "Mmm. And I forgot to update you guys on the Russells and the Mitchells. They can be crossed off, too. The Mitchells had court, and the Russells were at North Shore. Something about planning for an alumni fundraiser?"

I groaned. "About that—" I ran through the details of my meeting with Mrs. Lawson and my new plans for Saturday night.

"First, threats left in your locker, and now someone's messing with your scholarship?" Sabrina raised her brows. "This is getting a little too real."

"I told you earlier, I'm backing away from snooping. We can focus on the evidence we already have from Mr. Medina's flash drive. It has to all be there." I nodded over to Frankie. "You said you found something?"

He hesitated. I know he didn't like how quickly I moved past the subject. Sighing, he motioned for me to get up so he could sit at his desk, and then he booted up his laptop. "I got it unlocked this morning. I was waiting for you two. It's actually a lot easier than you would think, breaking an encryption. I mean there's different ways to do it, whether it's a zip or a .RAR—"

Sabrina waved him off. "Less talking. This sounds like school. No more school."

He rolled his eyes and stuffed another sandwich in his mouth. Within minutes, the folder was up on the screen, revealing scanned notes in Mr. Medina's handwriting and a few saved emails. One torn page listed five names, each followed by an Ivy League school and a four-digit number. Test scores.

MeiLing Zhao, Stanford, 1480
Alec Cole, Yale, 1510
Luce Peterson, Princeton, 1490
Charlie Samuels, Stanford, 1450
Joshua Morgensten, Harvard, 1460

"These names. I think these are students who graduated last year. I've seen a few in the trophy cases outside the guidance offices."

"How are we going to eliminate these people?" Frankie muttered. "They're all over the country."

"Social media, I guess?" said Sabrina. "But these students are long gone. Would they even have known what Mr. Medina was up to? Not to mention this isn't exactly hard evidence; it's scribble on a scrap piece of paper. I doubt Mr. Medina would approach their parents without something more substantial."

I nodded at the screen. "Well, what about the emails? It looks like one long chain."

From: Medina, Manuel
Sent: Friday, February 19, 9:54 a.m.
To: "Whiskey Blue"
Subject: I need your badge
g drta jmivrdzle wmm pmq ssp zr szjh rdbvap kfa tgpp

From: "Whiskey Blue"
Sent: Friday, February 19, 11:23 a.m.
To: Medina, Manuel
Subject: RE: I need your badge
fkn qk?

From: Medina, Manuel
Sent: Friday, February 19, 3:18 p.m.
To: "Whiskey Blue"

Subject: RE: I need your badge

chvapvb kwdetgwcq, ufsn smoj

From: "Whiskey Blue"
Sent: Friday, February 19, 7:02 p.m.
To: Medina, Manuel
Subject: RE: I need your badge

wkl ekk rk xgrv ka dmnv rdrl pyyr

From: Medina, Manuel
Sent: Saturday, February 20, 12:46 p.m.
To: "Whiskey Blue"
Subject: RE: I need your badge

wwe'r

From: "Whiskey Blue"
Sent: Saturday, February 20, 2:57 p.m.
To: Medina, Manuel
Subject: RE: I need your badge

wkl qpzjh yyrv rdvqa ymqeb zfeo?

From: Medina, Manuel
Sent: Saturday, February 20, 9:13 p.m.
To: "Whiskey Blue"
Subject: RE: I need your badge

5 39 33 | 4 59 28 | 12 51 60

"Whoa." Frankie sat up. "It must be a cipher. There are so many types, though, Caesar cipher, Playfair, even the Egyptians had their own—"

"Oh, and that one in *Skyfall*! Aiko made me watch all those James Bond movies, what was it called?"

"I don't think that one was real, Bri," I replied, skimming the letters.

She flipped through her phone. "Do you think Mr. Medina went the Benedict Cumberbatch route again? He played that British guy who cracked ciphers. The enigma code?"

"If you're referring to the movie we watched in history class, it was a cipher used by the Nazis. I don't think Mr. Medina would use that." Frankie shook his head. "No, it has to be a Caesar cipher. But how do we crack it?"

"Look at these letter groupings." I tapped on the "ssp" and then "wwe'r." "It must shift between letters. Can you think of a three-letter word that starts with repeating letters? And this one is a contraction, so we can assume that 'r' is a 't,' maybe even an 's,' but there's no way to know how many times it shifts or whether it's to the left or to the right."

"To the left. Or at least I think so. Mr. Medina was left-handed, so he would probably favor that side. Unless the person he communicated with set up the code." Frankie paused. "You're right, though. There's no easy pattern to even make a guess."

"And what about this note: '5 39 33 / 4 59 28 / 12 51 60'?" I pointed to the one cipher that differed from the others. "What's that supposed to be?"

Frankie shrugged, and Sabrina looked just as confused. There was something familiar about the string of numbers, but I couldn't put my finger on it. And the subject line: "I need your badge." What did that mean?

"Back to square one," I said. "I don't get it. The flash drive is just test scores, coded emails, and handwritten notes. How is this enough to kill over?"

"We'll figure it out," said Frankie, closing the laptop. "Until then, promise us one thing. Especially since someone *did* decide this was enough to kill over."

He didn't have to finish his sentence.

"No more snooping?"

Sabrina narrowed her eyes, and I held up my hands in surrender.

"No more snooping. I promise."

At least, I would try.

FIFTEEN

BLACK SLACKS, WHITE button-up, and a black clip-on bow tie. That was the uniform of choice for the sixteen scholarship students chosen to wait on North Shore's most elite alumni attending tonight's fundraiser dinner. The average student's goal: chat up donors in hopes of impressing one enough for a scholarship. My goal: track down Chief Ryan. And no, it didn't qualify as snooping.

I was running late, which was consistent of me. Surprisingly, as a private school kid, I didn't own a pair of black slacks. Reya had to drive me to Target for a last-minute shopping trip, and neither of us can go into that store and buy just one thing. With a trunk full of new hair products, a couple of books, and a pull-up bar, we were roughly an hour behind schedule for the setup call time.

"I hate when you tell me things and not your parents," she grumbled, responding to my update on everything I'd been up to.

"But that's what makes you so awesome. You can tell me how they'll react. Besides, I'm going to get my scholarship back tonight. There's no need to worry them about it." I fiddled with the clip-on tie in the passenger-seat mirror.

"After this, whether or not it works, you have to stop with this investigation. Your mom told me about your suspect list—"

I waved her off. "She's overreacting."

"And you're underreacting," she countered. "Jo. I've seen a lot of cases come through the state attorney's office that involve privileged kids and politicians. They always find a way to avoid the consequences. And you know who takes the fall?"

Julius's lopsided grin flashed in my mind. *The ones who can't afford to defend themselves.*

I closed the mirror. "How about this? *The moment* it gets to be too much, I turn everything over to you. All the evidence, all our theories." I gave her my pouty lip, which she never denied. "Please? Rey, we're so close."

She pulled into the school's long driveway, her knuckles turning white as she gripped the steering wheel. "You're done snooping? Only research left?"

I nodded. Not a lie, necessarily.

She shook her head but gave in. "Not *the* moment. The moment before *the moment*. You come directly to me."

I grinned. "The moment before the moment." I squeezed her tight before slipping out of the car.

"And, Jo?"

"Yeah?"

"The money trail. It always points to the one with the most to lose."

———

Stepping into the banquet hall, the room was dark and moody, its walls covered in gold embellishments and back-lit with a vibrant blue. Crystal chandeliers hung above, giving the illusion of icicles dripping with an ethereal light.

The event was already set up, twenty round tables the color of midnight covered with gold-rimmed plates, ready to host two hundred of North Shore's deepest pockets. A few other scholarship kids huddled in the corners, reading over notes scrawled across white index cards. I managed to sneak a look at the guest list, double-checking for Chief Ryan's name. Alongside his, I caught the names of Mr. and Mrs. Zhao, Senator Peterson, and Rosalyn Samuels—parents of the graduated students found in Mr. Medina's encrypted files.

Is this how they recruited Julius? At an event like this?

"Kelley Green Eyes."

Of course he's here.

I turned around to find Julius dressed identical to the other scholarship students, yet on him it looked less like an outfit he picked up from his local department store and more like he had it tailored to fit. Like he was meant to be here. "I didn't expect to see you here," I greeted. "Do the donors help with college, too?"

"They do, but I already have a full ride. Perfect SATs and all." He winked. "Though I'm guessing that's why you're here? I thought you already had a scholarship?" His eyes watched the door, and before I could answer, Chief Ryan entered with Maddie as his plus one.

Her eyes narrowed as soon as she saw the two of us together.

"One tip," he started, without taking his eyes off Maddie. "Corporal Andrews went to De La Salle, though her husband is an alum here. Tall, red hair, blue eyes. Mention that you transferred from there and you're good to go."

He didn't look back as he left. Instead, he sauntered over to Maddie, slinging his arm over her shoulder as he whispered something in her ear. Again, her eyes shot over to glare at me.

It wasn't uncomfortable at all.

I frowned looking after the two of them. *What is he doing with her?*

No snooping, I reminded myself. I was here to get my scholarship back. Though that was a flaw in and of itself. Chief Ryan was technically still on our suspect board.

"Jolene Kelley?" A familiar light-skinned boy walked up to me, black freckles dotted across his cheeks.

"That's me."

"Cool, I'm Tre Charles. Ms. Faiza told me to come find you. She said you're supposed to work as one of the servers and need to come to the back."

"Okay." I looked at the guests steadily arriving. With my attention on Julius and Maddie, I'd lost Chief Ryan to the mix of black tuxes and jewel-toned gowns.

Tre motioned for me to follow. "Are you coming?"

"Right." I scanned the room one more time before letting him lead me back toward the kitchen. *Hmm. Light-skinned with black freckles.* "You must be Lieutenant Charles's son, right? You look just like him."

"Yep."

"How did you end up here? Your dad said you go to Morgan Park."

"He cashed in a favor with one of his work buddies. You probably already know the tuition for North Shore is steep. But the chemistry focus here is amazing, and if I want a chance to attend next fall, I'll need a donor in addition to the financial aid the school offers. My dad gave me a list of people to talk to." He pulled a card out of his pocket, waving it for me to see.

I nodded, thinking back to Alderman Corben in Lieutenant Charles's office. This opportunity for Tre must've been part of the exchange for closing Mr. Medina's case so quickly.

"Ms. Faiza's over there." He pointed. "I have to go back inside with the greeters."

"Appreciate the escort. Make sure to mention that second-place ribbon at the science fair. That's sure to impress."

"Oh! I almost forgot about that. Thanks!"

After a lecture about timeliness from Ms. Faiza, and a quick lesson on how to pass out champagne while balancing a tray with one hand, I was back on the banquet floor. I felt as though there should've been a law against sixteen-year-olds handing out alcohol, and there probably was, but that didn't seem to faze anyone. I guess with Chief Ryan in attendance, anything goes.

Searching the crowd, I focused on finding my target. Julius seemed to have no intention of talking to any donors. He sat in the corner with Maddie and a few other society kids, laughing while sipping what I was sure wasn't sparkling cider. It was weird to see Julius like this. I'd never seen him with Maddie's crowd as school, but he seemed to fit right in.

Across the room, I spotted dark roots and frosted-blond hair packaged in a black tux. I made my way over, almost dropping my tray twice. Ms. Faiza forgot to mention the wobble that occurred every time someone lifted a glass. There was a science to this.

"Chief Ryan." I nodded to one of the few drinks I had left.

"Jolene!" He picked up a champagne, the raspberry bobbing up and down in the fizzy bubbles. "How are your parents? It's been a few weeks since I last saw you at headquarters. Are you wrapped up in a new cold case?"

"Something like that. Though I've hit a snag."

"Hmmm." He took a quick sip, his eyes sweeping the room behind me. "You already know, my doors are always open if you ever need to run a theory past me."

"Thanks, I might take you up on that for this case."

He was distracted, watching for someone. I tried to follow his gaze only to find Maddie glaring at me before whispering to Julius. It was more of a death stare, really.

"Actually, I do have a question—about my scholarship?"

He placed his glass down. "Yes, I assumed that was why you were here. Maddie volunteers with our scholarship board after school. She mentioned your status changed."

"She talks about me?" I wasn't quite sure how I felt about that.

"She's aware that we know each other. I bragged a little about you solving those two cold cases last spring. It's part of the reason I awarded you the scholarship in the first place."

"Are you aware that my status has changed unfairly?"

"Hmmm?" His attention was on me now.

"The GPA requirement changed without notification. I

checked the website. The requirement is still 3.5, yet the letter I got says it's 4.0. There's been a mistake. You mentioned Maddie is volunteering—"

"Well, I trust what the letter says."

I blinked, confused. "Excuse me?"

He didn't look at me as he spoke. Instead, he took another glass from my tray, leaving me to quickly adjust my grip for the change in weight. He finished it in two gulps. "It could be that you need to focus more on your schooling," he said coolly, his mouth tight. His kind demeanor had been replaced by something cold and frigid. "Pardon me, I see someone I need to talk to." And just like that, I'd been dismissed.

My mouth hung open.

"Lil Blue! How is that dad of yours?" Chief Ryan laid a heavy hand on Tre's shoulder.

Laughter sounded from Maddie's table, but I didn't look. Trying to ignore her, I turned to leave, nearly running over Alderman Corben.

"Oh, so sorry!" I managed to balance the tray as he caught a rogue champagne teetering on its edge.

"That's one way to serve a drink! And no need to apologize; that was all me. I rushed over to catch John but looks like I've lost him to a promising student. How are you doing? Are you here looking for a donor for next year?"

I glanced back once more to Chief Ryan, still in disbelief of what he said: another veiled threat. "I guess so."

"Well." Alderman Corben opened his arms.

"You want me to pitch myself to you?"

"If anything, consider it practice." He smiled his campaign smile. Still creepy.

I shrugged. "I'm a sophomore transfer from De La Salle. In all AP classes," I opened my mouth to say more but paused. Chief Ryan had moved back into my line of sight and was talking to Julius now, handing him a stuffed envelope, which Julius hurried to hide away. The latter caught me staring.

"You're being modest. Nic mentioned that about you."

I snapped back to the conversation. "Mrs. Medina?"

"I'm helping her with a remembrance project to honor her late husband. I'll let her share those details when the time is right. But I think any donor here would be happy to sponsor your next year. Corporal Andrews went to De La Salle; I'm sure she would love to speak with you. Have you taken your PSATs yet?"

I nodded. "Mid-1300s."

"Oh? And they say your SAT scores run a hundred points higher than your PSAT, don't they? Promising indeed." He grinned, and I tried to smile back.

What was in that envelope? Why were Chief Ryan and Julius talking?

"Ah, my wife is waving me over. It looks like she got cornered by the dean, and she despises the woman." He plucked a flower from a centerpiece at the table next to us. "Think this will do the trick?"

I managed a real smile. His assistant wasn't lying about their relationship. "I think she'll love it."

He winked. "Here's hoping. I wish you well tonight."

I nodded again. "Thanks, Alderman Corben."

Already wanting the night to end, I headed back to the kitchen only to find Julius waiting for me at the swinging doors. "You've chosen interesting company tonight."

"You spoke to the chief, too, if I recall, and Maddie. What was that about?" I eyed his pocket.

He grabbed the last glass from my tray. "Apparently she was in need of an arm piece for the evening."

I scrunched up my face. "And you just do whatever she says? I thought dating wasn't your thing."

"It depends on if it's in my best interest. Or in the interests of others I care about. Maddie wasn't always like this, you know. She's changed since her mother walked out last year. Her need for attention—I don't know. I don't think her dad is giving it to her."

"Oh." I frowned. "And what about the chief?"

"I meant what I said before: You don't want to get involved." He finished his glass and started to leave.

I clenched my jaw. I was getting frustrated with his vague responses. "Or what? Are you going to threaten me, too?"

He stopped and sighed but didn't turn to face me. "Just . . . don't. Trust me on this."

SIXTEEN

SUNDAY, MARCH 6, 1:24 P.M.

I SPENT THE rest of the weekend trying to forget the alumni fundraiser and counted down to the moment Sabrina would arrive and I could prepare her for a day of shadowing me at North Shore. We texted all day about it, though it was mainly her texting me, trying to figure out what she should wear to make the perfect first impression. This might have been a ruse, but she always took fashion seriously. On my shadow day, I wore fitted jeans, my mom's old Converses, and a hoodie that read, "Not Today, Satan." After that confession, Sabrina decided to confer with Aiko instead.

That afternoon, I tried studying for an upcoming test, but it was too hard to focus when I knew Sabrina and I would be crossing more suspects off our list the following morning via Operation Emile. (Sabrina's name, not mine.) I grew anxious, nervous about what the attendance records would reveal about Maddie and Julius. Saturday night had literally been a dinner full of present and past murder suspects. It was as if I was constantly surrounded by them.

"Mind if I come in?" My dad appeared in my doorway, a large envelope in hand.

I straightened up in my chair.

He stepped into my room. "I saw Mrs. Medina at church today."

I must've made a face, as it wasn't Easter or Christmas, because he immediately continued with "She had asked if I could meet her after Mass."

"Oh. How is she?"

"Good. As good as can be expected at least. She said Spain was beautiful. She got back Friday and went by the school yesterday to clean out Mr. Medina's office. She mentioned finding the fourth book of a collection she promised you. Those should arrive tomorrow."

I nodded. "I'll tell her thank you in the morning."

It was Dad's turn to nod. He fidgeted with the envelope. "There were a few other personal effects of Mr. Medina's she came across. This was one."

He turned the envelope over in his hands. *For Jolene* was scrawled across the front.

My breath hitched. I stood and crossed the room, only to

hesitate when I got close enough to grab it. "Do you know what it is?"

"I do." He paused, gauging what to say next. "Do you remember the deal I tried to make with you? About a four-year college?"

I nodded, keeping my gaze on Mr. Medina's handwriting.

"Well, I got the proposal from somewhere. Manuel had this idea about starting a nonprofit in Englewood, sort of like a community center for kids. He thought you might have an interest in that line of work—in addition to the private investigator thing." He handed me the envelope.

With a slow exhale, I lifted the sealed flap. Inside was a brochure for the University of Chicago and a handwritten note. Mr. Medina had listed a few programs with a focus on public policy, the words "Inequality, Social Problems, and Change" catching my attention. There was also a campus tour scheduled for a few weeks' time.

Jolene,

Before you start, it's a _great_ school. Just as great as some of the other schools kids at North Shore move on to. I arranged for you to meet a few people. Give it a chance, and if you don't like it, at least I tried. And don't be mad at your parents about this. This is me. So, if you hate it, well, this time you can be mad at me.

I almost choked. *Mad at me.*

"I can't—I can't think about this right now."

"Jo?"

My mind reeled. *I can't be mad at him. He's dead.*

I pushed the letter and brochure back into my dad's hands.

"Jolene—"

"Just, not right now." I crawled into bed, and after a minute, he shut the door behind him.

Emotions flooded my mind. The anger I'd pushed down whenever it flickered to the surface. I'd been mad for too long. Mad at anything and everything.

"Argh!" I punched my pillow. It was getting harder to box away my feelings. But I couldn't deal with them—not during my investigation. They would just get in the way. Still, my mind wandered back to Mr. Medina's words.

What would that make me, someone who gets mad at a dead person?

There's no point in being angry at him. It won't bring him back.

You're alone. Move on.

———

"Jo?" Sabrina pushed open the door a few hours later, Frankie trailing behind her.

"Seriously? Did my parents call you again?" I asked him.

He smiled, though it was a little weak. "Just here for

moral support." He went over to my desk, rooting through the bottom drawer for my candy stash. Sabrina turned on the TV, debating between which streaming service to boot up.

"What exactly are you two doing?"

"We already know you aren't going to talk to us," she started, switching on *True Detective*. "The best we can do is veg out and talk about cases." She scrolled through the seasons trying to pick one.

"Thanks, but we're stuck on those ciphers." I snatched the Red Vines from Frankie and narrowed my eyes. "Off-limits."

He grinned and took out his own pack from his pocket. "*Well*, maybe we can watch some stuff that has ciphers in it. What shows did Mr. Medina like?" He grabbed the remote from Sabrina.

"The classics: *Matlock*; *Columbo*; *Murder, She Wrote*." I plopped back down on my bed. "I don't know if those had a lot of ciphers, though."

"There was an episode of BBC's *Sherlock* that had something different. Something with a city guide book, remember?" Sabrina asked.

"A book cipher, but that's numbers—wait." I'd just watched an episode like that, too. I took the remote and found *Criminal Minds*. "The number sequence at the end of the email chain." I fast-forwarded the season two opener to Reid's aha moment and pointed to the screen. "Three numbers. Usually it's page, line, word. But you have to make sure whoever you are communicating with has the same edition of the book."

"The Hound of the Baskervilles." Frankie got up and started fumbling around my bookcase before moving on to my closet. He brought out a box labeled GRADE 8 and pulled out my copy of the masterpiece. "Here it is. But didn't he have a first edition?"

I paced. "Mrs. Medina is giving me his books, but they won't get here until tomorrow."

"He wouldn't have based it on his fancy copy. Whoever he was communicating with would need to have a first edition, too. What are the chances of that?" Sabrina pulled out her phone. "I saved a few screenshots of the cipher. First number is a five," she murmured.

Frankie started turning the pages.

"He would have adjusted the cipher to something you could use on any book. Try chapter five." I stood over his shoulder, heart racing.

"Line thirty-nine?" he asked.

I shook my head. "He wouldn't be able to control that. Lines would shift based on the book shape, right? What about paragraphs? We have to think of what *wouldn't* change."

Sabrina perked up. "Chapter, paragraph, word number!"

I grinned. After this weekend, I needed this. We were so close.

"Why is the type so small?" Frankie muttered. "Word number?"

"Thirty-three," Sabrina answered.

It took a few minutes, but after several restarts we had the three words.

"City Hope Scholastics." I sunk down to the floor.

"Mean anything to you?" Frankie asked.

"Not a damn thing." I ran my hands over my face. "We're running out of time!"

Frankie sat down next to me. "Hey. There's no ticking clock on this."

I rested my head on his shoulder. Of course he would say that. My recap of Saturday night didn't include the increasing number of threats. He didn't know.

I had to solve this before the threats turned into something more.

Like my blood on the tracks.

SEVENTEEN

MONDAY, MARCH 7, 8:26 A.M.

STEPPING ONTO SCHOOL grounds the next morning, I looked over to Sabrina as she took in a dramatic breath. She had opted for her own version of North Shore's uniform—a plaid, dark blue skirt and a crisp tucked button-up with some type of gold chain under the collar. Stars and moons hung down from the chain, matching her celestial earrings. Over her blouse—a dark blue boyfriend cardigan with orange accents. And for some ridiculous reason, she had ditched the usual double-layer tights we both always wore in the winter months and went with white knee-highs.

"It's cold as a mother—"

"You're the one who dressed yourself like that," I

countered as we walked up the steps and through the front doors of the administrative wing.

"I want Mrs. Medina to believe I'm taking this seriously. How's my hair?"

I glanced up to her two high buns on either side and fixed one of the loose curls she'd left out to frame her face. "Perfect. And the bronze eyeliner was a great choice," I added, knowing the next question would be about makeup.

She applied another coat of gloss to her lips and nodded. "Good. Okay. I'm ready."

We stashed our coats in my locker, and a few minutes later found ourselves in Mrs. Medina's office. Framed pictures filled her space, mixed in with blue-and-orange school paraphernalia. The photo she kept behind her had always been my favorite: a black-and-white still from her wedding, showing Mr. Medina lifting her up in an embrace. The smiles on both their faces were the biggest I'd ever seen. I kicked myself mentally for thinking there was ever an affair. Aside from my own parents, I used to believe love like theirs only existed in fairy tales.

Mrs. Medina got up as we entered, greeting us with the warmest hugs. "Jolene, Sabrina, so good to see you both."

"Thank you for doing this, Mrs. Medina. I never in a million years thought I could go here with Jo. I mean, I don't know how my mom will be able to pay for it—"

"Ah, don't worry about that, my dear. There are

scholarships available. Now sit down, both of you. Sabrina, we can finalize which fashion classes would be best for you to observe."

I sat in the chair by the door as the two of them chatted away about Spain and Textiles Through the Ages versus Fashion Merchandising. Mrs. Medina had her own book-case similar to the one in her husband's office, filled with some of the usual women's fiction classics like Jane Austen and Toni Morrison, a few titles by Amy Tan. Another shelf held what looked more like class-assigned novels; I recog-nized some books from my Gothic literature curriculum. Finally, a row of historical romances—I assumed her favor-ite genre based on how many I had seen in the loft. I pulled one from the shelf to find a note scrawled on the title page from Mr. Medina.

We had gotten so close last night only to hit another dead end. If we knew who he traded ciphers with . . .

"You and Mr. Medina met at a bookstore, right?" I asked, flipping through the pages.

She smiled. "Yes, about four years ago. Spotted him in the mystery section of course."

"Of course." I placed the book back on the shelf. "Did he ever talk about ciphers?" I asked lightly.

Sabrina met my gaze and nodded. "We found this cool one we know he would've loved," she added.

"Ah." Mrs. Medina's smile grew wider. "Did I ever tell

you that's how he asked me out for our first date? He slipped a note into that very same book one day while I was in line for coffee. I thought it was his phone number." She laughed. "A very weird phone number. But it was one of those ciphers he liked so much.

"I figured it out after three days," she went on. "It was a place for us to meet in Millennium Park. He told me that he had to be sure."

"Be sure of what?" Sabrina asked.

"Be sure I was the one," she said, a light smile in her voice. She stayed quiet for a minute, her eyes unfocused. She cleared her throat. "Well, you two are good to go. You can pick up your visitor's pass at the front office, Sabrina."

"Thanks, Mrs. Medina." Sabrina stood.

I hovered for a moment. "Did he ever write ciphers with anyone else?"

"Oh, not as much as he did when he was younger. I remember him telling me he had a friend who went into the force and they traded codes in high school. It drove his teachers crazy."

I nodded, letting that simmer in my thoughts. "Thanks again," I added as I closed her office door behind me.

Sabrina quirked up an eyebrow. "Way to be casual. Are you thinking what I'm thinking?"

"The emails with the ciphers. Whoever he was emailing

had to be someone he knew well and traded ciphers with before. Especially that book cipher."

"His high school friend. If we can figure out who that is . . ."

I nodded again. "Remember the subject line? 'I need your badge.' If it was someone on the force . . ."

Sabrina's eyes widened. "I have an idea, but we can talk more on it later. Time for Operation Emile."

Down the hall, we walked through the doors of the front office to a greeting I did not expect.

"Oh, this has to be her! Of course it is!" Emile stood from his desk and came around to give Sabrina a squeeze. "You are going to do our uniforms such justice."

Sabrina grinned.

I waited a beat to be acknowledged before I realized that wasn't happening. "I'll just go wait in the hall," I said to no one in particular, and went back out the door. Students walked back and forth, most of them chatting away with friends. Just about everyone had someone else here—except me of course.

Within ten minutes, Emile walked out the front office. "I need to get something from my car to show Sabrina. Don't go anywhere. I can get you two late passes for first period."

"I'll make sure she stays at your desk while you're gone," I promised.

He hurried off down the hall as I walked in to see Sabrina behind his computer.

She peeked over Emile's raised counter. "Whew, it's you."

"Did it work?" I asked, in a low voice.

"Well, he was already signed in, but I had to knock his mouse a few times to make sure the screen didn't fall asleep. I already checked Jhamal Russell's attendance for the morning of the murder. He has the most luscious dreadlocks I've ever seen, by the way. He's accounted for. So is his sister, Whitney."

"Did you look up Kehlani?"

"Also accounted for. I took pictures of their files for our records. But do you know who's not accounted for?" She tapped the screen and I walked around. Madison Ryan.

"Okay, then. This is getting interesting. How about Julius?" I bit my lip as Sabrina typed in his name. Absent. My eyes flicked to the front door. "Print out his file."

"Why?"

"Just humor me." I walked over to the printer nook off the front entryway. A few moments later, the machine came to life. I opened my backpack, sliding in each sheet of paper as it came off the press.

"Got it," Emile exclaimed as he walked back in the office—right as I stuffed the last sheet into my bag.

Sabrina smiled up at him. "Yes! That's the perfect swatch."

I leaned out of the nook to see Emile pulling various pieces of fabric out of a canvas tote, matching them together.

"And you have just the right alabaster complexion. You have to make it for your school's spring formal."

De La Salle didn't have a spring formal, but I stayed silent. The late bell rang.

"I'm going to have lunch with the department lead today. Don't worry." Emile winked to Sabrina. "You'll be here next fall."

"Thanks, Emile!" She waved, walking over to me as I ushered her out the door.

"Damn, forgot to grab the late pass," I muttered.

"What did you need Julius's file for?"

I riffled through the papers, looking for what I didn't want to find, but there it was.

"Julius had a disciplinary write-up? For swinging at Mr. Medina!" Sabrina snatched the paper from my hands.

"It was filed by Maddie. I thought she was lying." I read over Sabrina's shoulder.

"Lying? Wait, you knew about this?"

I shook my head. "Not exactly. She said something about a fight, but she isn't the most reliable source."

"Do you think Maddie made a fake statement? Faked this like she did with your scholarship letter?"

Student Disciplinary Action Form

Student: Julius James **Student No.** 443112 **Date of Warning:** February 4

Reported By: Madison Ryan ☒ Student ☐ Teacher ☐ Faculty

Type of Violation: ☐ Attendance ☐ Behavioral ☒ Violent Act

Action to be Taken: ☒ Warning ☐ Suspension ☐ Expulsion

Witness Statement:
Student witnessed heated argument and vulgar language exchange between Mr. James and guidance counselor, Mr. Medina. Mr. James became violent and swung, to which Mr. Medina narrowly avoided. Evidential by hole in office wall.

Mr. Medina clarified that Mr. James was upset about a personal matter and sought guidance from Mr. Medina. Mr. James purposefully punched wall to "blow off steam."

Recommendation:
30 Work Study hours in Guidance Department

Dean's Signature:
Margot Lawson

I glanced at the date. Two weeks before the murder. "I remember a hole in Mr. Medina's office wall. He said the bookcase slipped from his grip while he was rearranging furniture."

"This really changes things," Sabrina whispered. "Julius has a history of violence."

I flipped through other pages of his file. "It's the only write-up, though. And Mr. Medina disputed Maddie's claim. It doesn't necessarily mean he's violent by nature—"

I stopped. I'd reached his financial papers. "City Hope Scholastic Achievement Award."

Sabrina stood next to me, wide-eyed. "Well, that's convenient."

EIGHTEEN

MONDAY, MARCH 7, 1:22 P.M.

"FRANKIE. THIS ISN'T going to work."

"Why not?"

I stared at my best friend of twelve years as he munched on my sour-cream-and-onion chips. Never mind the fact that they were kettle chips and he was one of the loudest chewers I knew, but we were sitting in the library under a sign that read NO FOOD OR DRINK. North Shore Preparatory Academy Library to be exact. During my lunch period.

School was still in session.

This morning after making it through Ms. Taylor's class, Sabrina spent second and third period in the humanities wing getting an up-close look at the fashion and textiles course load while texting with Frankie outside our usual group chat. Frankie then took it upon himself to skip the rest of the day at De La Salle and sneak onto North Shore's campus so we could discuss this morning's developments—in person.

"The guard outside didn't even stop me. And the map online was very detailed. Found you two without a hitch."

I sighed, slouching back in my chair. "Just don't take off your coat."

"But it's hot," he whined.

"You're the one wearing a De La Salle pride sweater today," Sabrina pointed out. "It literally says 'De La Salle Pride' in bold print. If Grams were here, she could read it clearly across the room without her glasses."

Frankie slid off his coat, then proceeded to slip his arms out of his sweater so he could turn it around. "Fixed."

I shook my head. "If you're going to steal my chips, at least hand me my apple." I took a bite of the sweet Red Delicious, looking around the library to note who might also be around. It was relatively empty. Quiet rows of dark, wooden bookshelves reached well above my five-foot-five self. We were nestled in the back near a bank of windows, the light pouring in to warm our faces. The closest student sat at the far end near the librarian's desk, shouting distance at best.

"Okay, so what made you skip world history and trek up here?"

Frankie pulled out his laptop, typed in a few things, and swiveled the screen around. "Since we have more context, I was able to tighten our Google search on the words in Mr. Medina's cipher."

In front of me was the homepage for some political organization—the Future of Chicago. I frowned. "I don't understand."

Sabrina leaned over. "Tap the 'Community' tab."

I hovered over the menu and clicked. There was boiler-plate language about giving back to Chicago and the Lakeview neighborhood, which was to be expected. What caught my attention was a blurb with a "Learn More" link about investing in our youth. Clicking on that, I landed on the scholarship page, specifically the City Hope Scholastic Achievement Award Scholarship. And there, with one of those oversized checks for eight thousand dollars, was Julius.

"I don't understand. Is this some type of PAC?" I asked.

"I'm not sure. But it is a group that raises money, then awards it to various causes, campaigns, and scholarships. Scroll down to the next photo."

There, plain as day, Julius was posing with Maddie and Chief Ryan.

"This is one of seven checks he received for this school year," Frankie pointed out. "I found the names of the people who run the organization, and Chief Ryan's name isn't on it, and neither is anyone else from our suspect list. But all the parents *do* show up on the donor list—with identical donation amounts: eight thousand dollars each."

"Seven checks, seven students. This is the how." I skimmed the article. "Julius takes the tests and gets paid through a scholarship. Adding up all these awards, he was overpaid, really. That would be fifty-six thousand this year. Tuition is steep but not that high."

Frankie cleared his throat, shooting a quick look at Sabrina. "We think you should stop talking with Julius. This plus the disciplinary write-up means he has motive. And no alibi. I know you two have bonded or whatever, but you can't ignore the evidence."

I frowned. There was something about Julius that always made me hesitate. He was definitely guilty of being involved in the scam. But murder? I stared at the photo— his goofy lopsided smile. "Okay."

"Really?"

"Until we know for sure who left that note, I should probably avoid him. And Maddie."

Sabrina exhaled. "Oh."

The two of them exchanged glances. They obviously expected me to push back. "Is this why you came up here today, Frankie? You thought I needed some type of intervention?"

Honestly, maybe I did need one. At the very least, Julius was suspicious and vague and playing at something. But I had to know why. "My only interest in talking with Julius before was because he was a suspect. We just need to find the killer to make sure Mr. Medina gets the justice he deserves. Besides that, I don't need to get wrapped up with those two anymore."

"All right, then," said Frankie, satisfied with my answer.

"You sure?" Sabrina pried.

"No need to make her second-guess, Bri." He shifted the computer back to himself.

Sabrina caught my eye and frowned. Knowing her, the conversation wasn't over. She turned her attention back to Frankie. "So, eight thousand a test—five kids last year, seven kids this year. Tuition here is what? Thirty thousand? What did he do with the extra money?"

"I'm assuming he used it to make ends meet, bills and things," I replied. "He's his sister's guardian. This had to be part of his income. He implied his dad might not send enough for him and his sister to get by."

"Well, now we have possible evidence that the scholarships were how the parents got the money to Julius. But what's the arrangement between the parents and the ringleader— whoever it is?" Frankie questioned. "Is it Chief Ryan?"

My mind flashed to the stuffed envelope I saw him handing Julius. I opened my mouth to give my theory, then remembered I hadn't shared that part of the night with the two of them yet. Reya's advice popped in my head: follow the money trail. I needed to tell them about the envelope—

"Excuse me?" Behind us stood a middle-aged woman, modestly dressed, with a fire-red pixie cut. Ms. Cox, the librarian.

"I see your visitor's pass, young lady, but the gentleman with the backward sweater, I don't recognize you."

Frankie grabbed the rest of the apple from my hand, slipped his laptop into his pack, and picked up his coat. "Catch y'all later." With no hesitation, he ran out of the library as fast as his scrawny legs would take him.

"Wait. Young man!" Ms. Cox hurried after him. "Stop! I'll call security!"

I tried my hardest not to laugh. Sabrina had no such luck. She let out a snort, quickly covering her mouth. We cleaned up the crumbs left over from our lunch and headed out to the hallway, steering clear of Ms. Cox along the way. I didn't have to look to feel her eyes on me.

Outside the library, students fast-walked around us, a sea of midnight blue, crescent white, and pops of bright orange. There was one more minute until the next bell rang, but lucky for us, my next class was close by.

"We didn't mean to bum-rush you about Julius," Sabrina began. "It's more Frankie than me. He's worried you're going to shut us out and try to do your own thing, solving this by yourself."

"Never." I reassured her.

It hurt to lie.

After school, Sabrina ordered our rideshare as we sat outside on the stone steps of the main hall. She squinted up at the arch above us. "So, what's this building called?"

"Currently it's unnamed." I pointed to the brick where she stared, focusing on the spot where rust from the since-removed iron letters left a few remnants. "A couple of years ago, some students did a research project on the person it was originally named for and uncovered some iffy things about their family history. The school buried the story, but there were rumors."

"Like?" Sabrina waved her hand for me to continue.

"I don't know, I don't talk to these people."

"Jo." She shoved me. "You gotta put yourself out there. Like, who do you usually hang with? You didn't introduce me to anyone today."

I faltered a little. She didn't mean to, but her words only reminded me of a particular void in my life. I wrapped an arm around her. "I don't need to hang with anyone else. I can just keep sneaking you and Frankie in for lunch."

She opened her mouth to respond but was cut off.

"Aw, how cute," Maddie called out as she walked by, sliding into the back seat of a black Lincoln sedan. "Although, Sab, you don't want to start off on the wrong foot here."

Sabrina rested her head against mine. "Thinking what I'm thinking?" she whispered.

"Mm-hmm."

"Hey, Maddie," she yelled.

The back tinted window rolled down, and Maddie's pointed face peeked out only for her jaw to drop as she saw our grinning faces framed by our middle fingers up on both hands.

"Have a good evening," I called out.

She flipped her own finger back at us as her ride drove off, a red Ford Focus pulling up behind it.

"Oh, this is us." Sabrina stood up, and I followed her to the car.

"So, what now?" she asked.

"Want to try to cyberstalk those other five kids from last year?" I caught the eye of the driver in the rearview mirror, his brow cocked high in confusion. I smiled sweetly before looking back to Sabrina.

"Actually, Frankie and I texted about this earlier. We don't have any files on the other five kids, just names and test scores. Everyone's graduated and in colleges across the country. There's no real hard proof they were involved in this. Their part in the scam would be hearsay."

"Huh." I sat back in the seat, thinking it over. "Let's at least check their social medias to see if everyone is still enrolled. If Mr. Medina had tried to flag any of the kids from last year, the schools might have put the students on a suspension or something."

"Sure," she replied. "Good call. If anything pops up, I'll let you know."

"Thanks. We still have the other three suspects: Maddie, Chief Ryan, and Julius. None of them have an alibi. Maddie has her acceptance to Brown and her reputation at risk. Chief Ryan is bidding for the spot of police superintendent, so he can't risk a scandal, let alone jail/time. And Julius has custody of his sister to worry about."

Sabrina squirmed a little. "I was actually thinking we should take Julius's name off the list."

Now it was my turn to raise an eyebrow in confusion.

"It's just, it's most likely that Julius gave Mr. Medina the names of last year's students."

"Oh." Julius *would* know the names and the scores that he got for each person. "Did you run that theory by Frankie?"

She nodded.

"But that spiel about staying away from Julius—"

"I think you two just need to talk. You and Frankie." She looked down at her hands.

"Why?"

"Because even though you're telling us Julius is a suspect, he seems like your friend. You opened up to each other about how you met Mr. Medina. And he's doing for you what Frankie can't from De La Salle."

"What's that?"

"Look out for you."

I shook my head. "It's not—it's not like that." It wasn't. But it did feel good to talk to Julius. It took away some of the lingering emotions. But that was something I couldn't admit to Frankie or Sabrina.

My phone lit up with a new message.

Mom:

Come by my office on the way home.

"Excuse me, driver? I need to make a detour."

I flashed the text to Sabrina, and she pulled up the app to add in the stop.

"I'll talk with Frankie. I think you're right; Julius probably did feed Mr. Medina the names," I added. "But we don't have the evidence to rule him out as a suspect. And you know Frankie. He's more methodical and by the book than both of us."

"I know. Julius just doesn't feel like the guy. The ID in the dean's office, that could be her holding some type of leverage over him, keeping him from coming clean."

"There's still time for me to poke around if you're okay with me snooping."

Julius's disciplinary write-up did bring up some new questions about what really happened between him and Mr. Medina. I wanted answers.

Sabrina chewed her cheek. "Just be careful."

Fifteen minutes later, Sabrina dropped me at the public defender offices around the corner from city hall. I weaved through the building to my mom's office.

"Hey, Mom. What did you need—" I stopped.

Alderman Corben sat across from my mom's desk, a strained smile across his face.

I looked back and forth between the two, trying to think of the only logical reason for him to be sitting there right now. "We have our meeting coming up on Thursday," I noted, remembering my conversation with his assistant. I completely forgot to call back and cancel that. "Still looking forward to it."

"Yes, as am I, although I'm going to need to reschedule. But just ring Charlotte and she'll make it happen." Another strained smile.

I nodded, thinking that was the end of the conversation. I glanced over to my mom to see a steeled grin on her face. That was not the end of the conversation.

"Jo, I ran into Alderman Corben over at circuit court. He asked if you had connected with a donor Saturday night to help with your financial payment for school next quarter."

My stomach knotted. I had told her Saturday was girls' night with Reya. Not a complete lie. We did spend two hours at Target.

"I thought I could fix it before bothering you," I started.

"We can talk about it later." Mom had a smile on her face, but it was her *Wait until we get home* smile. "Alderman Corben was telling me he has a scholarship program he runs for students outside Lakeview who are attending schools in his district."

"Madison Ryan is my goddaughter," he explained. "She informed me of your status after she saw us talking."

"I see," I squeaked out. I had a feeling Maddie probably didn't say it so nicely. "Thank you for your offer."

"Of course. Think it over. I'll send your mother the

details. There are a few community service requirements, though they shouldn't be a problem. With your smarts, I'm sure you can fill those hours with a few tutoring sessions."

He stood up from his seat and shook Mom's hand before walking to the door.

"Wait. Um, do you know if Chief Ryan plans to award the Police Scholars Award to someone else next quarter?" I asked.

"Ah, not for next quarter, but he does have a candidate for the next school year. Lieutenant Charles's son. I believe the young man goes by Tre."

"Right."

"Let's talk soon. And my apologies, Mrs. Kelley."

"You have nothing to apologize for." Mom waved as the door closed behind him.

"He's a nice man," she noted. "You're lucky that all worked out."

"Yeah, I guess." I sat down in the open seat. But "luck" didn't feel like the right word. The revelation of his connection to Maddie alarmed me. I needed to steer clear of her at all costs. I learned her reach extended to her father Saturday night. Who else could she be manipulating?

A flicker of a thought crossed my mind. Maddie and her dad were both suspects. I had assumed the scholarship letter was Maddie's doing and her dad was playing along. But what if it was the other way around? Chief Ryan could be using his daughter. Julius mentioned Maddie wasn't getting the attention she needed from her dad. That would make her eager to help—do whatever he asked . . .

"You know, I didn't expect this from you."

I looked up at my mom. She had that quiet-anger expression, her lips pulled in a tight line while her eyes were narrowed on me.

"Expect what?"

"You letting your grades drop and losing your scholarship. I'm assuming that's what happened. Is this your plan to get back to your old school?"

"What? No! I wouldn't do that. The CPD—they changed the requirements. Or at least someone faked a letter saying they did." My words were coming out in a jumbled mess. "I might hate it at North Shore, but I wouldn't—"

"I don't know what to do with you anymore. You've been lying and skipping classes—working on your little investigations after I explicitly asked you to stop. Now you want me to believe the Chicago Police Department just up and changed their requirements without notifying you or your parents?" Her voice was getting loud.

"No. Well, yes. It was Maddie. It's this case—"

"Enough with the damn case!" Mom slammed her hand against the desk, and I flinched, my hand going to my cheek. "Jo." Her voice softened as she took in my reaction.

"You said you were trying," I whispered. "You aren't even listening."

"You have to stop with all this. I've already told you where it leads." She lowered her voice. "You're not doing this anymore. Not in my house."

I picked up my phone, texting her the two photos of the scholarship letters from Chicago Police Scholars. Her phone chimed.

"What's this?"

"My truth," I answered. I stood and walked to the door. "You know, it's okay, really. I don't need you to try with me anymore. I'll pick up my grades and graduate early like you want. Then I'll go to a fancy school just like you want, a thousand miles from here."

She didn't say anything, just stared down at her hands. She didn't see the tears streaming down my face. And she didn't need to.

I could see the ones falling down hers.

NINETEEN

AT HOME, I did everything to avoid my mom. I was over it. At least that was what I told myself. I didn't have the energy for our arguments anymore. I grabbed dinner to eat in my room, then spent what felt like a good hour pacing back and forth, contemplating how to bring up Julius to Frankie. I needed to explain how Julius was not the suspect we needed to focus on. Chief Ryan showed his true self Saturday night with his cryptic warning, not to mention taking away my scholarship. He was first on the scene—and possibly there—when Mr. Medina was pushed in front of the train.

The train's brakes screeched in my memory.

I inhaled, letting it out slowly.

I'll forget about it soon. Once this is over, it will leave my mind.

I stopped pacing and picked up my phone, tapping my nails against the back of the case. The three of us didn't keep secrets. I had to tell them what happened at the alumni fundraiser. But the exchange between Chief Ryan and Julius . . .

I couldn't work it out in my head why I still trusted Julius, despite everything we'd learned so far. I had to stay focused, by the book. If he was innocent, the evidence would prove it. Eventually.

Jolene:

Hey Frankie, I was thinking about earlier. And about Julius.

Frankie:

Yeah? Do you have something else?

Sabrina sent me a text separate from the group chat.

Sabrina:

👀

Back in the group chat—

Jolene:

A more promising suspect. We should switch our focus to Chief Ryan. At the alumni fundraiser when I spoke with him—he might've threatened me.

Sabrina in the group chat—

Sabrina:

👀

Frankie:

WTF?

I sighed, counting out five beats.

Jolene:

He all but admitted to knowing Maddie sent the fake scholarship letter. Then told me to "focus on my schooling." THEN there was the envelope he snuck to Julius . . .

Frankie:

He snuck an envelope to Julius? And you want us to switch our focus AWAY from him? What was in the envelope?

Jolene:

Idk. No snooping, right?

Frankie:

Damn it, Jo. What if that was a payment? Julius took a swing at Mr. Medina. Maybe Chief Ryan paid him to do something more.

I recoiled. That was not—no.
I sent Sabrina a separate message.

Jolene:

A little help?

Sabrina:

GIRL.

I threw up my hands, pacing the room again.
I texted them both.

Jolene:

He's not violent. Mr. Medina wouldn't cover for a student attacking him. And Bri has a theory that Julius was working WITH Mr. Medina, giving him the names of the students from last year.

Frankie:

...

Frankie:

I don't think you're seeing clearly on this, Jo.

Jolene:

What's your theory, then?

Frankie:

I don't have one. But he's staying in the suspect pool.

Jolene:

I never said to remove him from our list. Let's just switch our focus.

Frankie:

... fine.

My phone pinged with another text from Sabrina, privately to me.

Sabrina:

☹ That went well?

Jolene:

Yeah, thanks for the assist.

Sabrina:

You didn't tell me all that about Chief Ryan!

Jolene:

> I just need a break from all this. There's so much going on right now.

I stopped short of telling her what happened with my mom. I couldn't talk about that now without wanting to scream.

Sabrina:

> Let's give Frankie some time to cool down and take a day for the cold case. I found an old friend of Chloe's. Can you come with me to meet her for a late lunch after school tomorrow?

Jolene:

> Your treat? Otherwise I might have to just sip water. These Lyft rides are ridiculous.

It'd been days since I stepped foot on the train. My wallet had begun to take notice.

Sabrina:

> When you are ready to hop back on the CTA let me know.

Sabrina:

> But, no, not my treat. The friend's name is Hope and she offered to pay. She's up in River North. She wants to take us to a place called Hub 51.

Jolene:

> Sounds good. Meet you there.

Sabrina:

I'll have Aiko's ride. I can pick you up from North Shore and save you a few dollars ☺

I'd never been so happy to see Aiko's Volkswagen minibus pull into the front loop of the academy. Once inside, I took off my gloves to defrost my hands with the heat blowing from the vents. It was technically March, but that never stopped a random cold front. "Aiko didn't need her van?"

"Softball practice is starting again. It's only warm-ups today, so she won't need it until later tonight. Did you check out the menu?"

"I mean, we're meeting up with someone to talk about her best friend who was murdered thirty years ago. I don't want to take advantage. I figured we'd split something."

Stopping at the end of the drive, she locked eyes with me.

"Pulled chicken nachos," we said in unison.

When we arrived at the restaurant, a tall, curvy Black woman with a dark brown complexion waved us over. Her curls fell to her shoulders, a perfectly fluffed twist-out. "You must be Sabrina and Jolene! I'm Hope Michaels, Chloe's friend."

"Thank you for meeting with us." I reached out to shake her hand, just for her to pull me into a hug.

"Sorry, I'm a hugger," she said as she squeezed. "I think it's great what you all are doing. Digging into forgotten cases."

Sabrina smiled. "It's sort of a passion of ours."

I looked around, taking in the moody ambiance of dark wood, black leather, and flickering tea lights. The aromas made my mouth water, especially the sweet notes of maple from the table next to us. From the looks of it, they'd ordered a very late brunch. "How did you find this place?"

"Oh, I live up this way. I left Englewood in the early 2000s. But I still have lots of family there. A friend and I actually just bought a vacant lot on my uncle's street. We plan to turn it into an urban garden for families to grow their own produce."

"Wow." I raised my brows. "That's amazing."

"Always give back, right?" She smiled, her brown eyes twinkling.

We quickly ordered our food, with Hope insisting Sabrina and I get our own entrées and split at least one appetizer. I didn't argue.

"Tell us a little bit about Chloe," I started as our food arrived. "We found some of the old playbills. She must've been amazing."

"She was such a presence every time she walked on that stage," said Hope. "She was the type of girl who, when she entered the room, everyone flocked to her as if she was the only thing that mattered. Chloe had that pull."

"She sounds like a star," Sabrina replied. "We were shocked to find out that her case went cold."

"To be honest, I wasn't. Things were different then. Or should I say, not so different? Cops didn't give much mind to kids on the South Side. The two of us had saved up just enough to move out. She wanted an apartment by the theater, and with that new lead role and her new squeeze, everything was going well. But we were still not *from* this side—you know what I mean?"

I nodded. If that wasn't the truth.

"Her new squeeze—that was her fiancé, right? It must've broken his heart. He was an officer in the Marines?" Sabrina prodded lightly.

"Mm-mm." Hope shook her head as she finished her bite. "Not him. He was a sweetheart, but he broke up with Chloe right before he was deployed." Her eyes fell to the table. "It took him a while to move on after Chloe died. It took a while for a lot of us."

"We recently lost someone, too." Sabrina paused, stealing a sideways glance at me. "Both of us are dealing with it in different ways. He was an old mentor of ours. All I want is more time to solve mysteries with him. Honestly, it makes cases like Chloe's mean that much more to me— being able to carry on what he taught us."

I nudged her shoulder with mine. "I didn't know that."

She met my eyes, a soft smile on her lips.

"Sometimes, that's the best way to grieve," said Hope. "But Chloe's new beau, I never saw him at any of our memorials or the funeral. He didn't even want to sign our petition to have her case reopened. He just wanted to move on and forget."

Pain tugged at my insides. "Wanting to forget, that's— that's hard. But I can see how the pain could've been too much."

Sabrina chewed her lip, looking at me as if deep in thought, before turning back to Hope. "Did you ever meet him?"

"I met him after her opening night. He was mesmerized by her and proposed to her after a few months. He had big plans, too—wanted to have her star in all his shows."

"*His* shows?" I asked.

"Yes, he was the director."

My eyebrows shot up. "Oh."

Sabrina nudged me under the table, a quick *Fix your face* reminder.

I fixed my face.

The conversation turned to small talk, Hope sharing a few fun stories about her and Chloe growing up as we finished our meal.

"I'm so glad I got to meet you both and talk about Chloe again. And who knows, maybe someone will reopen the investigation. I would love to see the look on the beat cop's face when it happens. His lead officer was no different, but he really didn't seem to have much patience for any of us whenever we would check on the case's progress. He was a Black man, so I guess I thought he would've cared more. But he wanted to just leave his roots behind."

"What was his name?" Sabrina asked.

"Never will forget it: Wendell Charles."

I coughed, choking on my lemonade.

Sabrina slapped my back. "You okay?"

"Wrong pipe," I mumbled. Gathering my breath, I took another sip to clear my throat. "Thanks for your time, Hope. And this meal. It was amazing."

"Oh, anytime. I always thought Chloe would have loved this place."

Hope paid the check, and we all stood and said our goodbyes. She pointed her finger to each of us in turn. "You girls keep in touch."

"Yes, ma'am," we replied together.

"Call me Hope, I'm not ready to be a ma'am yet." With that she was out the door and around the corner.

"Well, that was interesting," I noted as we walked to the Volks.

Sabrina sighed, shaking her head. "I can't believe the beat cop from Chloe's case is the same cop who butchered Mr. Medina's."

"Lieutenant Charles isn't that old. This case is from over thirty years ago. But he is a junior, so it's probably his dad," I corrected, sliding into the passenger seat as Sabrina started up the engine. "Like father, like son, I guess. Still in a rush to just move on from things. Have you or Frankie tracked down the director in any of your other research?"

"Mm-hmm. He lives with his wife of thirty-five years in New York."

"Thirty-five? That would mean he was married when he became engaged to Chloe."

"Yep." Sabrina pulled up to a light, holding the brake as she looked at me. "Guess who he's married to?"

I knitted my brows together, then a thought popped in my head. "*No.*"

"The original lead actress."

"Wow."

The light turned green, and Sabrina continued down South Michigan Avenue.

"They were having an affair," I muttered. "Or maybe Chloe didn't know about his wife. That would be a new motive right there. The director could've lied about being married to get Chloe to star in his show. She finds out and confronts him. Chaos ensues. He most likely broke Chloe's finger trying to remove the ring he gave her. Dumped another in its place."

"Damn. She probably didn't even see it coming."

"Let's say that's what happened," I started. "You know the most messed-up part? All the cop had to do was spend more than five minutes on the investigation. If he had just listened to Hope in the first place, she could've pointed him in the right direction thirty years ago."

Sabrina nodded, letting the van fall silent.

I looked over to her. "How come you didn't tell me that thing about Mr. Medina? How our cases have more meaning to you now that he's gone?"

"You mean the same way you haven't admitted to me or yourself that you're throwing yourself into these cases so you can *not* deal with your feelings and just move on?"

I let out a breath. "Bri—"

"I think you and Julius should hang out."

I whipped my head around. "What?"

"You and Julius. I can tell from the way you talk about him you have a pull toward him, and he has one toward you, too. Frankie and I wanted to be the ones to help you through this, but I think you need someone else."

"I thought he was a suspect," I mumbled, turning my back to look out the window.

"I guess. It's more likely it was Maddie's dad. And there's no one else left to consider. I checked up on the students from last year like you asked. Everyone is still enrolled."

I didn't say anything.

"Hey."

I met her gaze.

She smiled. "Just live a little."

I shook my head. "Live a little with a murder suspect. You're such a bad influence."

Sabrina winked. "That's why you love me, though."

TWENTY

WEDNESDAY, MARCH 9, 10:31 A.M.

THE NEXT DAY, school was about as normal as it could be. With fresh theories about the director, Frankie wanted to turn Chloe's case over to authorities with our new lead. There was the partial print on the rope that was never identified along with the print on the champagne glass. We also learned the theater director had been arrested a few months ago after a reckless driving charge in New York. That meant his fingerprints would be in the system. The affair, his access to the stage and dressing rooms, and a possible print match came together to form the perfect argument for reopening the case.

I was texting Reya during AP Spanish for advice about how to present the evidence when an annoying voice whispered in my ear.

"Heard you lost your scholarship," Maddie goaded.

I ignored her, focusing on Reya's texts.

"You should stop trying to fit in here. Your parents aren't even real lawyers, and I don't think North Shore offers payment plans."

I groaned. "Seriously. What is your deal? Do you *not* have better things to do?"

"I want to make sure you don't forget why you're really here: a charity case for my daddy's tax returns."

I turned around. "You know, I've seen his office with pictures of all his kids, he even has photos of your mom still up, but I don't think I've ever seen one of you. Is that why you're so focused on me all of sudden? Is it because your dad, in the few times I've talked with him about cold cases, has spent more time with me than with his own daughter? Or is it because I actually deserve to be here, a sophomore who tested into all these AP classes filled with upperclassmen? And I didn't even have to pay someone to take the tests for me."

I bit my tongue at my last words. Too far.

Maddie leaned over her desk. "What did you say?"

Natalia's mouth hung open as she looked back and forth between me and her best friend.

"Nothing. Just—nothing. It's been a long few weeks, Maddie. That wasn't like me." I turned back around.

The bell rang, and Maddie walked around to the front of my desk, nostrils flaring. "You don't know anything about me." She shoved my books to the floor.

I sat frozen after she walked away, Mr. Perez calling my name a few times before I finally got up and left. *Damn it*, I thought to myself. I'd done exactly what I had warned Sabrina about a few weeks ago—gotten on Maddie's bad side. I didn't need her mean-girl drama right now.

I took the long way to class, ending up in an empty stairwell. It was quiet, though the silence was soon interrupted. Footsteps hurried behind me, followed by a sharp pain shooting through my spine.

No.

I lost my balance, tipping forward as my hands shot out to grab something—anything. I couldn't catch myself. I was falling, tumbling down the stairs, my hip knocking into the wall, my neck bouncing off the bottom step before my world went black.

———

Everything hurt.

Tears stung my eyes.

"Hey, hey!" a voice yelled.

I tried to focus on the blur in front of me as the dark spots clouding my vision faded. Julius.

"Did you trip?"

I slipped trying to sit up. Everything spun.

"Don't."

"I think I was pushed." I raised a hand to rub my neck. My mind raced, trying to piece together what just happened.

Footsteps rushing behind me. Before that, me leaving second period after getting into it with— "Maddie."

He took off up the stairs.

I rolled on to my side, a groan escaping me. The pain coursing through my body left me shaking. *My neck.* It was too sore to touch.

More footsteps. I flinched as they got closer.

"It's me." Julius stopped me from sitting up. "Stay still."

"Did you see her?"

"I didn't see anyone. I even checked the bathrooms— girls, boys, and uni." He looked me over with wide eyes. "I told you not to mess with her. You have to stop. You know what she spent the whole alumni dinner talking about? You. Jab after jab. The only reason she wanted me to escort her was because she noticed us talking a few times. She's obsessed."

"I can't stop now. I'm so close."

He shook his head. "You're going to end up like Mr. Medina."

His words echoed in my head, bringing up memories of the note in my locker.

"How did you find me back here?" I tried to look up the stairwell. There was no one there. When I started down the stairwell it was empty.

Julius didn't answer. He pulled out his phone and dialed a few numbers.

"Who are you calling?"

"Nurse's office. That was a serious fall. Falls like that can kill people. Just lay back."

He knelt down, and I leaned onto him, letting him take on my body weight. I was grateful he was here, but there was a small voice in my head that wondered if I was wrong about who had pushed me.

—————

I was lucky, the nurse said. A little banged up but nothing an ice pack couldn't heal. Still, she called my parents since that was school policy. I brushed it off as missing a few steps at the bottom of the stairwell—not the tumble down the entire flight of stairs. Dad went on a rant about "the younger generation being too engrossed with their phones to see where they're going." I had rolled my eyes but didn't correct him. All I could think about was what if I had landed at a different angle? Twisted the wrong way?

This investigation was nothing like a cold case. It wasn't a puzzle I could solve without emotion. It was real life, with real consequences. Threats on my life.

And everything was escalating.

The next day, Julius made sure to run into me before and after second period. That way, if I crossed Maddie in the hallways outside AP Spanish, I wasn't alone. I hoped my silence would lead her to think that I had misspoken, that she had gotten her message across, but she only got worse. Switching seats with Natalia, she sat directly behind me in class, spewing venom in my ear. I didn't respond. She'd won. I was too scared to say anything that might hint I was still working on the case, scared that I would give her a reason to lash out again.

Thursday, after school, the unanswered texts from Frankie and Sabrina piled up. I needed to tell them I wanted to stop working the case, but they had to keep going. Whether it was Maddie or her dad, I had been the focus of their threats. No one else knew Frankie and Sabrina were involved in the investigation. And I had to keep it that way.

But after my fall, I hadn't even been able to bring myself to talk to my friends, let alone meet up with them in person. I'd been wearing my hair down with scarves and high collars to hide the bruise at my nape. They'd see right through my act. If they knew what happened, they'd stop investigating, too, and no one would be left to solve Mr. Medina's case. I couldn't let it go unsolved.

He deserved more than that.

Frankie:

Still wrapped up in studying for all those tests?

Ah yes. The lie I told to avoid responding.

Jolene:

No, but I think I need to step back from the case for a bit.

Frankie:

Is everything okay?

Sabrina:

Did you get another note?

Something worse.

Frankie:

Jo?

I sighed and shot back a text.

Jolene:

I thought you'd be happy. You wanted me to stop snooping, remember? And stay away from Julius.

Frankie:

True.

Frankie:

I've been thinking on what you said about him. Once we can cross Julius off the suspect list for sure, we can go to CPD. We have enough to suggest foul play and ask them to reopen the case. Let the police take it from here.

Sabrina:

But go to who at CPD? Chief Ryan is our main suspect. And we don't really know anything about Lieutenant Charles. Do we trust anyone there right now?

At this moment, the only person in uniform I trusted was Officer Halligan from the records room. I tossed my phone across the bed and pulled the covers over my head.

We're so close to this being over. But I couldn't risk anymore.

A few minutes later my phone rang, BLACKPINK's "Ice Cream" instrumental interrupting the silence. Sabrina.

"You gave yourself a custom ringtone on my phone," I mumbled.

"Bet you knew it was me without having to look." I could hear the smile in her voice on the other end. "Are you okay? You stopped texting."

I glanced back through the texts I missed, the "Where'd you go" and question marks.

"I'm just really exhausted."

"It wasn't another note, was it?"

"I—I said something to Maddie—" I stopped. The pain still twinged in my neck. "I think she could be more involved than we thought. Maybe she's working with her dad and he's pulling the strings? I don't know. But I agree with Frankie. I'm ready to hand everything over to the police at this point."

Sabrina went quiet for a moment. "You're leaving something out. I can tell, Jo."

She knew me too well. Not wanting to keep secrets, I blurted out something else instead. I hadn't mentioned it to Sabrina before because I already knew what she would say. "Julius wants to hang out and talk."

"Yes!"

"Yes, what?"

"You're going! When? Where?"

I scrolled through my texts to find the one from him. He had sent it Wednesday, after everything with Maddie. "Saturday, Millennium Park. I'm not sure, though, Bri."

"Look, you aren't opening up to me and Frankie. You need this. It'll be cathartic. And hey, maybe you'll even learn something that will help us cross him off the list."

"If you say so," I muttered.

"Aiko and I will come, too."

"Bri—"

"We won't be with you guys, but we'll be at the park. That way if Julius makes you uncomfortable, you have backup."

"Sabrina and Aiko to my rescue. Didn't you quit jiujitsu after two weeks?"

"Yeah, but I got the basic leg-sweep takedown handy. And Aiko knows yoga."

I scrunched my face, unsure of what yoga brought to the table. "You're serious about this?"

"Yes."

I bit my lip, weighing the pros and cons. My eyes fell on the University of Chicago packet from Mr. Medina on my desk. Julius said he just wanted to talk. "I guess this is happening."

The next day before AP Spanish, I confirmed Saturday afternoon with Julius. I'd never seen him grin so big.

"Great. What's your shoe size?"

"I'm failing to see how that matters."

"Trust me on this. Shoe size?"

I pressed my lips together. "Seven and a half."

"Perfect. See you after class." He left with a wave, running to his own class before the late bell for second period had a chance to ring.

Settled at my desk, it took all of thirty seconds before Maddie was in my ear. "So, you two *are* dating. I guess charity attracts charity."

I shut my eyes and ignored her. My neck throbbed from the fall.

Just a few more days, I thought to myself.

It'll all be over soon.

TWENTY-ONE

SATURDAY, MARCH 12, 12:57 P.M.

I'D LIVED IN Chicago my whole life but can't say I'd ever hung out at Millennium Park. I'd seen the Bean, the gardens, and a few exhibitions on school trips, but that was the extent of it. I vaguely remembered the rock-climbing wall in Maggie Daley Park and wondered if that was what we were going to do. After I relayed the conversation to Sabrina, she knew exactly what the shoe ask was for but didn't feel the need to enlighten me.

Now here I stood in front of Park Grill like Julius had asked, layered up in my "Not Today, Satan" hoodie, fitted jeans, and lace-up boots, staring at a bunch of happy people skating in circles around an ice rink. Of course. This is Chicago, after all.

Aiko and Sabrina held hands as they went around, color coordinated in blush pink and soft lavender, their hair both up in Sabrina's favorite double high-bun style.

"Hey." Julius walked up in his own dark hoodie with a black bomber on top, distressed jeans, and Timberlands. He had his curls pushed off his face with a headband.

"Hey," I echoed back.

"You ready?"

I registered what he held in his hands: two pairs of skates.

"This is how you want to talk."

"No, this is how I want to break the ice—pun intended. Your guard is up high, and you need to learn how to relax."

I stuck out my tongue and reluctantly followed him to an empty bench.

"Do you know how to skate?"

I laughed. "My mom tried to take me to Midway when I was eight after I had watched the Winter Olympics. She lasted all of five minutes in the cold before we left. Winter is not her favorite season."

He reached over, tightening my laces. "Strange place to live and not like the cold."

"We have roots. My great-grandmother left Mississippi in the late fifties and came up here."

"Hmm. My dad grew up in Baltimore, which is where he met my mom, but we moved here when I was four. We actually lived not too far from the park. When he left us, my mom couldn't afford the place, so we moved to Chatham. Where are you, South Shore?"

"Englewood."

He finished another knot on my skates and stood up. "All right, now get up slowly." He held out his hands for me to hold and balance myself.

Forgoing his hands, I got up, stepped on the ice, and sped off.

"Hey!"

My hair whipped around me, and I couldn't remember the last time I felt like this. Free. I twisted around to skate backward, letting him catch up.

"You said your mom—"

"My mom hates the cold. My dad loves it and also loves hockey. He taught me to play. These skates are a little different, but I'll manage." I took off again, letting the cold air hit my face.

Before long, Julius fell in stride next to me. "You're a girl with many secrets."

"I could say the same about you." I didn't mean it as interrogation, but the hesitant smile on Julius's lips told me he wasn't quite sure if I was trying to dig.

I gave him a nudge. "Tell me more about your mom."

His mouth quirked up. "She was amazing. You would've loved her. She loved reading and telling stories. Taught English at Malcolm X. I think she's where I got my love of storytelling, except she preferred books, where I've always dreamed of the silver screen."

"Film school for you, then? Where are you going to go in the fall?"

"I was planning on USC. My dad is a few hours from there. Funny enough, he didn't care enough to try to get custody of Tati, but he's looking forward to being able to see her more often."

"Tati? That's your sister?"

"Yeah, she's seven. She thinks she's thirteen, though."

I laughed. "Sounds about right." And he was right about this place, too. We skated laps around the rink, passing couples out on dates, friends goofing off. Everyone grinning with the city skyline as their backdrop. The smiles were contagious.

"Okay. Icebreaker questions." Julius cleared his throat with dramatic flair.

"Seriously?"

He ignored my retort. "Scary movies or rom-coms?"

I gave in. "Scary."

"Really?" He nodded as though he was trying to make sense of my answer.

"Rom-coms are too formulaic."

"And scary movies aren't?"

"There's like a bajillion ways to execute a scary movie—thriller, suspense, jump scares. Rom-coms are limited. They feel basic."

"That's harsh."

I looked over to him. "I'm guessing rom-coms are your favorite?"

"Well, not anymore." He laughed. "Not trying to be 'basic.'"

"Okay, my turn."

"Didn't know we were taking turns," he muttered.

I pretended not to hear. "Favorite food?"

"That's the most basic icebreaker—"

I narrowed my eyes at him.

"Okay, okay. Feijoada. My mom was part Brazilian. She had this family recipe for it—it's like this stew that sticks to your ribs. There's black beans and pork. You haven't lived until you try it. You?"

My mouth watered. I loved stews in all forms, but they weren't my favorite. "My dad does this thing when we have cookouts and barbecues, and instead of hot dogs or a beef frank, he smokes this spicy sausage he makes himself. So that, with my Nana Josette's coleslaw on top, I can eat that every day. Even better on a pretzel bun."

"A girl who appreciates a fancy hot dog." He nodded with approval. "Okay, I got one." He skated around me, tapping his chin as if in deep concentration. "Zombie apocalypse."

"What about it?"

"What's the first thing you do? For me, I'm holing up in the closest Walmart."

"For rolling-back prices?"

His turn to narrow his eyes at me. "No. Lots of options for weapons and things to survive. Get me a lighter and some hair spray—instant flamethrower."

I held in a laugh. "You've put thought into this."

"I play a lot of video games. And I'm slightly obsessed with *The Walking Dead*. The graphic novels more so than the show."

"Mm-kay. Well, I guess I'm going to the police armory."

"Straight for the firepower. I feel like I've learned a lot about you in three questions, Kelley Green Eyes." He grinned his lopsided grin.

"I could say the same, Mr. Rom-Com."

Sabrina waved for my attention, flashed me a thumbs-up, and pointed to her phone.

Sabrina:

Looks like everything is going well? Aiko and I are going to grab a bite. Are you okay?

Jolene:

👍

"I got to meet your backup earlier." Julius nodded to the two. "But it was only Sabrina when she introduced herself. Who's with her?"

"Aiko, Bri's girlfriend."

"Ah. So, she's the Team Kristen Stewart friend. You didn't need backup, though."

"I know." Without realizing it, I reached for my neck.

Julius noticed. "You don't think . . ." He slowed to a stop. "You don't think I pushed you, do you? Is that why—" He looked back to Sabrina and Aiko as they sat and unlaced their skates.

"No, not at all," I replied quickly. "I mean, maybe only for a second? I don't know, Julius. I don't know what I'm even doing here."

He dropped his eyes to the ice, and after a few moments, he held out his hand for me to take. Wearily, I placed mine in his, letting him lead me off the ice. We settled on a bench, and he waited a few beats before speaking. "I didn't kill Mr. Medina."

"I know," I whispered. "I'm just in over my head. Someone pushed me down the stairs because I'm asking too many questions." I tilted my head up, closing my eyes. "There are so many emotions around it, too."

"And that's why I asked you here. To *talk*. You might not need to talk, but I know I do. Watching you throw yourself into this case and schoolwork, I knew you were putting on a mask and not dealing. Same as me. But we can't both keep doing that."

I met his soft gaze, not saying anything. The way he looked at me left me vulnerable in a way I didn't want to be.

"If you don't want to open up, at least listen to me for a bit," he said.

I fidgeted in my seat, then nodded.

"Mr. Medina was so much more than a mentor to me. He

started at North Shore during my junior year, and it was a rough time for me. My mom had just gotten her diagnosis after being sick for months, and I had this crazy hope that my dad would leave his new family and come back to be with us." He shook his head. "It was a stupid dream. He just did his usual and sent checks. But whatever the court had mandated he pay wasn't nearly enough. Mr. Medina started inviting me to his office and we would talk. It took a while for me to open up, and even then, I wasn't telling him everything. But he kept me grounded. And now that he's gone, I've lost that."

He hung his head. "I've lost that," he said again.

I crossed my arms around my chest, hugging myself. "He filled the void your dad left."

Julius nodded. "When he took me and my sister in, he and his wife were so good to us. They saw so much good in me, but I'm not a good person." His voice wavered. "I tried to be. And I still do. But he does that, right? Pushes you to be better."

"He did that," I whispered, correcting the past tense, more for myself than for him.

"Then it was like losing my mom all over again. It just hurts. I might try to mask it with smiles, but I'm struggling, just like you. I would've never done anything to hurt him."

I swung my legs back and forth, pressure slowly building in my chest. I knew he was telling the truth. "I believe you."

"Thank you. I just wanted you to hear me. I'll sit here until you're ready for me to hear you."

I didn't answer right away. I stared at a mother and a young daughter holding hands as they circled the ice, their smiles so genuine and innocent.

"I didn't want to come to North Shore," I said, dropping my eyes to the ground. "I was content with my life before that place. I got into a shouting match with my mom about it. Slammed the door in her face. It was . . . bad. She told me it didn't matter what I wanted. That I needed to grow up and stop treating life like some Scooby-Doo mystery. And my dad—he just stood there."

I stopped talking, my voice close to cracking. The anger was rising again, and all I wanted was to push it down again.

"Mr. Medina helped you through that?" Julius asked.

I shrugged. "I don't know that I'm *through* that. I thought I could just do a year there, maybe I could get back to my old school in the fall. Lunches with him made it a little easier. We talked cases and stuff."

I held myself tighter. The pressure inside was too much. A sob caught in my throat, and I closed my eyes. I didn't want to hold it in anymore. "But then he left me," I said.

Julius didn't say anything. He rested his arm on the bench behind me, shifting his body to me. His eyes burned on my skin.

He left me.

"He left me alone in the place he helped my parents drag

me to. What am I supposed to do now?" The tears flowed freely now. "I can't leave. That would be messed up after all he did for me. It's like I'm stuck. And I'm pissed. I'm pissed at a dead man for leaving me alone." The thoughts of the past few weeks swirled in my head.

Solve his murder, move on. Once this is over, I can forget about him.

But I'd still be alone. He took me away from the life that I had and left me alone.

Julius's arm pressed against my back, and I fell into him, my tears soaking his hoodie. I let everything out. All the pain I'd been holding in for the last few weeks. I'd let myself cry once on the day he died and felt so guilty about my selfish thoughts. But everything had just built on top of everything else. Nothing but a teetering pile of emotions, and it took feeling the wind against my face for it all to break.

"Is she okay?" Sabrina whispered above me.

Julius's body moved as he nodded. "She will be."

I stayed still, Sabrina lightly brushing my hair from my face. "It's okay to be mad after losing someone. I think he would understand."

I peered over at her. "How did you know?"

"Oh, sweetie, you're my best friend. I'll always know what's rattling around in that head of yours."

Another tear fell as I closed my eyes.

"You aren't alone, Jolene," Julius said. It was the first time I heard him say my name.

Sabrina stayed hunched by my feet, holding my hand, while Aiko squeezed onto the bench at my other side, lying against my back. "You'll never be alone. I know Bri well enough to know she'll never let that happen. She would burn the school down before that."

"Sure will," Sabrina quipped.

I managed a laugh. "Thank you."

"No prob." She squeezed my hand.

I inhaled, letting it out and counting to five.

Eventually, we all unraveled from the bench, and after checking to make sure I was okay a hundred times, Sabrina and Aiko left to finish their date. I dried my eyes as Julius left to buy us hot dogs with the works. I tossed the onions from mine into the closest trash can before taking a bite.

"Noted for next time," he said.

"So where to now?" I asked, ready to follow his lead. My eyes were still puffy, and I was sure I looked a wreck, but I felt lighter. No more anger simmering below the surface.

"Don't be mad."

I raised a brow as Julius held up his hands.

"Before you arrived, I talked to Sabrina."

"And . . ."

"And . . ." He stepped up to the corner and pointed across the street to the Washington/Wabash station. "Thought I would give you a ride home."

I froze.

He tugged my arm lightly.

"I know I just cried into your arms and all, but I'm not—"

"You're ready."

He waited for me to lead the way. I glanced down the block where a few rideshares waited. The light changed, the pedestrian signal indicating it was safe to cross. Holding my breath, I stepped off the curb.

We walked across the street, and I dug my blue-checkered Ventra card out of my wallet. It was tucked far behind everything else, seeing how it had almost been a month since I last used it. I waited as the person in front of me swiped their card, theirs a bright green.

"I go a couple of weeks without riding the train and the Ventra cards change colors?"

Julius eyed the person in front of us. "Oh, no, that's just a special edition, celebrating the river being dyed green. The CTA printed up a few thousand in late February but ran out within a week. You know how the city gets for Saint Patrick's Day."

"Ah. Yeah, my dad can't wait. He pretty much celebrates the whole month of March. Sabrina even made him a sweater to 'complement his eyes.'"

Julius grinned. "I need to see this sweater."

I pulled it up on my phone, letting him swipe through the photos of last Saint Patrick's Day.

"So, I think Sabrina is going to be my favorite friend of yours. I need to put in a sweater request."

On the platform, I inhaled, the smell of hot dogs and

pretzels mixed with the stale air of other trash assaulting my nose. But it was a familiar assault. And it didn't make my heart race.

The train honked softly as it pulled in. No screech of metal on metal.

Julius stepped into the last car. "And anyone ready to burn down a corrupt institution in the name of friendship is someone I want in my corner."

"You haven't even met Frankie."

He shrugged. "I'm sure Sabrina will still be my fave."

I rolled my eyes as the train shifted under my feet, pulling out of the station. "I'm on the train."

"Yep. Muscle memory. Let's sit on this side, I like to watch the city."

I joined him, taking the seat with the better view. My stomach eased. I was fine. Everything was fine. No flashes of Mr. Medina's death.

"You kept me talking on purpose."

He waggled his brows.

"Thanks," I murmured.

"Anytime. Mr. Medina told me to look out for you; it's the least I could do." Pain flashed across his face and he replaced it with his lopsided grin. "Promise me two things."

"What's up?"

"First, no more pent-up anger. Don't go to sleep mad at anything or anyone, and don't try to hold it in. It's not healthy, and life's too short for that shit."

"I'll give it a try. What's the other thing?"

He gazed out the window, eyes fixated on the city lights. "Hug your mom. Every night. Do it for me."

I blinked. He didn't look back at me.

I rested my head on his shoulder. "Promise."

TWENTY-TWO

SUNDAY, I WAITED in the kitchen for my mom to get back from running errands with a recipe ready. Keys jingled in the front door and I exhaled. "Hey, Mom."

She dropped her purse onto the table and looked around. "What's all this?" Across the counters I had laid out Roma tomatoes, garlic, celery leaves, and yellow onions. Cubed beef defrosted in the sink.

I held up the Ziploc in my hand, the plastic protecting the paper inside from the oil on my fingertips. "I thought we could make Sunday dinner together. Like we used to with Nana Josette."

Mom read the recipe to herself. "This was your great-grandmother's grandmother's recipe. That sheet of paper is so old." She shook her head to herself. "Nini Lo's Red Stew. You have the Scotch bonnets?"

"Frankie's mom had some in her fridge."

Mom smiled. "I would love to make Sunday dinner with you."

We spent the next couple of hours in the kitchen, side by side, letting the seasoned beef simmer with the other spices. With things so tense between us these last few days, we didn't say much at first. But I had to find a way to let go of my anger. I made a promise to Julius yesterday, and it was a promise I intended to keep.

Eventually, Mom and I stopped tiptoeing around each other and some of the tension left the room. Mom was first to loosen up, sharing tales about her adventures in Chicago as a young teen learning how to juke. It was great hearing her laugh and learning about her life from when she was my age. She had her own passions and dreams I never knew about. It made her more relatable in a way. She was carefree once.

"Enough about me. I'd like to hear more about the cold case you're finishing up. Reya was raving about how clever you and your friends were with this one."

My brows went up. That was the last thing I expected her to ask about. Not after our last conversation. "A lot of the cold cases we choose really just need fresh eyes on them. They're cases no one had the patience for, mostly from the neighborhoods around here. There are some from forty years ago with partial prints, and technology today would easily be able to match and identify new suspects. That's what happened with this victim, Chloe St. James. The police took one look at the body, thought they knew what happened, and never even questioned the new suspect we have."

Mom smiled. "You three really are good at this."

"Yeah." I hesitated. "I know you don't like that I work on them, though. We can talk about something else—"

"I can't even imagine the sense of closure you're bringing her family. That's just . . . it's amazing, Jo. I know it might not seem like it after our last . . . talk, but I'm proud of you."

"Thank you," I said quietly. I swallowed, unsure of what else to say.

Mom stared, looking me over before opening her mouth to speak.

"You know those two sayings your daddy is always spouting off, 'voice to the voiceless' and 'speak your truth'?" she asked. "Well, he stole those from my daddy—your grandfather. Those sayings have been in our family for generations, and I know you're carrying that on. But the profession has never been kind to us. You never got to meet your granddaddy or my brother. I want you to have a full life—one they didn't get to live."

I dropped my eyes to watch the pot in front of me. "I know."

"That . . . *conversation* we had earlier this week, I don't want that to be us. I don't want to lose you. It's hard to be your mother and see so much of your uncle in you. He was my best friend. He wasn't on the force for a full year before . . ." Her voice cracked.

I knew the story well. His partner was a dirty cop and left him alone during a sting that went south. He didn't call for backup. He thought he could do it on his own.

"Just be careful, Jolene. Don't get too deep into anything. As soon as you find yourself in trouble, you ask for help. There's no shame in asking for help from those you trust. I don't want you to get hurt, too."

I rubbed my neck. "I'm taking a step back for a little while. But I do hear you. Moving forward, I'll always hear you."

Mom pulled me into a hug, and I squeezed her as hard as I could.

It wasn't long before the side door opened and Frankie's voice rang out. "My moms said you're making red stew for dinner?"

Needless to say, Frankie stayed over.

"That was a wonderful meal, Mrs. K and little K." Frankie nodded to us.

"Are you staying for dessert?" Dad asked. "You just about wiped out the stew."

"I'll have to take that to go. Bri will be here in a minute."

I perked up. "Sabrina's coming over?"

"Yeah. We had a few things we wanted to revisit before turning the case over to the police. Meet you upstairs?"

Frankie got up, and I reached for a slice of pound cake only for my mom to slap my hand playfully.

"Nope. You go finish up that case."

I glanced over to Dad.

"I learned a long time ago not to argue with your mom."

So I didn't. I went up to find Frankie sitting at my desk, his feet perched on the edge of my bed.

I bowed. "Please make yourself comfortable."

He gave a half smile. "So I hear I missed the fun yesterday."

I closed my door. "It was nothing."

"Sabrina had a different recollection. Honestly, I can't tell you how happy it made me to know you finally opened up."

"Even if it wasn't with you?"

"I know I've been taking my big-brother role seriously lately, but yes. Even if it wasn't with me. I just want you happy, or as happy as your little moody ass can be."

I rolled my eyes. "I'm not moody. And I'm older by six months."

He opened his arms, and I fell into them for a hug. "If you trust Julius, I trust Julius. But you know we can't just cross him off the suspect list without proof."

"I know."

The doorbell rang, and I moved to sit on the bed as footsteps bound up the stairs to my room.

"Hey." Sabrina opened the door and looked between Frankie and me. "All made up?"

"All made up. What did you two want to go over? I thought we were finished with Chloe's case. We're going with the motive of an affair gone wrong. I already sent a copy of everything to Reya for her to take into the office."

Frankie nodded. "We wanted to talk about the other case."

I sunk back in the bed. "I was serious about stepping away from it."

"We know," Sabrina said. "Just run through these scenarios with us."

I sighed. "Fine."

"Okay." Frankie clapped his hands together. "Let's start with the events that led up to that morning. You both had a point about Julius probably giving Mr. Medina that list of names for the students last year. But whether it was by Julius or someone else, Mr. Medina was clued in to the scam and started asking questions. He approached the first proctor. I'm thinking Mr. Callahan fleeing the country put others on edge. Then Ms. Taylor proctored once, but she didn't know what she was getting into. She did the last test, which was for—"

"Antonio Garcia." I interjected. "That's the ID in Mrs. Lawson's file on Julius. There's a good chance that Ms. Taylor took it off him during the test and reported him to the dean. The dean could've tried to bring Ms. Taylor into the scam, but she wanted nothing to do with it."

Frankie nodded. "And from there Mrs. Lawson would have to tell the others involved that everything had to stop until they found a replacement. There are still three more tests before summer. More parents could've been lined up.

"Somewhere in the mix, someone must've figured out that Mr. Medina was poking around. Everyone would've been on high alert after the first proctor left town. And someone in on the scam left Mr. Medina a threatening voice mail the night before he died."

"'I protect what's mine,'" I quoted. "Based on the words and what we know, it points to Chief Ryan protecting Maddie or his job. Then, the next morning, Mr. Medina goes to meet his old friend from school he exchanged ciphers with."

"This is where I have something," Sabrina interrupted. "I had asked Mrs. Medina about going over to the loft to look at Mr. Medina's old books. I found his high school yearbooks in the library."

"Did you figure out who the friend was?"

She nodded. "Lieutenant Charles."

I sat up. "Lieutenant Charles? *Our* Lieutenant Charles? You're sure?"

"Yeah, he went by Blue back then."

"Whiskey Blue. The email address Mr. Medina traded ciphers with," I murmured. "'Whiskey' is 'W' in the phonetic alphabet. His first name is Wendell. It fits."

"Okay, so we know who he was talking to. But we still don't have the cipher code," Frankie reminded us.

"Actually, I think we do. Pull up the police report."

Frankie pulled it up on my laptop, and I pointed to the lieutenant's star number. "The email subject line was, 'I need your badge.' Before, we thought it meant Mr. Medina was just looking for an officer he could trust. What if it had a double meaning—using Lieutenant Charles's badge number as the shift? Two-four-nine."

Sabrina went to my closet, grabbing the white board. "I'll write out the alphabets. Frankie, you split up the emails."

Frankie scribbled a few of the ciphers down and handed them to me. "Let's start with shifting left, so for 'e' and the number two, you should end up with 'c.' Then apply the four to the next letter, nine to the next—"

"Then repeat." I finished for him.

We sat silently, each consumed with the ciphers we'd been assigned to break. After ten minutes, the letters on the board were replaced with a conversation.

MM: g drta jmivrdzle wmm pmq ssp zr szjh
rdbvap kfa tgpp
I have something for you but it will affect the city

LC: fkn qk?
how so?

MM: chvapvb kwdetgwcq, ufsn smoj
elected officials, your boss

LC: wkl ekk rk xgrv ka dmnv rdrl pyyr

    you got to give me more than that

MM: wwe'r

    can't

LC: wkl qpzjh yyrv rdvqa ymqeb zfeo?

    You still have those hound dogs?

MM: 5 39 33 | 4 59 28 | 12 51 60

    City Hope Scholastics

LC: Monday 10 a.m. Bring everything.

"So, Lieutenant Charles knew Mr. Medina had something on his boss." I nodded to the board. "Whiskey Blue, Lil Blue," I mumbled.

"Who's Lil Blue?" Sabrina asked.

"His son, Tre. At the alumni event, he said someone owed his dad a favor; that's how Tre was able to attend. I had assumed it was Alderman Corben who owed him the favor, for his help getting the case closed quickly for Mrs. Medina. What if it was Chief Ryan? What if Lieutenant Charles gave him a heads-up about Mr. Medina's investigation?"

I sat on the bed, the cogs churning in my mind. Chief Ryan rushing out the building that morning, being first on the scene, and knowing about the camera placements.

"Chief Ryan has a lot on the line with his bid for police superintendent. It's a big political move. If Lieutenant Charles told him about Mr. Medina's plans to drop off all his evidence that morning, Chief Ryan could've gone to the train platform and waited for the right opportunity. Purposely stayed out of sight."

"Do you think Lieutenant Charles betrayed Mr. Medina, though?" Sabrina frowned. "They'd been friends since they were our age. Could Lieutenant Charles have let the info slip by accident?"

"I'm not sure. This is good, though." Frankie took a photo of the board with his phone. "I can include this with the rest of the evidence we hand over."

Sabrina raised her hand. "*I* still think it was Maddie. It had to have been Chief Ryan who left that message, but Maddie could have overheard her dad on the phone. My theory has more what-ifs, *but* what if, after hearing her dad leave the voice mail, Maddie saw Mr. Medina leaving the school with the files the next morning? She realizes this would ruin her. No more Brown, probably expelled from North Shore. She could've followed Mr. Medina, confronted him, and pushed him onto the tracks. Then she called her dad afterward so he ends up first on the scene to get her out of there."

I nodded to myself. I'd run through both scenarios multiple times in my head. Maddie's queen-bee reputation and anger in class last week showed me she was more than capable of violence. And it wouldn't be the first time she'd pushed someone.

"This is all conjecture, though. What we *can* prove is the scam. Frankie, did you save screenshots linking all the parents to the campaign donations?"

"Yep. It's circumstantial, but all of them made an eight-thousand-dollar donation to the City Hope Scholastic scholarship fund a few days before their kids' exams."

"And we can prove the cipher was meant for Lieutenant Charles, which will lead the police to check any call records between him and Mr. Medina." I stood up. "We can't do much else. We've narrowed down the pool as much as we can."

"We didn't run through a scenario for Julius," Frankie said quietly.

It bothered me that I couldn't take Julius out of the suspect pool. I thought about what Reya said last week—how the privileged always found a way to avoid the consequences. Right now, our money trail pointed directly to Julius. There was no hint of another ringleader or anyone else getting payments.

I stared at the whiteboard. With only three names, Frankie had used one side of it to list out clues along the way. "We forgot about something."

Frankie frowned. "What's that?"

"The mystery book club that me and Julius were supposedly attending. That's our proof that Julius's name comes off. He was feeding Mr. Medina information and meeting with him after school. They probably used the work-study hours to talk through their plan."

"Jo, we need proof—" Frankie shook his head.

"I'll ask him. He basically knows what we're investigating. I'll just ask him at school tomorrow."

"Sweetie, you said you didn't want—"

"It's not him, Sabrina. I know you know it, too. After this, it's done. We turn over what we have. Deal?" I looked between Frankie and Sabrina.

"Deal," they both said.

TWENTY-THREE

MONDAY, MARCH 14, 11:47 A.M.

I WAITED UNTIL after third period to approach Julius. There were so many emotions running through me, knowing we were so close to handing over all the evidence. Anxiety was at an all-time high. I stood at the doorway, bouncing on my heels. Finally, Julius walked out of class.

"Hey."

"Kelley Green Eyes. Are you escorting me to *my* classes now?" He bumped my shoulder with his.

I tried to smile. "I can. I thought we could talk about that thing I'm not supposed to be investigating."

Julius frowned.

"I know it wasn't you," I rushed out. "I just—I need to talk about it."

"Okay. Yeah, we can do that." He tugged on his backpack straps. "It's going to be longer than the five-minute walk between classes, though. How do you feel about coming over? After school?"

"Sure. Meet you on the steps outside?"

"See you then."

The rest of the day was slow. We met on the steps like we agreed. The conversations we held on the way to his house were light and guarded, my body growing tense. We reached his neighborhood, and it looked a lot like mine. Some might say the homes looked old and unkept, but I always saw the history. These houses had seen a lot of things, sheltered and provided for a lot of families.

A school bus waited in front of one with a pale yellow door. "Give me a sec." Julius jogged over to the bus and out of sight. When he stepped back into view, he held the hand of a little girl with the same dark curls and almond-brown eyes as her brother. "Say hi, Tati. This is my friend Jolene I was telling you about."

She waved with a smile that went from ear to ear. "You're so pretty!"

"You're prettier." I smiled back. "I'm jealous of your curls."

She giggled, running into the house.

I pointed to the old blue Honda Civic in the driveway. "You stay with someone else?"

"No that's mine, technically. It was my mom's. Public

transportation is cheaper, though," Julius answered, leading me through his front door. The living room was small and quaint, Tati already sprawled out on the floor in front of the burgundy couch, snacking on chips and watching cartoons. "I'll be in my room with Jolene, okay? Come get me if you need anything."

Tati nodded, not peeling her eyes away from the screen.

Julius's room was the last door on the right. Movie posters filled his walls: *Goodfellas*, *Lord of the Rings*, and Jordan Peele's *Us*, being just a few of the ones I recognized. Most were older and in black and white.

He dropped his backpack at his desk and started typing on his computer. "You know what, let me get us some drinks and snacks first. Any requests? I buy the groceries, so the junk food selection is amazing here."

I smiled. "Water with crushed ice is fine. Not hungry yet."

"Got it." He slipped back into the hallway.

Not wanting to sit on his bed, I sat in his desk chair and continued to take in his room. He had a corkboard on the wall with USC paraphernalia pinned all over it. I spotted his acceptance letter and the financial aid papers. He had gotten some grants and scholarships, enough for a full ride like he said.

At the edge of his desk, there was an envelope from the Future of Chicago Organization. I stared at it. It was the same group that awarded him with all those "scholarships." Every bone in my body told me to snoop.

I should wait, just ask him up front.

The letter sat there, the previously sealed flap already ripped open.

I gave in.

FUTURE OF CHICAGO ORGANIZATION

February 24

Dear Julius James,

The Future of Chicago Organization is pleased to award you the City Hope Scholastic Achievement Award in the amount of thirty thousand dollars. Congratulations on your acceptance to the University of South California, School for Cinematic Arts.

Go Trojans!

Charlotte Mackenzie

Charlotte Mackenzie

Scholarship Chair, Future of Chicago Organization

I stared at the date. The same day Mr. Medina's case closed. I did quick math in my head. Julius already had enough in scholarships for USC. Anything over the school's tuition fees—wouldn't that result in a cash payment? At least, that's how it worked at North Shore. The school would send the student a check with the balance, right?

I looked up to the corkboard. At the bottom of the

financial aid papers for USC, there was a login to Julius's account.

Getting up, I tiptoed to the hallway. Tati and Julius were still talking in the kitchen.

I can't believe I'm about to do this.

Rushing back to his desk, I typed in the URL, then his username and password. I clicked on the financial aid section.

USC *FAST*

| Application Status | Financial Aid Summary and Tasks | Aid Status |

Academic Year

Estimated Cost of Attendance	**$60,275**
Gift Aid **Grants**	**$92,775**
Estimated Federal Pell Grant	$2,500
USC Trustees Scholarship	$60,275
City Hope Scholastic Achievement Award	$30,000

"Hey, sorry that took so long."

I shot up from his desk.

He handed me my water with knitted brows, looking from his lit computer back to me. "Did you go through my things?" He walked over to his desk, spotting the scholarship letter and where I had navigated through to his USC student account. His nostrils flared.

I backed up to the closest wall. "You got paid by the Future of Chicago Organization *again*. After all the other checks. I know that's how the parents paid you for their kids' SAT scores. But this—" My heart beat hard against my ribs.

Julius gritted his teeth, his fists balled at his sides. "I can't believe . . . Dammit, Jolene . . ."

"Did you do it? Did you push him and someone paid you for it? *Rewarded* you?" My voice cracked. "Because that's— that's what it looks like."

He shook his head. "I told you to stop with this. I put the note in your locker, hoping to scare you off—"

No. I blinked, tears forming.

He took a step toward me, and I did the only thing I could think of—I threw the ice water in his face and ran.

"JOLENE!"

Outside his house, I turned up the street, back the way we came, and didn't stop running.

It's him.

It was all I could think as I willed my feet to carry me far away from his house. I had left my backpack and my phone in his room. I had nothing, no way to call anyone.

Shit. Shit. Shit.

I turned another corner, ending up on an unfamiliar street.

"Shit!" I cried out. *Which way? Which way?*

A blue Honda Civic pulled up beside me.

"Get in the car."

Tears streamed down my cheeks, but I didn't stop running. The car revved, popping up the curb to stop in front of me. Julius stepped out, his shirt and face still wet. "I didn't kill Mr. Medina. If you get in the car, I'll explain. I need you to listen." Behind him, Tati sat in the back seat, buckled into her booster seat. Of course he couldn't leave her. Still, the sight was jarring.

She smiled up at me.

I looked back up and down the street. I was turned around now—nowhere else to go. Walking to the passenger seat, I slid into the car, wiping my face.

"Sorry about that," Tati quipped. "Jules really can't drive." She smiled again and went back to playing the game in her hands. My backpack and phone lay next to her across the seat.

I glared at Julius. Was he really using his sister in this moment?

After a minute, I realized we weren't driving back to his house. He dropped off Tati with a neighbor, and then it was just the two of us, sitting in silence. He drove for a while, and I started recognizing the streets as my own neighborhood. Pulling into the parking lot of Kershaw Elementary, Julius shut off the engine.

"Sophomore year, I took a bunch of those practice SATs

with the guidance counselor before Mr. Medina. My scores always came back 1580, 1590. The guidance counselor wanted me to humor her. She scheduled me for a SAT exam that winter. I got a perfect score. Then she introduced me to Alderman Corben."

My mouth dropped. "Wait—what?"

"Let me finish. It'll come together at the end. The conversations were innocent. He wanted me to tutor his son, Matt. Said his scores weren't good enough for Yale. We met all through January, February, but Matt wasn't trying. There was a kid that he used to pay to do his class assignments, so he was far behind. One day I joked and said, 'You should just pay me to take the exam.' He took it literally."

He paused for a minute, eyes focused on something outside the window. "At first I said no. Then, in March, my mom got really sick. The bills—we couldn't afford the bills. So I went back to Matt and said yes. I wish I could say I tried to back out before we went through with it, but I didn't. The alderman found out what Matt and I did and sent me to the dean. I thought I was being expelled. But instead, I started getting invited to those alumni fundraiser dinners. Parents wanted to pay me to do their kids' homework, midterms . . . college admissions tests.

"It feels weird to say I did it for my mom, but that's what it was. Junior year started, and her diagnosis was official. Dad wasn't sending us enough to cover the chemo. We needed the money. I needed it. Then, after my mom passed away in September, I had to find a way to get custody of Tati. Our dad had made it clear he didn't want us. I couldn't stop taking the tests. I knew it was wrong, but . . ." He sighed, wiping at his eyes.

"You had to take care of Tati," I murmured.

He nodded. "Then Mr. Medina saw me at one of the SAT sites in October and noticed a score never posted for me. At that point, I was living with him. Taking advantage. I just—" He shook his head. "The guilt was there. I knew he would start poking around sooner or later, so I confessed."

Julius ran his hands over his face, his knees bouncing with nerves.

"I told Mr. Medina about the five tests I took for kids during my junior year and the seven lined up for this year. He told me he would find a way to get me out of it. But I had already tried before Mr. Medina ever found out. I spoke to the original proctor, Mr. Callahan, before he bailed, but he didn't want to hear it; the tests were already lined up. Then I started receiving threats. Mrs. Lawson keeps the IDs I used. For blackmail, I guess. She rescinded her recommendation letter for me. Chief Ryan promised another payment if I saw things through, stayed quiet. But I didn't want the money anymore.

"Mr. Medina and I agreed I would finish taking the tests that were scheduled through the end of the semester. Then he would take all the information I had and find hard evidence to back it up. About two weeks before he died, I got nervous. He had reached out to someone at the police station, one of the bureau chiefs, and ended up with a death threat on his voice mail—a different one from the one you heard. I assumed it was Maddie's dad. Mr. Medina and I already knew we couldn't go to the dean since she was part of it, and now the police station wasn't a safe bet, either. We argued about him continuing with his investigation. I actually punched a hole in his wall." He chuckled.

"But he wanted to keep going?" I asked quietly. "Even with the threats?"

Julius nodded. "He didn't want to back down, though he did have some reservations. He wanted to do it in a way that didn't involve his wife. To keep her safe. So we met a few times after school during my work-study hours to go over how we could approach the police. He made a few ciphers and passed them back and forth with a different cop he felt good about, someone he knew from high school. That morning . . ."

Julius stopped talking. He took in a few breaths, but it only made him shake more. Getting out of the car, he started pacing back and forth. His cheeks wet, his eyes red.

I got out to walk over to him, but he kept his head down, avoiding my gaze and clenching his fists until he couldn't hold it in. Tears streamed down his cheeks.

"We were going to meet at the school and ride the CTA to the police station together, but I was late. No one's fault but the trains running slow. He said he would meet me at the station instead. I remember standing at the doors as the train pulled into Thirty-Fifth and Bronzeville, and then being jerked back off my feet. That sound, the screeching."

I knew the sound well—metal on metal.

I covered my mouth. "You were on the train."

He nodded. "I was on the train that killed Mr. Medina."

Broken, he dropped to the ground, his head in his hands. I sat next to him, crying my own tears. Neither of us said anything for a long time. The sky grew dark, and after a while, Julius walked me back over to the passenger side and opened the door for me. Back in the car, he drove to my house, me speaking only to give directions.

"The payment you saw earlier on my USC account—the thirty thousand—I declined the check. Chief Ryan tried to give it to me in cash, you saw that at the alumni fundraiser, but I returned that, too. I gotta find another way to take care of Tati."

"I'm sorry. I didn't think you killed Mr. Medina. I just needed to be able to prove the scam existed. When I saw the letter—"

"You jumped to a reasonable conclusion." He turned the last corner onto my street.

"Do you know who did it?" I asked quietly.

He tilted his head to the side and frowned. "I have theories, like I'm sure you do. When they let us off the train, I had to catch a ride home. On the corner by the train station, I saw Maddie standing with her dad by a black Lincoln."

My breath caught.

"It's not this house, is it?" He pointed to my redbrick.

"This is it." As soon as the words left my mouth, I saw what he had noticed: There was a black Lincoln parked right outside.

TWENTY-FOUR

AS SOON AS the car was in park, I ran into my house, Julius trailing close behind me.

"Mom?" I stopped short. At the kitchen table, Maddie sat with my mother, sipping on glasses of iced tea. My whole body went cold.

"There you are, Jolene! I was just about to leave. I guess you forgot about our project for Mr. Perez's class?"

I clenched my jaw. This was too far.

"We tried texting and calling," Mom said. "You didn't pick up."

"My phone slid down under the car seat. I just found it a few minutes ago," I lied. "I didn't know you were coming over today, Madison. I must've blanked on the assignment."

"Oh, it's not due for a while, but you know me. I don't like to push things off to the last minute. I did that once, and it didn't end well for anyone." Maddie stood from the table and leaned down to give my mom a hug. "Thank you so much for the hospitality, Mrs. Kelley."

"Of course, Madison. It was nice to meet one of Jo's classmates."

Maddie sauntered over to me at the door and tugged lightly at the scarf at my neck hiding my bruise. She smirked. "Your mom mentioned everything worked out with your scholarship. First my dad helped you, now my godfather." She paused, lowering her voice. "I wonder what would happen if they knew you were snooping in the dean's office and hanging out with this scum. I don't think they'd want you to talk to *anyone* anymore."

She stepped around me and out the front door, letting it slam behind her.

I let out a breath, falling into the nearest chair.

"Is everything okay?" Mom asked, looking from me to Julius.

Eyes watering, I turned to her. It was too much.

"I need help."

I began to tell her everything, only for her to stop and call Dad so he could hear it, too. I texted Frankie and Sabrina to come over. Before long, my parents, Sabrina, and I sat at the table while Frankie and Julius leaned against the counters.

"You three are handing everything over to the police in

the morning. And, Jolene, you are not to go to school until Maddie is removed," Dad ordered.

Mom pulled out her phone. "I'm going to reach out to Hal to make sure there's an officer we trust with you. You're going to have to hand everything over to Lieutenant Charles—"

"But he ratted out Mr. Medina the first time," Sabrina interrupted.

Frankie nodded. "He's part of it."

Mom put the phone to her ear. "We don't know for sure that he is, and until we can prove otherwise, the evidence has to go to the case's original supervising officer. We'll keep copies of everything, too. And I can send a copy directly to the state attorney's office. Whoever is behind this, they won't be able to hide." She stood from the table, taking her call in the living room.

"Your mom and I both have court at seven tomorrow morning, but Reya will meet you. Do not walk into that station without her. We'll be there as soon as we can."

I nodded.

"I'll go to school," said Julius. "I think if Maddie sees us both missing, that might cause her to think something is up."

"I'm so sorry," I mumbled.

Mom walked back into the room. "Don't apologize." She pulled me to her and wrapped me in her arms. "You asked for help, which is all I wanted. Though, next time, ask a little sooner." She gave me a squeeze. "Hal will be waiting in the lobby at nine thirty. He'll leave a message for Lieutenant Charles requesting a meeting, but he won't mention the case. I should be able to meet up with you all by ten."

I turned to Julius. "What does this mean for you?"

"I promised Mr. Medina before he died that I'd give a statement, and I still want to. I know what I'm risking." He leaned up from the counter, checking his watch. "I have to pick up my sister, though."

I nodded. "I'll walk you out."

Outside, I grabbed my backpack and phone from his car. "I'm sorry again."

"For what?"

"Not trusting you. This could've gone differently if I had. If I wasn't so focused on just closing everyone off—"

Julius held up a hand. "You tried to solve a murder while grieving and dealing with emotions you weren't ready to handle. And you almost did it. Don't beat yourself up for that."

"Thanks." I tugged my backpack onto my shoulder. "I wish you had tried to be my friend sooner. Before all this."

A smile tugged at the corner of his lips. "I'll talk to you tomorrow. Try to stay out of trouble until then."

Back inside the house, only my parents remained in the kitchen.

"Bri and Frankie are waiting for you upstairs," Dad said.

"Jolene?" Mom tapped her fingers against her glass of tea.

"Yes?" I stepped toward the kitchen, bracing myself for the repercussions.

"Asking for help can be hard. I'm proud of you. We can talk about this more later—when we're prepping Sunday dinners together." She smiled. "We'll call it our safe space."

I let myself smile, too. "I would like that. I'd like that very much."

"I just can't believe we let that little monster into our house. You really think she did it?" Dad asked.

"You'd be surprised what the kids in that school would do for some Ivy League clout."

TWENTY-FIVE

MONDAY, MARCH 14, 8:02 P.M.

"HOW ARE YOU feeling, sweetie?"

I slumped onto my bed, Sabrina next to me and Frankie at my desk, both of them looking at me expectantly.

"I'm ready to turn everything over. We don't have hard evidence on the killer, but the cheating should be enough to have Maddie expelled from school, right?"

"I hope so," said Sabrina. "I wish you would've told us about the fall at school before now. She went too far."

"I wasn't really thinking. I knew I needed to step back from the case, but I thought you guys would've wanted to just throw the whole thing out. I didn't want to do that. Mr. Medina died over this."

"Yeah." Frankie caught my eye. "He *died* over this. We

aren't going to let that happen to you. I'm glad you finally spoke up."

I nodded. "Me too."

Frankie sighed. "I guess we should go over everything one last time before we hand it over."

"Well, we have everything on the flash drive: test scores, recommendation letters, and proctor schedule." Sabrina counted off on her fingers. "Then there's the scanned notes that Julius can confirm with a statement, and the email ciphers that will show Mr. Medina was in touch with the police."

"And, Frankie, you have the time stamps of the others we eliminated and all our notes on their alibis?"

"Uh-huh. Everything on the money trail, too. And I made up the suspect profiles for our final three—Julius, Maddie, and Chief Ryan."

"Can't we take out Julius at this point?" Sabrina asked. "That's why you were with him today, right? And he's agreed to be a witness."

I turned to Frankie. "If you hack into the platform cameras again, you'll see Julius get off the train that was stalled on the platform."

"Wait." He sat up. "The one that hit Mr. Medina?"

"Yeah. You can check if you need peace of mind, but I don't think handing over the hacked footage would be good. We can give the police a very precise time frame to check."

"Wow, Jo. Shit, I'm sorry—"

"You had good reason to suspect him. Believe me, there was a moment today when I wasn't sure, either."

I glanced down at our final two suspect profile cards.

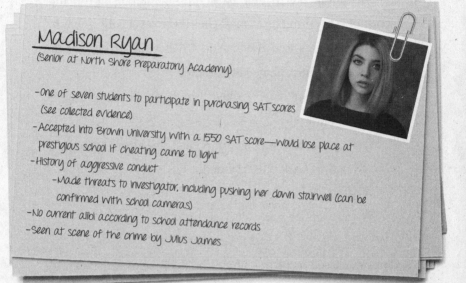

Madison Ryan
(Senior at North Shore Preparatory Academy)

- One of seven students to participate in purchasing SAT scores (See collected evidence)
- Accepted into Brown University with a 1550 SAT score—would lose place at prestigious school if cheating came to light
- History of aggressive conduct
  - Made threats to investigator, including pushing her down stairwell (can be confirmed with school cameras)
- No current alibi according to school attendance records
- Seen at scene of the crime by Julius James

Chief John Ryan
(High-ranked official in Chicago Police Department)

- Money trail to confirm he paid for Julius James to take SAT for his daughter, Madison
- Seen rushing from headquarters prior to Mr. Medina's death and was the first officer on scene, reporting two minutes after the incident
- Left threatening voice mails for victim—police to confirm with phone records
- Running for Police Superintendent—scandal would ruin family and personal reputation, as well as result in jail time

"Frankie?" Dad poked his head into the room. "You ready to head out? I want the girls to get some sleep. I know it's going to be a restless night."

"Sure thing, Mr. K." He packed up his laptop. "I'll print a copy of everything and email the files to everyone, including your parents and Reya. And I'll have a backup USB. This is happening. They can't stop us."

"Thanks, Frankie." I walked him to my door, closing it slowly behind him.

"Well, your dad was right about one thing." Sabrina plopped herself back onto my bed.

"What's that?"

"No one's getting any sleep tonight."

***

Chicago passed by us in a blur. The three of us sat smushed together on the Green Line on our way to Thirty-Fifth and Bronzeville. Sabrina checked and rechecked all the evidence we printed out while I tried to stop my legs from bouncing.

It's almost over.

My phone buzzed.

Julius:
You're not going to believe this.

Julius:
I just got suspended.

I nudged Sabrina and Frankie so they could see the text.

"Think Maddie knows what we're doing?" Frankie looked at me.

Jolene:

What happened?

Julius:

Mrs. Lawson called me into the office once I got in. She said a student approached her and said I'd been selling homework assignments. I'm suspended until further notice.

"That's definitely Maddie's doing," said Sabrina. "And didn't the dean already know that?"

"She's probably just trying to cover for herself." I shook my head.

Jolene:

Are you going back home?

Julius:

I mean I can't stay here. Maddie made sure she was in the office talking to Ms. Faiza when it happened.

Now Sabrina bounced her legs. "What do we do now?"

I placed a hand on her knee. "She's still at school. She can't do anything else."

The train pulled into the station, and the three of us got off. My phone buzzed again. I answered the call from Reya, putting it on speaker. "We're almost there, Rey. Just hopping off the train."

"Don't. Lieutenant Charles canceled the meeting."

I stopped walking. "What?"

"He canceled it. Said he was unavailable."

"Is he there?"

"Yes, and that alderman we saw in his office a couple of weeks ago was there, too. He was leaving as I walked into the building. Lieutenant Charles was already in the lobby to turn me away."

"Why is the alderman there?" Frankie asked. "I thought everything with him and his son was a one-off before the scam really started. He's the one who first tried to turn Julius in."

I frowned, replaying everything Julius said to me. "We missed something. Matt still went to Yale. He had to have still used the SAT score Julius got him."

"Jo." Sabrina elbowed me, her eyes locked on something farther down the platform. Alderman Corben stepped onto the northbound train, sliding a bright green card into his pocket.

"I'll call you back, Reya." I hung up. "Did you see that? The card he slipped into his pocket?"

Frankie nodded. "What about it? It's a Ventra card."

"Ventra cards are blue. Unless . . ." I searched my memory. *What did Julius say about the green cards?* A voice came on overhead as the doors of the train warned they were about to close. Without thinking, I slipped back onto the train, three cars down from Alderman Corben, the doors shutting behind me.

Frankie slammed his fist on the door. He reached into his pocket for his cell.

Frankie:

WTF JO

The train pulled away, and I found myself thinking the exact same thing.

TWENTY-SIX

I PACED BACK and forth in the train car. The green cards for Saint Patrick's Day—the CTA printed up special Ventra cards to celebrate.

Frankie:

Get off at the next stop. Bri is freaking out.

Frankie:

JO

Sabrina:

Please, Jo. Come back.

I swiped the messages off my screen and navigated to the CTA's website.

"'Limited Edition St. Patrick's Day card to celebrate a

beloved tradition,'" I muttered. "The cards were available starting February fifteenth but were sold out by February twenty-second."

Jolene:

Did either of you look at the photos from the crime scene?

Sabrina:

Yeah?

Jolene:

I noticed a Ventra card on the tracks when Reya and I went to the station to give my statement. Was it in the photos? If the crew cleans the tracks Sunday nights, it would have had to fall down there between Monday morning and then.

Frankie:

Where are you going with this?

Jolene:

I just saw Alderman Corben slip one of those new limited-edition cards into his pocket. He would've had to place the order in mid-February in order to get one. And when I went to his office, there was mail from the CTA on his assistant's desk.

Sabrina:

Frankie's pulling up his laptop to find the photos.

I sat down in an empty seat as the train passed a second stop.

Sabrina:

There's a card . . .

Jolene:

Is it backside up? Can he run the serial number to see who it belongs to?

Sabrina:

He's doing it now.

My heart raced and blood pulsed in my ears. I didn't know why I jumped back on the train. My body just reacted to seeing the alderman, seeing that card. His assistant's calendar entry for the press conference said, "No Driver Requested," so he could've taken the train that morning. But Thirty-Fifth and Bronzeville was one stop too far, past his destination. He had no reason to be there.

Frankie:

You're right, it was his card.

Frankie:

Get off the freakin' train.

Sabrina:

I'm texting Aiko. We'll get the keys to her van and come get you.

The train pulled into the next stop, and I stepped off, my breaths short. I leaned against one of the columns, willing my heart to slow down.

Jolene:

I'm off.

Frankie:

That card places the alderman at the crime scene on the day of the murder. We can go from there and check the cameras for when he arrived. He must've hidden somewhere out of sight on the platform.

Jolene:

We never checked his alibi when we looked at the press conference video, since we had no evidence he and Mrs. Medina were having an affair.

Frankie:

Let me look now . . .

Sabrina:

He shows up at 9:40 a.m.

Jolene:

8 minutes to run from the crime scene to the convention center. Even in the chaos he could've made it.

Got him. I made my way to the platform exit.

Jolene:

I'll meet you guys at the street. We have what we need.

Sabrina:

What station did you get off at?

"Miss Kelley!"

My blood turned to ice. That voice.

"Alderman Corben," I replied with a forced smile. I glanced over to the station sign. I'd gotten off right by his office.

He grinned. "Playing a little hooky today?"

I opened my mouth, then closed it. "Actually, I was on my way to your office. I never rescheduled with Charlotte."

I tried to text Sabrina and Frankie without looking, but after a quick glance it was just a jumbled mess of words.

"Perfect timing. And I owe your mom that scholarship information packet. You can pick it up for her. After you." He gestured for me to take the first step.

Shit.

I took a step, walking out of the station as he followed close behind. I needed to get myself out of this. I ran through possible scenarios in my head. Do I run and scream? Play along? What do you do in the presence of a murderer?

Within minutes we were at his office, entering the lobby. The French-vanilla scent slapped me in the face. I never hated a smell so much. My stomach turned, bile rising in my throat.

Just play it cool.

"Hold my calls, Charlotte." Alderman Corben took off his coat and placed it on a hanger. He reached for mine.

"Oh, no need, it's just a quick pickup. I can wait out here."

"Nonsense." He helped me out of my coat and took my bag with our extra set of evidence. I slipped my phone into the back pocket of my jeans and pulled my sweater over it.

Once my coat was hung up, and he saw my hands were empty, he led me back to his office.

"Can I get you anything?" he asked.

I glanced around, searching for an out. An exit sign flashed near the kitchen at the end of the hall, but that was where he was headed. If I tried to leave, would Charlotte stop me?

I smiled. "Water, and if you have crushed ice that would be great, too."

He nodded, leaving me alone while he walked down the hall. Pulling out my phone, I dropped my location into the group chat, then dialed Reya.

"Jo?" Reya's tiny voice said from the speaker.

Footsteps approached and I sat in the chair opposite the alderman's desk, hiding my phone under my thigh.

"Thank you." I took the glass from him. "Your office is amazing, Alderman Corben. Nice view of Lakeview." The decor was similar to the lobby: navy walls and bamboo hardwood. His desk was made of the same wood and spotless, only a discreet desk phone. Awards and honorary degrees hung on the wall, along with photos of him shaking hands with high-ranking officials. Everything a show of power.

He glanced out the window, his lips curving. "I like to keep an eye on what's mine." He opened a desk drawer and pulled out some papers. "Let me find that application."

The desk phone rang, the name Charlotte Mackenzie flashing on the screen.

"I asked you to hold my calls," he answered.

Charlotte Mackenzie. I swallowed, trying to steel my face. That was the name on Julius's letter from the Future of Chicago Organization. Charlotte—his assistant.

We never did figure out the ringleader of the SAT scam. I guess now we know.

I looked up to see Alderman Corben watching me.

"Tell him I'll call him back in a few minutes." He hung up the phone.

I cut my eyes away, scanning the room again. In the wall behind him, there was a cutout for a door. "Where's that go?" I asked, curious.

He looked over his shoulder. "A service elevator that goes down to the garage. It makes it easy to sneak out sometimes," he joked. "Maddie did say you ask a lot of questions."

I sipped on the water.

"She thought you were trying to do something to keep her from attending Brown."

I took another sip, avoiding his gaze. *If he leaves the room again, I can go down to the garage. Find someone to help me.*

"You didn't deny it."

I snapped back to attention. "What?"

"I said, she thought you were trying to keep her from Brown—that you knew she paid for test scores. You didn't deny it."

"And you didn't mention the test scores the first time."

"Mmm." He got up, walking to a small table at the side

of the room. A few tumblers and a bottle of amber liquid, Scotch, sat on a mirrored platter. He picked up an empty glass.

"I'll admit," I started. "I didn't know it was you. Not until this morning when I saw you get on the train."

In my head, I screamed at myself for goading him. But I needed him to talk. I needed to give Frankie and Sabrina time to get to me.

Please find me.

"What exactly did I do?" he asked. He picked up the bottle of Scotch but placed it back down, seeming to have decided against it.

"Kill Mr. Medina," I replied plainly. "I had thought it was Maddie."

"Well, you weren't wrong. I've always found my god-daughter a little extreme. She's been lashing out more and more for attention since her mother left. I thought I had cleaned up her mess at the train station. No one saw what she had done. But Maddie being Maddie couldn't leave it alone. Couldn't stop bragging about how she had gotten away with murder. I believe that's when you got involved? You overheard something?"

"She told me she planted that scholarship rejection in Mrs. Lawson's inbox to scare you. I thought it was a bit much. But it did give me an opening to fix things. Then she told me about your fall, and, well, I knew that was sure to set off alarms."

"You're really going to try to pin this on Maddie? *You* killed him. You left evidence behind at the scene. We can place you there."

I bit my tongue.

"We?" Alderman Corben glared for a moment, then adjusted his collar with his free hand. "You and Julius, you mean? You know it wasn't hard to get Mrs. Lawson to suspend him as a warning. One phone call. Another one and I can have you both expelled." He paused, looking me over. "But that won't stop you, will it? No, you have that connection at the state attorney's office."

He walked to stand behind me, and I let out a slow breath.

Just keep him talking, I told myself.

As I opened my mouth to speak, I caught movement in my periphery. He raised the empty glass and brought it down with a crack that reverberated through my skull. My sight went black, and I fell forward.

Then nothing.

TWENTY-SEVEN

I WOKE WITH a groan.

Alderman Corben paced over me, his phone pressed to his ear. "I thought you said you cleaned this up with Julius. . . Well, remember that favor you owe me for getting the aldermen to rally behind you for superintendent? I'm calling it in."

My phone laid on the floor in front of me, but I couldn't move. My head throbbed, pressure building behind my eyes. Everything blurred and swayed. I tried to push myself up only for my hands to slip in something slick and warm. Blood. My blood.

"I have a skeleton in my closet that I need help with." Alderman Corben's eyes fell to me, a wicked grin spreading across his face. "Well, soon-to-be skeleton. I'll let you kill this one." Spotting my phone, he stomped with his heel, shattering the screen.

"No," I whispered. "HEL— Oomph!" My scream got cut off with a swift kick to my gut.

"Text me a place where we can meet." He hung up the phone and reached down to yank me up by my hair. "Let's go for a ride."

"Ah!" Black spots dotted my vision. I clawed at his hands, trying to get him off me. Blood, wet and sticky, ran down the side of my face, more of it at the base of my neck. *How much was I losing?* "Please. You don't have to do this."

He dragged me to the back hallway and called for the service elevator. I kicked my legs, but I couldn't gain any footing. My limbs were heavy. Weak.

"You did this to yourself, Miss Kelley. Trying to play detective. Like Lieutenant Charles, bless him. He didn't even know his call to warn me about possible dirt on my scholarship program led to his old friend's death. All he knew is that it was the same scholarship I promised for his son. And he needed that money. Lucky me."

"City Hope Scholastic. How long have you been running the Future of Chicago Organization through your assistant? I saw Charlotte's name on the organization's letter to Julius."

"Ooo, you almost got it. I don't run it. Do I control where the money goes? That's the question you're looking for."

"So, what you did for the conductor—getting him that

nice retirement package—you were protecting yourself. Not helping getting closure for Mrs. Medina."

"Nic didn't know a thing about her husband's makeshift investigation, but I had to make sure. It was hard following her around like that. She was so sad. We're old friends, you know. I almost felt guilty."

"You *are* guilty!" I tried to pull away again only for him to tighten his grip.

"Yet no one saw me on the cameras. I even tracked down the tourist couple who left with me before the police arrived. Made sure they never went back to make a statement placing me there. And you, you didn't recognize me then, either. Everything was perfect."

My head ached as the scene flashed in my memory. "The man in the double-breasted coat."

"Oh, you do remember?" He pressed the button for the elevator again. "Looks like we're taking the stairs."

I twisted around, pulling my legs underneath me. "Let me stand, I'll cooperate. Ow!"

He jerked me by my hair again, letting my head hit the wall. "What's another concussion or two," he muttered. A door creaked and fire shot through my spine as he pulled me backward down the flight of stairs. "I've worked too hard for this. I have the perfect social-climbing wife, the caring son who *will* graduate from Yale. You know some people are even talking about how I should run for governor." He laughed to himself. "The office is as good as mine."

Another door swung open. My sight came and went, though the smells burned my nose. Car exhaust and wet asphalt. The garage.

"Please don't do this," I rasped.

"Your guidance counselor almost ruined it all. I gave him chances, warnings. I learned my lesson, though. Should've killed him sooner. With you, sure, you're a kid, but—" He stopped, pulling me up to stare into his eyes. All I could make out was that bleach-white smile. He grinned. "I'll survive."

A car door beeped, and there was a pop of a trunk. Everything was too loud, distorted. The steady drip of a leaking pipe overhead sounded like rushing rain.

He lifted me up, shoving me into a cramped space. He hovered with his arm raised, ready to slam the trunk door. Then his head whipped to the right. Tires squeaked on the concrete, and the garage grew brighter and brighter.

Headlights.

"JO!" a voice screamed.

Sabrina?

The alderman ran, slipping in the puddle of the leaking pipe before regaining his footing. He didn't get far. Sabrina braked a second too late, the neon Volkswagen minibus slamming into his back. He fell down to the ground.

"Jo! Jo, are you okay?" Frankie grabbed me from the car trunk, pulling me to his chest. He held me close, shaking.

I squinted, just enough to see Sabrina run over to pick up a groggy Alderman Corben by the shirt collar, pull back a fist, and knock him out, cold. The Alderman's once stark-white button-up now stained red with blood dripping from his nose.

She hurried over to me and Frankie.

"You ran someone over for me," I mumbled.

"Shhh. It was more like a tap of the bumper. Though I could back up and try again." She pressed her lips to my forehead. "I didn't even think when I saw you as we turned the corner."

I shuddered. *If it had taken them one more minute, one red light—*

"It's okay, sweetie." Sabrina brushed my hair off my face. "Frankie, call an ambulance."

He nodded, pulling out his phone as Sabrina took his place, sitting at the car's edge to hold me tight.

I let myself breathe in Sabrina's embrace, the aches and pains dulling at her touch. The sight of another vehicle approaching caused me to draw a sharp breath. A police cruiser. My thoughts flashed to the alderman calling Chief Ryan for a favor. *Help to get rid of a skeleton. I'll let you kill this one.*

Kill *me.*

My whole body went rigid.

The tires screeched, and I exhaled at the beautiful faces stepping out of the car—Reya and Officer Halligan.

Reya rushed over to me and Sabrina. "Jolene." She cradled my face.

"Did you hear enough?" I whispered.

"Alderman Corben plotting to kill a sixteen-year-old and confessing to murder? Yes, I heard it." She laughed, holding back tears. "Though, I did panic a little when the call went dead. I'm just so happy you're okay. Happy you knew to call for help."

"Well, I'm not alone, right?"

"Never," she murmured, pressing her forehead to mine.

"Jolene Kelley. Private investigator." Hal shook his head as he dragged Alderman Corben, handcuffed and looking two seconds away from falling unconscious again, to his cruiser. "Are you okay over there?" he called over.

"Could be better. I'm grateful, though—having all of you come to my rescue."

"Of course. Sorry, I didn't get Ms. Morales here faster. I had to arrest my boss's boss. I could really use a pastrami from Manny's after a morning like this."

"I think I have a concussion, Hal. But rain check."

More police cruisers pulled into the garage, followed by an ambulance. I shielded my eyes, the blinking red and blue lights making me light-headed.

"She has a gash at the back of her head. There are bits of glass in her hair, too," Reya said, waving over an EMT. Sabrina squeezed my hand before moving to give the EMT some room.

I flinched. "The lights . . . it's hard to focus."

"Close your eyes," said Reya.

There was a light touch at my nape and a snap of hard plastic as the EMT put me in a neck brace. I kept my eyes closed, listening to the sounds of the scene. Police officers questioned Sabrina and Frankie not too far off while another recited Miranda rights to Alderman Corben.

My body lifted, and the hard ground beneath me was replaced with something slightly less hard. Buckles and metal locks clicked in place. A gurney. I was on a gurney. I winced as it rolled across the bumpy, cracked concrete, the voices and chatter of the garage soon replaced with the sounds of Chicago traffic. Doors opened, one more big rock to the gurney and then quiet.

"Wait, that's my daughter!"

The ambulance shifted as a new voice entered the back cabin and a warm hand weaved its fingers with mine. I opened my eyes. Tears streaked my mom's face, yet she still smiled. She cupped my cheeks and I leaned into her touch.

"Mom?"

"Save your energy, baby."

An EMT got into the back with us, closing the doors.

"Is she going to be okay?" Mom asked quietly. She didn't take her eyes off mine.

"She'll be fine, ma'am. From what I heard outside, she's quite the hero catching a murderer."

Mom nodded. "That's my daughter," she repeated. A single tear fell. There was no anger in her expression, only pride. "I'm so proud of you, Jo. You did it."

EPILOGUE

SUNDAY, MAY 22, 9:14 A.M.

THE DAY AFTER Alderman Corben was arrested, seven students were expelled from North Shore Preparatory Academy. Mrs. Lawson was removed, though it turned out her file cabinet had more than just dirt on Julius. Evidence of the five students Julius took tests for last year also came to light, and now those kids would never become Ivy League alumni, including the alderman's son, Matt Corben. Mrs. Lawson even kept receipts that showed the donations parents made to Alderman Corben's campaign through the Future of Chicago Organization—his cut for setting everything up. And Maddie, in addition to being expelled and losing her spot at Brown University, caught a Class A misdemeanor charge for pushing me down the stairs. As my dad put it, no one touches his daughter.

Over the following weeks, other parents resigned or were removed from their positions of power throughout the city. Deputy Mayor Khara quietly stepped down from office. Lieutenant Charles lost his pension. Julius cooperated with police, and while his suspension was lifted, he was encouraged to take the remainder of the year off for his role in the scam. He'll be back with me in the fall as a proud super senior.

"Scooch your boot." Frankie bumped me with his hip as he joined my table at Manny's. It was May, it was getting hot, and I was just relieved to not be cold. Sabrina slid into a seat on the opposite side.

Frankie stole a bite of my French toast. "Julius is coming, right?"

"Yep," I said, snatching back my food. "He's bringing the morning paper. Should be front page."

"Good. Well, I have news." Sabrina pulled out an envelope with the North Shore crest. It was addressed to me.

"How'd you end up with my mail?"

"Your mom gave it to me. Open it."

Breaking the seal, I pulled out the letter. "Miss Kelley, we are pleased to inform you— STOP." I read it all the way to the end. "A full scholarship?"

Frankie nudged my shoulder. "Check out the scholarship name."

"Manuel Medina Young Voices," I whispered. "Damn. I'm gonna cry. I don't know what to do."

"You can accept it. I know your parents said you can come back to De La Salle next year, but this . . ." Frankie pointed to the letter.

I nodded, unable to form words.

"You're going to have to learn to socialize on your own," Sabrina pointed out.

"I think I'll manage. You can give me a few more lessons in how to properly gossip." Tears gathered in the corner of my eyes as I reread the letter, signed by the new dean, Nicolette Salvatore Medina.

"Someone ordered a pastrami to go?" A waiter walked over, bag in hand.

I waved him down. It took a couple of months, but I *finally* got Hal that sandwich.

Frankie eyed the to-go bag. "Grabbing a new case? I still can't believe how Chloe's case turned out."

"Well, the director wasn't going to take the fall for his wife," Sabrina replied. "As he put it in his confession, it was her idea to spike Chloe's drink."

"Well, they're both behind bars now. And school is almost over. So yes, it's time for a new case. Found one that I think you would like. High school reunion, late nineties . . ." I wiggled my brows at Sabrina.

"You already know what I want to say, don't you?" she replied.

"Go for it."

"This is giving me—"

"Okay, make room, young folk." Julius walked up, tossing a few copies of today's paper on the table.

I grinned. "Best. News. Ever."

Julius sighed. "I'll be happy to just get through the next year and graduate with nothing else happening."

Frankie quirked up a brow. "What else could happen?"

"I'm sure De La Salle has its own drama, so you might think you know what it's like," Julius started. "But North Shore . . . things are different up there."

"Well, I know one thing." I leaned back in my chair. "I'm done snooping."

Frankie shook his head. "No, you're not."

"Yes, I am."

"Sweetie, I thought we agreed you'd be honest with us moving forward?"

"Well . . ." I looked around the table at everyone with knowing smiles on their faces. "Maybe a *little* snooping here and there."

ABOUT THE AUTHOR

A. M. ELLIS is an author and a lover of all things steeped in mystery, magic, and mythology. Hailing from the suburbs of Washington, DC, she lives with her husband and three kids while working as a senior brand and creative manager for a nonprofit focused on ending childhood hunger. Her stories are often inspired by her adventurous daydreams and the characters in her life, blended with her own experience as a Black woman with neurodivergent children. If she's not writing or designing, you can find her nose deep in a book or playing video games with her family.

ABOUT HUNT A KILLER

Since 2016, Hunt A Killer has disrupted conventional forms of storytelling by delivering physical items, documents, and puzzles to tell immersive stories that bring friends and families together. What started as an in-person event has now grown into a thriving entertainment company with over 100,000 subscribers and over four million boxes shipped. Hunt A Killer creates shared experiences and community for those seeking unique ways to socialize and challenge themselves.